GHOUL STRIKE!

Andrew Newbound

Chicken House
SCHOLASTIC INC. / NEW YORK

Text copyright © 2010 by Andrew Newbound
All rights reserved. Published by Chicken House, an imprint of Scholastic Inc., *Publishers since 1920*. CHICKEN HOUSE, SCHOLASTIC, and associated logos are trademarks and/or registered trademarks of Scholastic Inc.

www.scholastic.com

First published in the United Kingdom in 2010 as *Demon Strike* by Chicken House, 2 Palmer Street, Frome, Somerset BA11 1DS.

www.doublecluck.com

Library of Congress Cataloging-in-Publication Data Available
ISBN 978-0-545-22938-8

10 9 8 7 6 5 4 3 2 1   10 11 12 13 14

Printed in the U.S.A. 23
First American edition, October 2010
The text type was set in ITC New Baskerville.
The display type was set in Sodom.
Book design by Elizabeth B. Parisi and Kristina Iulo

For my beautiful wife, Sue, who has been a constant source of understanding, encouragement, and inspiration during the long journey; we got there in the end.

1

Alannah Malarra's mobile phone buzzed in her hand like an angry wasp. The twelve-year-old had disabled the ringtone hours earlier, but its electronic spasms still pierced the night's silence. She quickly flicked her wrist to open the handset, killing the noise instantly.

"You're late," Alannah hissed into the phone. "You were scheduled to call two minutes ago. Do we have a problem, Wortley?"

Five hundred feet away, clinging desperately to the lowest branch of an age-twisted oak tree, Wortley Flint struggled to suck air into his lungs. With both arms occupied, he'd had to rely on voice-activated Bluetooth technology to speed-dial his business partner's name the moment he yelled it out loud. His leg muscles burned as if they'd been set on fire and his heart was pounding against his chest like a jabbing boxer. Beneath him, two sets of bone-crushing jaws rose in tandem to snap hungrily in the air just below his blood-soaked back-pack. The word "problem" hardly seemed to do the eleven-year-old's predicament justice.

"Bring . . . me . . . more . . . bait!" Wortley spluttered.

"Why do you need more bait?" Alannah demanded to know. "I gave you enough to knock out two large dogs!"

The smell of raw meat invaded Wortley's nostrils as the jaws snapped shut beneath him, this time only a breath away.

"They're . . . not . . . dogs," he gasped, arching his back to avoid another ferocious lunge. "They're hyenas!"

Wortley's earpiece stayed silent for three long seconds until Alannah spoke again.

"Say that again," she ordered. "For one ridiculous moment I thought you said hyenas."

Alannah had been meditating. She always liked to build up her psychic energy before a ghost hunt, and had found a nice secluded spot at the base of an oak tree. She had been in the middle of a particularly rest-ful trance when Wortley had disturbed her, and she was far from happy.

Wortley's job was a simple one: All he had to do was break into the manor house undetected. He was a burglar—one of the best, too—and it should have taken him no more than a few minutes. But things weren't going according to plan.

"I did," Wortley snapped. "Look!"

The young burglar waited until his two attackers had launched another air-bound assault. Then, as they tumbled back to Earth like falling boulders, he swung his head to the right and pointed the Bluetooth video camera, loosely attached to one of his large stick-out ears, straight at them.

Alannah gawked at her phone's tiny screen. The image flickered with interference whenever Wortley moved his head, but she could clearly see that two wolf-sized wild animals were prowling the ground beneath him.

"Fool!" she hissed, scolding herself for not casing out the old manor house first. It was the kind of mistake a professional ghost hunter should never make. Alannah was getting sloppy!

It had sounded like such an easy job. The Earl of Pittingham's email had dropped into Alannah's Hotmail inbox three days earlier. Like numerous clients before him, the desperate earl had found the young ghost hunter's website — *www.goawayghosts.com* — at the very top of the first Google search page. Alannah paid a lot of good money to a lot of shady people to make sure she always appeared at the top of any ghost-related Google search. And her guarantee to rid any house of any ghost meant that her site always attracted a lot of traffic.

Typically, she would receive thirty new emails every

day. The majority were from time-wasters, like neurotic new mums who thought their babies were possessed, or overimaginative children who believed that monsters really did live under their beds. But occasionally an email would appear that Alannah would take seriously. The earl's was one of them:

> Please help us!
> We are under attack and need your services.
> Ghosts are surrounding us. They're in the cellar, behind the walls, under the floorboards. They're everywhere!!! And more are coming every night. They cackle and scream; one even growls. I'm sure that they want to kill us.
> I'll pay you extra! Come quickly!!
> Yours desperately,
> The seventh Earl of Pittingham

There was an address and a phone number, too, but Alannah knew better than to call. She never made appointments. In fact, the first any client knew of Alannah's involvement was usually when the haunting stopped. And the young ghost hunter rarely charged for her time. The ghosts always paid. Usually with priceless treasure.

"Are you going to help me or not?!" Wortley screamed.

Alannah sighed and climbed to her feet; treasure-hunting would have to wait. Her friend was in a hyena-shaped pickle and it was all Alannah's fault. The least she could do was to give the kid a hand.

Luckily, she had come prepared. There was an emergency supply of bait stashed in her backpack. All she had to do was feed it to the hyenas and the extra dose of animal tranquilizers would put them to sleep within seconds. But it did mean leaving her post and abandoning her well-planned schedule. She sighed. Ah well, that's what friends are for!

"Simmer down, Worts," she replied as she shuffled her rucksack into a more comfortable position. "I'm on my way."

Alannah had Wortley in her sights. She could see him hanging wearily from the tree branch, desperately hugging the bark with his skinny arms each time the hyenas launched an attack.

As she edged closer, she could actually hear them snarling and gnashing, grinding their teeth and snapping their powerful jaws together. Anything that got between those jaws would be history. And Alannah had absolutely no intention of getting any closer than she had to.

The hyenas had other ideas. They stopped circling Wortley and switched their attention to something far more interesting. Alannah's mouth suddenly went dry. She could sense a different hunger emanating from their cold, dark eyes and, as her stomach began to churn like a washing machine on its spin cycle, she had the ominous impression that their new prey looked a lot like her.

Stubby noses investigated the night air as the hyenas followed an invisible, scented wisp that led straight to Alannah. A gentle breeze made her scent even stronger and, as the two animals broke into a trot, bungee ropes of drool dropped from their jaws to the ground.

Within seconds they were running. Strong legs carried them easily across the ground, and growls like a dragon's snore grew louder with every stride. Alannah could smell their foul breath as they approached, yet she chose not to move a muscle.

Wortley's relief at no longer being on the hyenas' menu was short-lived. Only one thing on Earth could drag a hyena away from an easy meal—an even *easier* meal. And in this case the main course was Alannah Malarra.

Helpless, he watched as the animals switched to full hunt mode. It was pure instinct and impressive to watch. While the lead animal made a hurried beeline for where Alannah was obviously hiding, the second animal veered to the right, circling at amazing speed to cut off her only escape route.

The situation looked hopeless. Alannah seemed doomed.

"Run!" Wortley yelled. "Get out of here!"

Alannah didn't move an inch. She didn't even blink. Instead, she stared straight into the oncoming hyena's eyes as it bounded hungrily toward her. It seemed to be grinning at her, its growls replaced by a laughing yelp. Little did it know that Alannah would have the last laugh.

Hyenas don't leap. They simply keep on running at high speed until they catch their prey. Nothing stops them. Except, perhaps, a loaded gun. Or a ten-foot-tall, triple-strength, reinforced, interlocking wire fence.

Alannah had taken a risk and bet her life on two probabilities: First, that the gloom of night would prevent the hyenas from seeing the fence that circled their master's home. And second, that they were too dumb to realize that Alannah was behind it.

When the first hyena slammed into the fence, Alannah didn't think her gamble would pay off. A hyena-shaped bulge actually appeared in the wire, and the creature's jaws were two chomps away from its target, splashing Alannah with a shower of saliva. But then the fence did its job, snapping back into shape and repelling the hyena like a rock from a catapult.

The second hyena struck the wire moments later and suffered exactly the same fate. Alannah had been right; they hadn't seen the barrier. And their repeated attempts to run through it proved they were every bit as dumb as she'd hoped.

Slowly, she climbed to her feet and dropped the backpack off her bony shoulder. When she opened the flap, the smell of fresh meat filled the air, stopping the hyenas in their tracks. Now she really did have their full attention.

"Hungry, are we?" she asked, waving the meat under their noses. "How about a little snack before bedtime?"

"Are you sure they're out?" Wortley asked. "I mean, really out?"

He was still clinging to the tree branch like a sloth, and refused to move until Alannah had prodded both of the sedated hyenas with a stick.

"They're sleeping like babies," Alannah assured him. "And they've got full stomachs, too. So you're off the menu."

Gingerly, Wortley dropped to the ground. His arms and legs hung off his thin body like lead weights. All he wanted to do was go to bed.

"Can't we do the job tomorrow?" he pleaded.

"No!" Alannah barked, tapping her watch. "We're already behind schedule. Besides, all *you've* got to do is get me inside. I'll do the rest."

Wortley sighed. He knew his business partner was right, as usual. But she had been wrong about the guard dogs, er, hyenas, hadn't she? And that had almost cost him his life. He wondered what other nasty surprises were waiting for them inside the old manor house.

"I don't know," he mused. He ran his hands through his closely cropped blond crew cut and tried to straighten his ill-fitting clothes. "There's something not right about this one. Why don't we come back tomorrow, during daylight, and do it legit?"

"'Legit'?" scoffed Alannah. "Legit gets us fifty bucks to split two ways. My way could get us fifty thousand. You know full well that ghosts guard treasure. Taking it from them is what makes this job so much fun. It's easier than taking lollipops from babies! But I can't very well do that while the owner of the house is looking over our shoulders, can I? Technically, any hidden valuables still belong to them."

"But that's *stealing*," Wortley pointed out. "I know I always say it, but it's true."

"No, it's not! The treasures we find are either lost or forgotten. Nobody knows they're here. Think about the ruby ring we took from that old inn in York last week. According to the ghost of the demented highwayman, it had been stashed at the bottom of the well since 1726. The current landlord had no idea it was there, and he has even less idea now that it's gone. So who, exactly, did we steal it from? The last time I checked, there were no laws against pilfering from ghosts. Besides, everyone gets exactly what they want: The client gets a ghost-free house, and we get stinking rich."

"What about the poor ghosts?" asked Wortley.

"We're doing them a favor," said Alannah. "Do you actually think they *want* to be stuck on Earth?"

"It's just that they seem pretty happy to be here," Wortley countered.

"That's because they don't know any different," growled Alannah. "They were mean and greedy people when they were alive, and they're still mean and greedy now. Why do you think they go *down* instead of *up* once we've taken their treasure?"

Wortley shrugged; he had absolutely no idea. Until a couple of years ago, he hadn't even believed in ghosts. He still hadn't seen one, and that's exactly the way he liked it. They frightened him, and he quivered like trembling Jell-O whenever he knew they were around. An obvious drawback for a ghost hunter's assistant. In fact, the only things he'd figured out about them were that they made the air cold and they were all scared of Alannah. Part of him almost felt sorry for them.

"I can't imagine it's particularly nice down there, that's all," he said, pointing to the ground beneath his feet. "Maybe we should try to help them."

Help them? Why couldn't Wortley understand that

ghosts weren't nice? And they certainly couldn't be helped. Alannah really didn't have time to explain everything again. It would take way too long. Besides, there was a lot about ghosts that even she didn't understand. All she knew was what her parents had told her, which wasn't much.

She still clung to the memories of the first ghost-hunting mission they'd taken her on, and remembered how amazed she'd been to see her first actual ghost.

"Don't be scared," her mum had calmly whispered as a snarling seventeenth-century cavalier waved its razor-sharp sword inches from their faces. "It can't hurt you, I promise. But it doesn't belong here. It's trapped by its selfish love of earthly possessions and now it's our job to send it on its way."

Alannah couldn't recall if her mother had ever actually got around to explaining where it was they were supposed to send the ghost. All she remembered for sure was seeing a huge flash, hearing an even bigger bang, and then spotting a particular look on the ghost's face the second before it was banished. It was a look she'd seen on the face of every banished ghost ever since: a look of absolute dread.

Wortley sighed as he saw the faraway expression in Alannah's eyes. She was thinking about her parents again. That happened a lot, usually when he and Alannah were arguing, and at times like this there was just no getting through to her, although that rarely stopped Wortley from trying.

"Maybe the earl's onto us," he said. "Maybe he's rumbled your scam and he's waiting inside right now with a loaded elephant gun. It could be a psychic sting operation?"

Alannah tossed her long red hair behind her shoulder with a sweep of both hands and rolled her green eyes. Wortley was a good burglar, probably the best, but she'd met jellyfish with more backbone, and his lack of courage had sabotaged missions in the past. There was too much at stake to let him jeopardize this one.

"Let's go through it one more time, shall we?" she said wearily. "The earl thinks his house is haunted and there's a good chance that he's right. He's asked me—sorry, he's asked *us*—to do whatever it takes to exorcise the ghosts. And for that, he'll pay us the princely sum of fifty British pounds."

Wortley looked up at Alannah and fixed her with a poisonous glare. "We've got more money than we'll ever need; I'm tired of telling you."

"And *I'm* tired of reminding *you* that we'll *never* have enough—how else can we search for my mother and father?"

For the briefest of moments, Alannah felt her eyes well with tears. She hadn't seen her parents since they'd disappeared in the Scottish Highlands over three years before. And nobody could tell her whether they were alive or dead. According to the authorities, their official status was MISSING. Although they'd been among the best ghost hunters in the world, nobody was trying to find them. Alannah knew she'd have to do that herself. And searching was expensive, so she needed money. Lots of it.

Wortley knew better than to argue anymore. It annoyed him that Alannah always played the "My Parents Are Missing" card, but she did have a point. He couldn't begin to understand what it would be like to have no one around to look after him. Wortley loved his mum and he'd be a gibbering wreck if he ever had to face life without her. But Alannah was different. She seemed to be made of tougher stuff.

And now her eyes had acquired a steely look that the young burglar knew only too well. He'd seen it before, many times. And he'd rather face a house full of rampaging elephants than one of his boss's tantrums. So he decided to save his retirement speech for another day.

"All right," he said meekly, pulling a specially customized screwdriver from his backpack. "Meet me around the back of the house in . . ." He checked his watch. ". . . forty-five seconds."

Alannah smiled.

"Make it thirty-five. We're already running late, and I'm in the mood to scare some ghosts."

Flhi Swift felt a heavy shove in her back and the thick rubber sole of a size-ten combat boot across her behind as she was bundled into the briefing room. Then the door slammed shut. She looked up and gasped.

Flhi was in serious trouble. Already stripped of her trooper's badge, she'd now been thrown in front of the largest collection of high-ranking officers she had ever seen in one place. She scanned the lapel badges and read them in awe: captain, colonel, squadron leader, senior flieutenant, and . . . she gulped as her eyes came to rest on the highest-ranking badge of all. Sitting directly opposite, on a chair that seemed far too small for his muscular frame, was Flhi Swift's worst nightmare.

Over the desk, a grimace appeared on Commander Rage's angular, leathery face. He didn't like Flhi Swift. He had little time for troopers who bent his carefully constructed precinct rules, and Swift regularly tied them in knots. His disdain for her was legendary.

"Per . . . per . . . permission to speak, sir?" Flhi squeaked. Her silver pigtails seemed to quiver.

The commander's top lip curled into a snarl, then he nodded.

"Why am I here?" Flhi asked.

"Good question," Rage answered gruffly. "If I had my way, you'd be driving a garbage truck and working the graveyard shift."

"I don't understand."

Rage thumped the small table that separated him from Flhi. For a moment, it looked like he was preparing to leap across it. Boy, was he angry.

Bravely, one of the other senior officers intervened. His badge told Flhi he was a captain. "Your behavior hasn't gone unnoticed, Swift. We've been watching you for some time and . . . well . . . we've seen that you have specific talents."

"You're trouble, Swift!" spat Rage, jumping to his feet. "With a capital *T*." At least a head taller than most Evanescents, his towering presence carried an air of menace.

This time a colonel stepped forward. He dropped something onto the desk and slid it toward Flhi.

"From time to time, the precinct has uses for troopers with your abilities."

Flhi reached out to take the object, but Rage beat her to it. His hand whipped forward with the speed of a striking snake, slamming onto the desktop and covering the item.

"I want it on the record," he growled, "that this is against my better judgment."

The colonel looked nervous but stood his ground. Although Rage outranked him and every other officer in the room, this was a joint project, sanctioned by them all. "We agreed, Commander. To serve our greater goal . . ."

It took Rage several moments to compose himself. But eventually, he relaxed, slowly took his hand away, and sat back down. His cold gray eyes never left Flhi's, though. If looks could kill!

The colonel bent close to Flhi and whispered into her ear. "The commander is right, Flhi. You are trouble. Think of this as your last chance. Mess up, and your career is as good as over. Geddit?"

Flhi nodded. The officer's breath was revolting, and she was relieved when he finally moved away.

With all eyes on her, Flhi Swift picked up the object. She recognized it instantly. It was her old A.N.G.E.L. Patrol wallet and badge. At least that's what she thought, until she opened it up.

"What the . . . ?"

Instead of her carved diamond trooper's badge, the wallet contained a gleaming block of engraved platinum.

The words etched into the precious metal leapt out at her: INSPECTOR.

Ever since she'd been able to crawl, Flhi Swift had longed to join Evan City's A.N.G.E.L. Police Force, or, to give them their full title, the **A**ttack-ready **N**etwork of **G**lobal **E**vanescent **L**aw-enforcers — the Higher Dimension's elite army of protectors. She'd only graduated a few eons ago, and her record wasn't exactly unblemished. Yet now they were promoting her?

"Promotion? How?" she spluttered.

Rage shook his head. His thick locks of unruly white hair visibly bristled.

"There's a special mission we need you to complete," said the captain. "You'll be assigned a team to command. And as you know, no A.N.G.E.L. below the rank of inspector can command a fellow trooper."

Special mission. Flhi liked the sound of that. A hundred questions jostled in her mind.

"Why me?" she asked.

"You've shown a particular aptitude for getting in and out of places unnoticed," explained the officer with bad breath. "That skill could be pretty useful where you're going."

Flhi sniffed. Urgh! What was that stink? Sour fruit? Out-of-date yogurt? Unwashed hiking socks?

"Where am I going?" Flhi asked, trying not to breathe in the smell.

Rage seemed to snicker. "The Earthly Dimension."

Flhi gasped. "Down there? With all those . . . humans?"

The room full of high-ranking A.N.G.E.L. officers nodded. Most grinned wickedly. They all looked at Bad Breath to explain more.

"There's been some unusual activity at a hot spot we monitor. Our sensors may have picked up a hostile presence before they suddenly went off-line six hours ago. They've recorded low temperatures and exceptional levels of ectoplasm that might indicate more than a basic haunting." He seemed a touch nervous, and glanced at his colleagues. "It's probably nothing to worry about, but it needs checking out. And fast."

"Which hot spot?" Flhi enquired. She rubbed a slender finger across the platinum badge. Wow, an inspector.

Bad Breath looked to Rage for support. He received none.

"Um." He seemed reluctant to give Flhi an answer. "An old Fleshi dwelling . . . in Sector . . . Eight."

Sector Eight. That rang a bell. And an alarm bell, to be exact. Flhi remembered her history lessons from second year at the A.N.G.E.L. Academy. Sector Eight was located on a small, damp island that Fleshies — or humans, as they called themselves — called England. It was also home to a very important portal that had to remain closed. At all costs!

"Are they back?" Flhi gasped.

"Of course they're not *back*," rasped Rage. "The portal is closed and the Gargoyles are trapped in the Dark Dimension forever."

His fellow officers nodded in agreement. Although a few had winced at the word *Gargoyle*. They were clearly scared.

"It's probably a software blip," Bad Breath tried to reassure Flhi. "You know what the tech guys are like—too proud to report a malfunction. We just need someone to check it out and set the City Elders' minds at rest."

"And that someone is me?" said Flhi.

Bad Breath nodded.

"Why? Because I'm dispensable?" Flhi asked. She suddenly saw the bigger picture. "You want to know if the Gargoyles are back, and you don't mind sacrificing me to find out."

Rage coughed. "Sounds like a fair deal."

"I prefer to look at it as a chance to redeem yourself," said Bad Breath. "It's an opportunity to do something meaningful and get your career back on track."

"Hmmmm," mused Flhi. "But if I run into trouble and get killed, nobody sheds a tear. Right?"

Rage just smiled.

Flhi took a deep breath. It was nice to know exactly where she stood. In a way, it was kind of liberating. And she'd be in charge of her own mission.

"Sounds good to me!" she announced happily.

Rage eyed her suspiciously. He knew the little trooper was smart. Very smart. And there was something—well, quite a lot, actually—about Flhi Swift that he didn't trust. What did she have up her sleeve this time?

"I'll do it!" Flhi confirmed, thumping the little table to drive home her determination.

The officers mumbled approvingly. One of them reached for a briefcase he had cleverly concealed behind his back. He tossed it onto the table.

"Comes with the rank," he said coldly.

Excited, Flhi unzipped the case and reached inside. Feathers. Could it really be?

Gingerly, she pulled the contents from the case. Wow. She flashed a smile that stunned the officers. Flhi Swift was pretty, but when she smiled, she was beautiful.

"They're new," said Bad Breath. "Expensive, too. So take good care of them."

But Flhi didn't hear him. She was too busy holding up the beautiful white-feathered A.N.G.E.L. inspector's wings. Her first pair. A smile stretched wide across Flhi's face. She couldn't wait to try them on. Did life get any better than this?

Rage couldn't take any more. He kicked his chair away and jumped to his feet again.

"I'll be watching you, Swift!" he barked. "Sneeze in the wrong direction and I'll pull you back to Evan City in a second and rip those puny wings right off your shoulders. Understand?"

Flhi dramatically stood to attention and offered her commanding officer a mock salute. "Loud and clear, Commander Rage. Loud and clear."

Rage turned to Bad Breath and glared at his fellow officer. "I want her fully briefed and prepped for the mission. When she fails, I want her to have no excuses. None!"

Without giving the officer a chance to reply, Rage pushed by and stormed from the room. Everyone breathed a sigh of relief.

Bad Breath turned to a colleague and snapped his fingers. "Fetch troopers Yell and Gloom," he ordered. "It's time Inspector Swift met her new team."

Breaking into old houses was surprisingly simple.
The alarm systems were almost always broken or switched off, and the one protecting Pittingham Manor was no exception. Even before Wortley shimmied up the rusted drainpipe to disconnect the fuse, he knew that the box on the wall was little more than an ornament. When he tugged on the wires, they crumbled apart.

Wortley smiled. He scuttled back down and checked his wristwatch. Ten seconds to go. Any longer and Alannah would have another excuse to moan. And he didn't want that.

His trained eyes scanned the back of the house. It was a huge, sprawling building that had once been quite magnificent. Now, though, it was definitely long past its prime, and if the owner neglected the house, perhaps he neglected other things, too.

Two large French doors led from the house onto a paved patio area that was as big as a tennis court. Wortley crept toward it and noticed a lush film of moss carpeting the flagstones. It looked as if the patio was rarely used, and the young burglar smiled again. As he stepped toward the doors, he pocketed his screwdriver. A hunch told him he probably wasn't going to need it.

At first, the brass door handles wouldn't budge. Clearly, they hadn't been used in years and had rusted solid.

Five seconds to go! thought Wortley.

Calmly, he reached into his rucksack and pulled out a can of industrial lubricant. Even in the dark of night, his aim was good, and the jet of fluid scored a direct hit on the door handles. He counted to three, then tugged the handles again.

"Time's up, Wortley," Alannah's voice whispered into his earpiece. "Ready or not, here I come."

On the second tug the handles finally twisted and Wortley heard a reassuring *click*. As he had suspected, the doors were unlocked, and just before Alannah appeared at his side Wortley eased them both open.

"Bravo," said Alannah. "You really do have quite the talent for breaking and entering."

Wortley blushed. He had no intention of telling her just how easy it had been.

"Now step aside," Alannah said, shoving past her friend. "It's time for the real work to start."

The old manor house was definitely haunted. Alannah could sense a spirit's presence and it was strong, which meant it was close. The hairs on the back of her neck bristled and a torrent of excitement gushed through her body. She never felt more alive than when she was tangling with the dead.

Wortley hurried to catch up with her. Ghosts could cause trouble. Alannah had rescued him from scary situations on more than one occasion, and he knew it paid to stay close.

"Can you see anything?" he whispered, hoping the answer would be no.

Alannah shook her head. The ghost had yet to show itself, but that didn't matter. She could hear it, and it was coming straight toward them.

"Ring around the rosies, a house full of ghosties," a spectral voice sang cheerfully. "We scare you! We scare you! You all leave town. . . ."

Alannah's fingers began glowing brightly. A single flick from any one of them would send a dart of energy whizzing across the room. To other humans, these darts were invisible and harmless. But they were dangerous weapons against ghosts. A direct hit banished them forever—leaving their treasure for Alannah.

Her parents had promised to teach her how to use

this energy, but that was before they went missing. Now, as the months turned to years, Alannah found that she was becoming more and more powerful. These days she could also create glowing balls of astral light that would fizz around a room like heat-seeking grenades. One day soon, she hoped to be able to harness her powers and control them. But for now, that ability was beyond her. All she knew was that whenever she got angry or upset, her attacks became stronger.

The manor house ghost knew none of this. It didn't even know that a ghost hunter was on the premises. And as the spirit of the third Earl of Pittingham's gamekeeper danced through the old house, merrily slamming doors and knocking vases to the floor, it had no idea that a fate worse than exorcism was lurking a few shadows away.

"Ten priceless ornaments sitting on a shelf. Ten priceless ornaments!" the ghost sang. "And if one of those priceless ornaments should happen to fall . . ." The spirit flicked a delicate porcelain statue off a shelf and watched it topple to the floor. *Smash!* "Oopsy! Nine priceless ornaments sitting on a shelf!"

Alannah stepped out from the shadows as the ghostly gamekeeper entered the room by floating through a wall. He was dressed in dirty tweeds and carried a very old, polished hunting rifle. Half his face was missing, which suggested he had lost his life in an accident. Or perhaps he had been murdered.

"Urgh!" gasped Alannah. "You've got to be the ugliest ghost I've ever seen."

"Who . . . what . . . ?" spluttered the ghost. He almost jumped out of his spectral skin when he spotted Alannah, and shock bounced him from one wall to the next.

It took a few seconds for the gamekeeper to regain his composure. Then he bellowed, "Get out of this house!"

"Oh, do shut up," Alannah ordered. "Your haunting days are over."

"Says who?" the ghost asked scornfully.

"Says these," Alannah replied, flicking two fingers and firing a couple of astral arrows toward the ghost.

He ducked at the last minute and managed to avoid the first arrow. But he was too slow to dodge the second, and it blew a hole clean through the butt of his rifle.

"You'll pay for that," the gamekeeper hissed as he examined the smoking remains of his weapon.

"Wrong," said Alannah. "It's you who's going to pay. Now hand over the treasure before I blast a great big hole in you."

The ghost shrugged innocently. "What treasure?"

Alannah sighed wearily. Ghosts were so predictable. "Look, I know you've got something valuable hidden in this house. It's why you're here. And now you know I know. So if you know what's good for you, you'll stop wasting my time and tell me where it is."

The ghostly gamekeeper looked confused and spent the next few seconds trying to figure out what Alannah had just said to him. When he finally got it, he started to back away.

"You're a thief. A lousy, poaching thief," he snarled. "And do you know what I used to do to poaching thieves?"

Alannah rolled her eyes. "I couldn't care less. Now give me the treasure."

"Never!"

Alannah wiggled her glowing fingertips.

"Okay, you can have it," the gamekeeper suddenly conceded. He looked a little scared. "But there's one condition."

This was a first. Alannah had never encountered a ghost that wanted to bargain. And there was a mischievous glint to the gamekeeper's eye that she didn't quite trust. But what the heck . . .

"Name it."

The gamekeeper laughed. "You'll have to catch me first!"

He was quick, and before Alannah could fire off a fresh volley of astral arrows, the gamekeeper had outfoxed her, disappeared through a side wall, and escaped.

Flhi loved nothing more than hunting for Ghouls,
Gargoyles, and Gnarls from the shadowy depths of the
Dark Dimension. She stalked them across the precinct's
simulators like a house cat, lying patiently in wait until
her prey made one fatal mistake. She had a rare skill for
it that had initially marked her out as one of the academy's finest students and a candidate for officer rank.
Perhaps she shouldn't have flouted the rules so much
since graduation. Still, at least she was an inspector now,
even if it was only so she could take on a mission no one
else wanted.

And now here she was in Pittingham Manor, once an
important strategic location during the first Great Spirit
War between Evanescents and Malevolents. This was the
site of the Door of Souls, an ancient seal covering
the vortex that connected all three dimensions. Of

course, Commander Rage could be right and the sensors were malfunctioning. But if they weren't, if the seal was broken, that would spell bad news for everyone.

Flhi Swift stretched her new wings nervously. They still felt a bit stiff. It would be several eons before the ecto-moldings on the joints loosened, and she adjusted the high-tech shoulder strappings to make them more comfortable. After a solitary test flap she quickly folded them away. Okay, so they weren't the beautiful golden feathers of a sentinel, or the silken plumage of a guardian, but Flhi felt she'd been born to wear them.

She gave the billiard room a final visual sweep. Nothing moved. There was no threat here. How boring.

Yell, do you copy? she thought into the telepathic communicator. *Give me a status report from Zone Two!*

Trooper Yell's reply boomed into her ear, reminding her that his parents had chosen his name well; he was loud even when speaking telepathically. *All's quiet in the dining room, ma'am. Do you want me to go scouting?*

Flhi's wings twitched angrily. *Negative, Trooper. Do not walk through any walls until you receive my instructions.*

Affirmative! Yell bellowed, almost short-circuiting his inspector's receiver. *No wall walking.*

When Flhi had been introduced to her team, she'd immediately realized they were combat first-timers whom other inspectors had refused to enlist. Yell, whose voice made him a liability. And Gloom, whose miserable disposition could sap the joy from a lottery winner. Her enforced promotion had been on the condition that she took these rookie A.N.G.E.L.s under her new combat wings. They might be raw, inexperienced, and hugely unprepared, but they were her troopers now and that was all that mattered.

Gloom, any movement in Zone Three? the inspector asked.

No, a sad voice responded. *The study is quiet as a church. But what did you expect? Nothing exciting ever happens to me.*

There's a first time for everything, Gloom. Remember what I said about positive thinking?

I've tried it, Gloom responded sadly. *Now I'm positive things will only get worse.*

Flhi's silver pigtails danced like tree branches in a storm as she shook her head. Would Gloom ever cheer up? She sighed and turned her thoughts back to the mission. Hopefully, she would discover a malfunctioning sensor and could get out of there without having to test her troopers' battle skills.

Her telepathic communicator suddenly bellowed into life again.

INSPECTOR! Yell shrieked excitedly. *We've got company in Zone Two. There's a renegade ghost, and a . . . a . . .*

Go visual, Flhi ordered. Instantly, she received a tele-pathic broadcast from Yell.

Fleshi children, she gasped. *What are they doing here? The sensors only picked up two older Fleshies in the house.*

Told you things were going to get worse, Gloom moaned.

Button it, Gloom! Flhi hissed.

He's right, ma'am, Yell shouted. *Things have just gotten worse.*

What do you mean? Flhi asked, trying to hide the panic that goose-pimpled her shimmering ecto-skin.

I think the girl can see me! Yell screamed.

Oh no, blubbered Gloom. *A psychic!*

Moonlight poured through the dining room windows, painting everything with an eerie silvery sheen. Alannah and Wortley picked their way silently through a forest of cluttered furniture. Wobbly stacks of books rose like desert cacti from the floor. One wrong move and the piles would collapse around them.

Alannah caught a glimpse of a shadow moving in the corner of the room. Clearly, there was more than just the ghost of an old gamekeeper roaming the old manor house. Something else was lurking in the dining room.

Staring into the dark, she could see it was about the same size as a small chimp, yet there was something unnerving about this strange new entity; it was holding what looked like a weapon.

Suddenly, she noticed that splashes of ectoplasm were everywhere. Swollen puddles of the stuff wobbled on the polished wooden floor. It was splattered across the walls, too, and hung off door frames like trolls' drool. Only a gang of ghosts could make that amount of paranormal slime. And, because it was fresh, they were obviously close by.

"I think we've hit the jackpot," Alannah whispered to Wortley. "Something big is hidden here."

"Yeah, well, I hope it's not too heavy," Wortley grumbled. "And is it me, or is this carpet sticky? I can hardly lift my feet."

Alannah looked down. Wortley had been splashing through the puddles and his shoes were covered in huge glowing blobs.

Intrigued, she pointed her finger downward and shot an arrow of burning light from beneath her painted nail. *Zing!* Her first blast bounced away, barely even scorching the ectoplasm. She frowned and concentrated her energies to fire a second blast. This time the gooey puddle melted. Clearly, this wasn't the ordinary gloop she was used to dealing with; there was something different about this place.

"Stay close," Alannah warned Wortley. "We're not alone."

She watched the armed entity through the corner of her eye. It was different from the ghosts she usually encountered. Earthbound spirits like the gamekeeper were often deranged—driven loopy by an eternity of boredom—yet this new entity was calm and hovered perfectly still. It was also dressed in a military uniform and carried its weapon with confidence. It was clearly no ordinary being, and Alannah sensed trouble. But its presence supported the idea that there was major booty somewhere in the old manor house. Perhaps even under her nose. And if a team of ghosts was patrolling the floors, their hoard could fetch a six-figure sum. All she had to do was persuade them to give it up, which usually meant having some real fun.

"There's another ghost in the room, isn't there?" Wortley asked fearfully.

"Sshh!" Alannah hissed. "I don't want it to know it's been spotted. And try not to go to pieces on me this time, Wortley. One just got away and I might need your help."

That didn't sound good to Wortley. He got them into the house and Alannah dealt with the ghosts. That was how they always worked together. Why did things have to change now?

"Can't I just hide under a table until you're finished?"

"No! You're going to have to earn your money tonight."

★ ★ ★

Flhi watched Yell's telepathic broadcast with increasing alarm. The way the young girl had melted so much ectoplasm in seconds gave her particular concern. That was serious firepower, certainly much more than her troopers were equipped to deal with. Flhi had to get to Yell's zone, fast.

After she'd heard where she was heading for her first mission, Flhi had dug out her old academy textbooks and quickly swotted up on the Earthly Dimension. She had always wondered why the Fleshi inhabitants called it Earth, but it seemed that the whole place was covered in a trillion tons of stinking mud! And if the Fleshies weren't growing strange-looking food in it (yuck, those long orange roots looked particularly disgusting), they were digging it up and using it as building materials, or burning it for fuel. The Evanescents had never done anything quite so primitive. They'd always had the sense to dig a little deeper and mine the energy-packed crystals. Diamond seams had been powering their world for hundreds of eons, and would power it for hundreds more. Yet to the inhabitants of the Earthly Dimension, diamonds were little more than decorative trinkets.

Urgh, Fleshies were so backward! Perhaps someone should tell them.

Of course, that someone would not be Flhi Swift. The Third Vow of the Evanescent Code strictly forbade lowly A.N.G.E.L. inspectors like her from making any kind of contact with Fleshies whatsoever, something her briefing had made absolutely clear. She would be thrown in a Level Five holding dungeon for an eon or two just for sniffing the odor of a Fleshi. Speaking to one would see her court-martialed, or worse, banished to the Dark Dimension.

Flhi shuddered at the thought. The Malevolent realm, occupied by snarling Ghouls, Gargoyles, and ferocious Gnarls, was no place for an Evanescent—even one armed to the teeth with a high-tech ecto-blaster.

Flhi was hoping it was a fate she wouldn't have to worry about. The Evanescents had been making routine patrols around the Earthly Dimension for hundreds of Fleshi years, and they rarely attracted so much as a puzzled glance from the slow-witted inhabitants. Occasionally, a psychic might sense their presence, or catch a fleeting glimpse of an Evanescent, but the Fleshies always dismissed these encounters as nothing more than ghostly visitations. Yet instinct told Flhi this Fleshi girl was different, and she needed to ensure the safety of her troopers.

Yell, prepare a landing cloud, Flhi ordered. *I'm switching to wings.*

At last, Flhi would get to try her new inspector wings in live action. With a single telepathic thought, she triggered the sensory-control module and unfolded them. Another thought set them flapping, and soon she was hovering in the air like an attack helicopter. The power was incredible, and Flhi could feel the wings straining to be unleashed. She reached just above her head, where a silver halo hovered in the air, pressed a hidden sensor with her fingertip, and felt the halo buzz into life immediately. Seconds later a protective veil of transparent energy wrapped itself around her head; the ecto-visor was deployed. Wow, Flhi really did love Evanescent technology!

Yell, that cloud had better be ready.

Negative, ma'am! Yell screamed. *We have a no-go on the cloud.*

Oops! Flhi had already unleashed her wings and was hurtling toward the nearest wall at meteoric speed.

Deploy now! Flhi ordered. *Inspector coming through.*

Yell saw the wall buckle and tossed his last two landing grenades over his shoulder as he flung himself to the ground. They immediately exploded, filling the corner of the dining room with two billowing ecto-clouds. The substance solidified on contact with air and immediately turned into a pillow of milky jelly.

Flhi Swift crashed through the wall at twice the speed of sound. The warm ectoplasm wrapped around her body, gently stopping her in her tracks.

"Well done, Trooper Y—"

Yell responded by grabbing his pretty inspector around the waist and pulling her body onto his. A court-martial offense!

Flhi heard the thunderous explosion that ripped her landing cloud apart and explained Yell's indiscretion. She whirled around and fixed her attacker with an angry glare. It was the Fleshi girl. Now that she was closer, Flhi could see that she was tall, willowy, covered in the kind of freckles that adults probably thought were cute, and with a head full of long red hair that flapped around wildly. Her appearance was striking, but it was the Fleshi girl's eyes that really caught Flhi's attention. They were green and piercing, and they were looking straight at her.

Yikes, this Fleshi really could see them! It was also armed and extremely dangerous. Why did this have to happen on Flhi's mission?

The Fleshi offered the A.N.G.E.L.s an unfriendly grin, then spoke to Flhi. "I'll make this easy for you. Show me where the treasure is and I promise not to hurt you."

"Oh no!" Yell wailed. "Now it's talking to us."

"Be quiet," Flhi ordered. "If we ignore it, it might go away."

The Fleshi girl laughed. "Ignore me? That's a new one. No ghost has ever tried to ignore me. Did someone give you a knock on the head before you died?"

Yell gulped nervously. "It doesn't sound like it's got any intention of going anywhere."

Psychics had not been covered in Bad Breath's briefing.

Rage and his officers had mentioned not engaging with Fleshies, but that was just the standard health and safety warning given before every earthly mission.

The inspector groaned. She knew she should probably retreat, but Flhi Swift had never taken a backward step in her life.

Light sparked from the young Fleshi's fingertips as she fired up her weapons. It was clearly a threat. The Fleshi was hostile.

Flhi Swift didn't panic. Her mission was clear: Defend her team, collect vital intelligence, then report back to A.N.G.E.L. headquarters. It was simple enough and she wasn't about to let a Fleshi girl get in her way. It was time to do what Flhi Swift did best: ATTACK!!

"Let's teach this Fleshi child to respect authority," Flhi spat, pulling her twin-barrel ecto-blaster from its holster. It had four settings: SHOCK, STUN, FREEZE, and EVAN-SENT. The last setting was designed to send even the toughest Ghoul or Gargoyle spinning straight back to the Dark Dimension. In this situation Flhi doubted shock would be enough and flicked her weapon to STUN.

"Not so fast!" Alannah growled. She raised both arms and pointed her slender fingers straight at the new winged arrival. Her digits sparked dangerously.

Flhi had no choice. She aimed both barrels at Alannah and took a deep breath. Yell closed his eyes and dived for cover beneath a walnut coffee table.

"Looks like a stalemate, Fleshi," Flhi said. "I'd leave now if I were you, for your own safety."

"We're not going anywhere without the treasure," Alannah said. "You can give it up the easy way, or the hard way."

"What treasure?"

"Don't play dumb, ghoul. Your friend the gamekeeper has already admitted it's here."

The Fleshi girl seemed to be talking in riddles and Flhi was bewildered. Who on Evan was the gamekeeper?

Alannah was losing patience. "Just tell me where it is and my assistant will collect it."

Flhi smiled and flicked off the blaster's safety catch with her thumb. "Ah, your assistant. Would that be the young man in the custody of Trooper Gloom?"

Alannah turned to where Wortley had been hiding. He was now hanging like a startled bat two feet above the ground, suspended by his knee from the hand of a third specter.

"Is this what you meant by having fun?" he squeaked.

Ah! She'd been outthought, outflanked, and now she was outnumbered. It was three against one, and her opponents were armed with a sophisticated array of spirit-world weapons, whereas Alannah had only her bare hands. It hardly seemed a fair fight.

Flhi and her team didn't stand a chance.

Perhaps if he'd had the time, Gloom might have considered using Wortley as a shield. But Alannah's attack was so swift that the trooper had no opportunity to think, never mind take evasive action. One moment he was holding the Fleshi boy aloft like a hunting trophy, the next he was rolling around on the floor trying to douse the fires that raged across his armored plasma suit. Five energized darts had struck him, setting fire to his suit's ecto-coating and igniting him in a fountain of sparks.

"Help!" he bawled, scrambling for cover behind a pile of toppled books. "A.N.G.E.L. down."

Yell peered out from beneath the coffee table. The smoke from Gloom's smoldering ecto-suit made his eyes stream. He quickly picked up a large leather-bound ledger and began to swat out the flames. Gloom yelped and thought he was under attack again: This was not a good day!

Flhi pulled the double trigger on her ecto-blaster and launched two high-powered bolts straight at Alannah, who scrambled for cover behind a chair just in time.

Flhi had no intention of letting her first-ever mission end in failure. The Fleshi girl was good, she had to admit that, but Flhi had years of academy combat training to fall back on. All she had to do was figure out how to turn the situation to her advantage, and fast!

Alannah was enjoying herself. Tracking down treasure wasn't usually this much fun. Ghosts rarely fought back. And if they ever did, it was only in a desperate attempt to escape. But these three had ambushed *her*, and their leader had wings like an albino pterodactyl's and a halo for a helmet. What, or who, were these guys? Shame they weren't on the same side. A team of combat-skilled entities would certainly come in handy if Alannah ever decided to expand the family business.

She was still imagining the possibilities when a small cloud of steam floated past her eyes. It was followed moments later by another, and then another. The room temperature had suddenly dropped and she wondered whether this was yet another enemy assault.

One look at the entity with silver pigtails told her that it wasn't. She seemed to be frozen solid, and the look in her eyes was one of absolute terror. Something was scaring her.

Flhi had noticed the drop in temperature a second too late. Her instincts had let her down. Now she was trapped. Her ecto-support system would react shortly and send a warming pulse across her body, but she was a sitting duck, and so was the Fleshi girl. Neither of them was fast enough to escape the hundreds of sticky plasma threads that had begun to coil around their bodies, wrapping them tighter than flies in silk and dragging them upward.

Alannah couldn't move. She was pinned to the ceiling and could only gaze down at the gang of new arrivals with a mixture of repulsion and awe.

They were like nothing she had ever seen before. These entities had made no effort to take human form. Instead, they had molded their semi-frozen plasma skins into the shape of gargoyles, and each one was different. The largest wore the folded wings of a demon. Another had thick stalactite fangs that dropped as far as its knees. Others displayed pointed ears, hooked noses, and hairy witches' chins. Together, they looked like a gang of goblin pirates and were as close to pure evil as Alannah had ever encountered, with a dark power that was straining to be unleashed. Alannah had no intention of being anywhere near when it broke free.

"Does your weapon work on these ugly things?" she whispered to the female entity strapped to the ceiling beside her.

"They're Gargoyles," whispered Flhi. "And of course my weapon works on them. It's designed to reduce Malevolent soldiers to slush—without their plasma skins they're harmless. The blaster doesn't kill them, it just sends them packing back to the Dark Dimension."

"Gargoyles? Malevolent soldiers?" Alannah sounded curious.

"Yeah, demons from the Dark Dimension. They're our enemy," Flhi reluctantly explained. "But don't ask me anything else. I've told you too much already."

This was incredible. Alannah had just discovered a whole new breed of creature she could exploit. She'd hit the jackpot!

But before she could cash it in, she first had to escape. And to do that, she needed the little female's help. "How about I cut you loose and you show me what that gun of yours can do?"

Flhi smiled thinly. "It'll be my pleasure."

Sparks of white light fired across Alannah's skin, only this time not just from her fingertips. Light erupted from every pore, engulfing her body and burning through her sticky bindings in seconds. She severed Flhi's restraints with a brief blast of fire and together they dropped to the floor, landing bang in the middle of the gang of spitting beasts. Bull's-eye!

"You take the ugly ones," Alannah instructed.

"They're all ugly," Flhi pointed out.

"Then shoot them all."

Flhi needed no further encouragement and pumped a round of Evan-sent ecto-bolts into the nearest beastie. It vanished in a cloud of hissing steam as searing heat reduced its softly frozen plasma suit to a pool of boiling gloop. Naked and exposed, its Malevolent energy spun into a whirling cloud of gas that danced defiantly before retreating through the floorboards, as if being sucked underground by a vacuum cleaner.

Snakes of icy plasma surged toward Flhi as three more Gargoyles launched an all-out attack. Alannah hit them with forks of white light and they exploded into a million hissing droplets of mush.

"Nice shooting, Fleshi," gasped Flhi.

"Will you stop calling me Fleshi?" Alannah growled, pointing her fingers at another monster. "My name's Alannah."

But Flhi wasn't listening. Teaming up with the Fleshi girl had been fun, but she'd taken her eye off the ball and forgotten about her primary responsibility—Yell and Gloom. She had assumed they were safely tucked away, hiding somewhere secure. Only they weren't, and now a Gargoyle had sniffed them out.

"Gerroff!" squealed Yell. He smashed the barrel of his ecto-blaster against the razor-taloned claw that swiped a hairbreadth from his face. "Eek, that was close."

"Hold on there!" Flhi yelled. She flapped her wings and swooped toward the attacking creature. Before the Gargoyle even sensed the little A.N.G.E.L. approaching, she had rammed the soles of her combat boots into the back of its skull. *Wallop!* The Gargoyle collapsed, unconscious.

"I thought we were dead," admitted Gloom.

"Not on my watch," Flhi reassured him. "Now find somewhere more secure and power up your blasters. If a Gargoyle gets close, give it both barrels."

The troopers both nodded obediently. "Yes, ma'am."

Alannah was having a great time. The remaining creatures were fast-moving and really tested her aim. She was finding them hard to hit and sparks from her fingertips were ricocheting off the walls, leaving scorch marks everywhere. This was getting messy.

Finally, she had one of the monsters in her sights. She watched it scuttle across the ceiling, tracing its journey with a glowing fingertip. She was about to fire off a flare when a familiar voice coughed from across the room.

"Um . . . when you've finished playing with ghosts, I could do with a little help."

Wortley! In all the panic, Alannah had forgotten about her best friend. And now it was too late. He was already wrapped tight as a spider's meal and stuck to the wall just below the ceiling, with one of the Gargoyle demons standing guard.

"Thtupid Fleshi boy," it lisped aggressively. "You're gunna thuffer when Krot arriveth. Krot'th real nathty and he loveth hurting little wretcheth like you."

"Not half as much as I love melting Gargoyles," said Alannah.

The Gargoyle spun its head like an owl to scowl at Alannah.

"Reckon he'th gunna enjoy making you thuffer, too," it snickered.

Alannah paused just as long as it took for a nervous thought to skip through her brain. These Gargoyles were ferocious, mean, and utterly fearless. Yet now it seemed there was another creature on its way that was even nastier. A nagging voice in the back of her mind told her to get the treasure and leg it. She didn't want to be around when the Krot arrived. Two new species in one day was enough for anyone.

Grenades of spitting light exploded from her upturned palms. The Gargoyle howled in panic as first one orb and then another detonated against it, splashing a gluey hail of green plasma skin across the room.

Alannah kindled a fiery fingertip and sliced the flame

through Wortley's restraints. He dropped to the floor and crab-scuttled his way behind an upturned table, using its tilted top as a shield.

"I told you we should have gone home," he complained.

"Stay there and wait for me," urged Alannah. "We're not leaving here without the treasure."

"I'll settle for leaving in one piece," said a muffled voice from behind the table.

Flhi had spotted the two remaining Malevolents. She popped a fresh plasma cartridge into her blaster and engaged her flight wings. As if suddenly filled with helium, she rose into the air and gently floated toward the ceiling. As she'd hoped, the Gargoyles remained blind to her presence. She could easily sneak up and apprehend one of them.

Capturing a Gargoyle for her superiors to interrogate would make the mission a success. After all, the presence of demons from the Dark Dimension was probably what had triggered the sensors' abnormal readings. There was no malfunction at all. The Gargoyles were back, and returning to Evan City with intelligence like that might just be enough to rescue her career. Heck, she might even get to keep her new rank. All she had to do was bag a live one.

It was a pity, then, that at that precise moment Flhi's astral communicator burst into life.

"Inspector Swift, this is Evan Precinct," an irritated voice barked. It was Rage himself. "Your initial status report is overdue. Report or abort. I repeat, report or abort!"

Flhi winced. She could almost hear the glee in his voice.

"Report or abort, Inspector," the commander barked again. "This is your last chance."

Flhi had two minutes, no more. Any longer and Commander Rage would log the mission as FAILED. And that would definitely mean the end of her career.

She raised her blaster, switched the setting to STUN and aimed at the biggest and ugliest of the two remaining Gargoyles. "Gotcha," the A.N.G.E.L. whispered as she hooked her slender fingers around the weapon's double trigger. Her brain told her finger to shoot, but before the message was processed, Flhi's target exploded into a trillion droplets of boiling ectoplasm.

"Bull's-eye!" yelled Alannah gleefully. She prowled beneath the last remaining Gargoyle. It was an ugly little brute with a face that could have been carved from a turnip, and the look in its eyes told Alannah it was terrified.

She fired up her fingertips and beckoned the spirit toward her with a single curl of her finger. "Come down here, little ghostie, and you might get out of here in one piece."

Flhi had other ideas. "Step away from the fugitive, Fleshi," she ordered. "That Gargoyle is under arrest and it's coming with me."

Alannah turned angrily to face Flhi and found herself staring into both barrels of the A.N.G.E.L.'s ecto-blaster. "I thought you and I were on the same side."

"You're meddling with something you don't understand. Just leave now, while you still can."

"Oh, very clever. I leave and you force Ugly into handing over the treasure. Well, think again, soldier," Alannah flexed her fingertips menacingly. "I'm here to claim whatever treasure this demon is guarding and you'd better not get in my way."

"Treasure, what treasure?" Flhi had no idea what the Fleshi girl was talking about. "I'm not here looking for trinkets. I'm scouting for enemy Malevolents and that one is now my prisoner."

"Well, it looks like your prisoner is trying to escape," Alannah smirked.

Flhi spun to look at the fleeing Gargoyle. She quickly altered the setting on her blaster to FREEZE and fired. Instead of an ecto-bolt, a plasma-web exploded from one of the barrels and hurtled toward the Gargoyle. It didn't stand a chance and was instantly tied up like a fisherman's catch.

"Very impressive," a menacing voice snarled. "But

I thinks you'll find that's my property you're bicker-ings over."

Alannah and Flhi both looked over their shoulders. The ghost of the dead gamekeeper was pointing his spectral shotgun at them and jumping up and down gid-dily. But that's not what alarmed them. There, behind the bouncing gamekeeper, lurked something much larger and altogether more terrifying.

6

Flhi gasped. This entity was huge and growing larger by the second. From a vast shadowy mass, a shape began to emerge. And that's when the combat A.N.G.E.L. realized she was in serious trouble. The creature was a Gnarl. But surely Gnarls had been banished from the Earthly Dimension eons ago. The Door of Souls had been sealed shut to keep them trapped forever in the Dark Dimension. If a Gnarl was here now, that could only mean one thing . . . the portal had somehow been breached!

Flight or fight? According to her mission directives she should back away immediately, return to Evan City, and make a full report. But when had Flhi Swift ever done as she was supposed to?

Still, eons of academy training told her that the idea of taking on a fully grown Gnarl was as ridiculous as a toddler wrestling an elephant. Gnarls were twice the size of even the biggest Gargoyle, and ten times as strong. Single Gnarls had, in the past, been known to attack and defeat an entire squadron of combat A.N.G.E.L.s, just for fun. One ordinary A.N.G.E.L. wouldn't stand a chance.

Only Flhi Swift didn't consider herself ordinary. She was just about to pull an ecto-grenade from her pocket when Rage hissed an order into her ear.

"Tell your troops to pull back and get out of there. NOW!!"

"You mean retreat?" Flhi asked.

"Yes, and fast," Rage demanded.

Flhi was surprised by Rage's reaction. Did her commander really care about her welfare? "I thought this was what you wanted," she said. "The mission was to find out whether the equipment was faulty. Well, I think we can safely say it isn't. You can see the place is teeming with Gargoyles—and one huge Gnarl. There, you've got your intelligence. Why would you care if I lived or died?"

There was a moment's silence before Rage spoke again. "According to those busybodies in Internal Affairs, leaving you in the field would be classed as murder."

Flhi couldn't help grinning: good old Internal Affairs. She'd always known they must be good for something.

"Now move your skinny butt, Swift," bellowed the

commander. "That thing you're thinking about taking on is Fugitive 1635. You'd need an entire army to get past him."

Fugitive 1635! Flhi shuddered. The legendary four-digit number meant only one thing: Krot! And there wasn't a combat A.N.G.E.L., active or retired, who didn't fear the name.

Krot was the only prisoner ever to have escaped from a Level Five maximum-security holding area, Evan City's deepest underground dungeon. Captured Malevolents were usually left there to rot. The combination of unbreakable enchantments, floor-to-ceiling diamond-dampening walls through which no dark magic could pass, and round-the-clock vigilance from the Higher Dimension's elite sentinel fighters, meant that escape was virtually impossible. But Krot had managed it.

Now he glowered at Inspector Flhi Swift. Strings of slimy saliva dripped from his fangs as he sized up his foe, and when he dropped into an attack-ready crouch, razor-sharp tips extended from claws as big as shovel heads.

"Activate Academy Rule Eight," came Rage's voice. "Retreat and regroup. Abort your mission! I'll be held responsible if anything happens to you, and I'm not prepared for you to sacrifice my career along with your own. ABORT NOW!"

The cocktail of anger and panic in her commander's voice told Flhi she had to act fast.

"Yell! Gloom! Do not engage the enemy. Pull back behind the walls and retreat to the exit portal. If I'm not there in ten seconds, make your own way to the precinct."

"What about you?" inquired Yell, his voice unusually quiet.

"I'll be there as soon as I've secured the area. Now go!"

The troopers didn't argue and slipped quickly behind the walls, out of harm's way. Flhi edged slowly away from Krot with every intention of following them.

"Where do you think you're going?" Krot growled. "I've been waitings a long time to capture a combat A.N.G.E.L. likes you. And if those things attached to your back are what I thinks they are, I'd says I've just captured an officer."

"Hands off, Señor Ugly, she's with me," barked Alannah, stepping suddenly between Krot and Flhi. "And if you don't cough up some treasure right now, I'll make you wish you'd never died."

Krot sniffed the air with an alpha predator's hunger. "Ah, so I did smells Fleshi blood after all. Looks like you chose the wrong night to come ghost huntings, little girl."

"And you should have stayed in your grave, specter," Alannah hissed defiantly.

"Let the Fleshi leave unharmed." Flhi moved forward,

her arms raised above her head. "And I'll surrender."

"No!" Rage yelled into her ear. "Don't be so stupid."

"I don't need your help," said Alannah.

"You saved my life earlier. Now I'm saving yours," Flhi explained, dropping her blaster to the floor and kicking it away. "This makes us even."

"How civilized," mocked Krot. "But aren't you forgettings something, A.N.G.E.L.?"

Flhi thought hard for a moment, but there had been nothing in her academy training about second-guessing a Gnarl.

"I don't plays by A.N.G.E.L. rules," he spat contemptuously. "And I don't wants an interfering little Fleshi to poke its nose into things that don't concerns it."

Krot opened his jaws wide and a howling wind erupted from deep within his chest. It was icy cold and as strong as a gale, and when it struck Alannah, it propelled the young ghost hunter backward and pinned her to the wallpaper, splashing her wild red hair across the wall.

The gust of foul air only stopped when Krot paused to refill his chest, allowing Alannah to slide slowly down the wall and onto the floor. She was dazed but unhurt. The impact had knocked the wind from her lungs and she was panting for breath, but she had no broken bones and she was still conscious. She was also very angry.

"Is that the best you can do?" Alannah snarled. "Low-grade apparitions attack harder than that."

She thrust her arms forward. Krot had no time to get out of the way as two huge balls of boiling energy slammed into him with the force of a water cannon. No ordinary spirit could survive such an assault, but Krot was no ordinary spirit. He was a master of the Dark Dimension's darkest powers. He knew spells and incantations that could repel even the pure power of a sentinel, and Alannah's most ferocious attack was little more than an irritant to him.

Alannah couldn't believe it. "How . . . ?"

Krot just laughed. "You can't hurts me, little girl. All that flesh absorbs your power like a sponge. I'll rids you of its burden so you can join me in spirit. Then I'll shows you how to really use your powers."

This time, Krot began to draw shadows from the darkest corners of the room, pulling each one toward him as though it was attached to an invisible string. He gathered them into a swirling cloud of hostile blackness that seemed almost alive. It was tugging and fighting, pulling against invisible restraints like an angry dog and, when Krot finally released his grip, the black cloud lurched violently toward Alannah.

It gripped her with the strength of a giant anaconda and she could feel her ribs beginning to buckle. Breathing was impossible, the blood slowed in her veins as her heart struggled to beat, and a heavy curtain began descending across her eyes. There had to be something she could do.

"Meditate!" Flhi knew Alannah had only one chance to escape. "Meditate and go astral. You have to leave your body."

Alannah closed her eyes, but not in meditation. Blood was no longer carrying oxygen to her brain and her body was rapidly shutting down. She was slipping into a coma.

Then suddenly she was free. The cloud squeezed so hard that she shot from the cumbersome restraints of her flesh and bones with the speed of an arrow. Krot's spell had somehow triggered a power in her that even she didn't know she had. Energy pulsed through her as though she was hooked up to the national grid. Seconds ago, the room had been a forest of darkened shapes, yet now it was bathed in a golden light that made even the shadows glow. And then Alannah realized where the light was coming from. Her! She was the light. Psychic energy seemed to pour through her and when she looked over at Krot she saw that the Gnarl was cowering from the glare.

"Burn him!" Flhi shouted. "Use your astral light to destroy him."

Astral light? Was that really what it was? Alannah didn't have a clue why she had it or even how to use it, but as she floated toward the Gnarl she could see why he hated it. The light was actually burning holes in his scaly ecto-shell. Krot's skin bubbled and steamed, ripping apart to create vents that spewed jets of spectral gas. He was slowly being destroyed.

The gamekeeper didn't stand a chance before Alannah's energy engulfed him. "Oh dear . . ." was all that the ghost managed to splutter before he spiraled down into the floor and vanished.

No Malevolent had any defense against astral light, and that included Krot. But how was the girl able to use it? Only sentinels could summon such powers, and even then it took them hours of concentrated meditation. Yet this girl seemed to be made of the stuff. All the Gnarl could do was retreat. And if he wanted to win this war he would have to seek out the one person on Earth with powers to match hers. He had to find Horrad.

Twenty-eight, twenty-seven, twenty-six . . . Wortley had finished counting to one hundred and was now counting backward to zero. If the room was still silent by the time he'd finished, he would think about taking a look around. Or maybe he'd count to a hundred again, just to make sure.

. . . *five, four, three, two, one, zero.*

He waited, listening hard. When he heard nothing, he lifted his head and peered out from behind the upturned table. What he saw made him wish he'd stayed hidden.

"Alannah!" he cried and began crawling toward her.

Alannah's skin was as pale as vanilla ice cream, and when Wortley touched her she was just as cold.

"Check for breathing, check for breathing," he muttered to himself, lowering his ear to her chest. "Come on, Alannah. Breathe!"

But she didn't. There was no trace of a heartbeat, either, but when he gingerly lifted her closed eyelids and gazed at her pupils he saw the tiniest flicker of light. His business partner wasn't dead. At least not yet.

"You're not leaving me here by myself, Alannah Malarra," Wortley suddenly raged. "You got us both into this mess and you can get us both out." Boiling with anger, he clenched his hands into fists and hammered them down onto his lifeless friend's chest. "Get up!" he ordered, striking Alannah's body again and again. "Get up!"

Every one of Wortley's frenzied blows landed just above her heart. At first they had no effect. But then he started to thump even harder and his punches actually began to pump the blood in and out of Alannah's vital organs. Something else happened, too. Each thump was sending sparks of Alannah's ebbing life force high into the air and when they floated back to Earth they showered across Wortley's arms. Pure astral energy was circulating between them.

Without warning, Alannah's spirit was tugged backward through the air. It felt as though a rope was fastened between her shoulder blades and someone had just pulled it. Then it happened again. And again. In fact, every time Wortley drove his fists down onto her body Alannah's soul was yanked backward.

"It's working," Flhi cheered. "Your cord is still attached."

"What cord?" Alannah's spirit twisted and turned like a shark on a fisherman's hook as she tried to catch sight of the cord.

"The one that connects your soul to your body! It's not been severed, which means you can still go back." Flhi watched as Wortley's punches began to reel in Alannah's spirit.

Alannah finally saw the cord. It was wire-thin and almost invisible, but when the light reflected against it at just the right angle it glinted brighter than a rainbow. It was beautiful.

"There's something you need to know," Flhi told Alannah as she was yanked backward to within inches of her body.

"What?"

"I think it's going to hurt."

Commander Rage paced the debriefing room with the
menace of a caged jaguar. Gargoyles and Ghouls were
running amok on the Earthly Dimension, his nemesis Krot was back, the Malevolents were meaner than
ever, and their close proximity to the Door of Souls was
clearly no coincidence. Something big was happening;
something bad! His warrior spirit told him to put an
elite strike force together and secure the manor house,
ASAP. But it wasn't that easy. There was a Gnarl on the
loose, a fierce Gnarl Rage knew only too well, and it
would take an eon of training to get even his best troopers ready for combat. His blood boiled with frustration.
He wanted to fight NOW!!

"Idiots!" Commander Rage made Yell's voice seem
like a squeak. His voice ricocheted off the thick glass
walls of his office. "What were you thinking?"

He looked down at Flhi with a glare of withering contempt. The task of protecting every single inhabitant of Evan City clearly weighed him down; in fact, most people assumed that his notorious bad temper was a product of stress. Unlike other A.N.G.E.L.s, Rage was never off duty and wore his huge white wings 24/7. Right now they were bristling angrily, and the commander's cheeks were so red that Flhi seriously thought his head was about to go up in flames.

"We neutralized an entire gang of rogues and almost apprehended our most wanted fugitive," Flhi pointed out. She sounded a lot braver than she felt. "And we discovered what had been causing the unusual readouts, which was the objective. Under the circumstances, I think we performed quite well. Sir."

Rage finally exploded.

"QUITE WELL? Do you think breaking the Third Vow and engaging with a Fleshi is doing quite well? Is being outthought and outfought by a human girl doing quite well? And I suppose having to rely on that same Fleshi to save your sorry plasma skin is also doing quite well?"

"That's not how it happened," Flhi responded.

"That's exactly how it happened, *In-spec-tor*. I've got your sensory logs to prove it. And I haven't even reached the bit where you ignore every single directive I've ever issued on dealing with Fugitive 1635. I'd say you racked up at least half a dozen court-martial offenses."

Flhi was doomed. There was nothing she could say or do to change Rage's opinion of her, and she knew it. He'd won. She'd lost. Inspector Flhi Swift was a thing of the past and she'd be lucky if she was allowed out on litter patrol this side of the next millennium. Then something happened that she didn't expect.

Gloom raised his hand.

"What do you want?" spat Rage.

"She saved our souls, sir," Gloom said miserably as if Flhi had done something terrible.

"She did what?"

"Inspector Swift saved us," repeated Gloom, this time with a little more conviction. "She covered our backs while we retreated to safety."

"She did everything an inspector should," Yell added loudly, backing up his colleague. "And more besides. So if you demote her, you'll have to demote us, too."

For a moment Rage looked confused. "I can't demote you two buffoons," he scoffed. "The rank of trooper is as low as you can go. Unless, of course, you're volunteering to be traffic wardens."

The two troopers looked at each other but said nothing. Secretly, Yell had always wanted to be a traffic warden. He loved the bright green ecto-suits they wore and thought their peaked hats were divine. It was certainly a lot less dangerous than being a combat A.N.G.E.L. Perhaps demotion didn't sound so bad.

Beside them, Flhi was almost bursting out of her combat suit with pride. Her team had just risked their own careers to defend her, and their display of loyalty brought a lump to her throat. If she got out of Rage's office with her wings intact, she would never doubt her two troopers again.

"In any other circumstances, I'd reward your loyalty," Rage seethed. "But on this occasion it's just another example of your poor decision making. As I expected, you've let me and my senior officers down. However, you've proved that you're a team so we'll punish you as a team. Hand over your combat badges. As from now, all three of you are suspended pending court-martial proceedings."

Flhi felt as if her soul had just been torn apart. She had expected Rage to take away her wings, even demote her. But her combat badge meant everything to her. It was her identity, her reason for being, and having it removed felt almost like losing a limb. It was then that she realized just how much her commander hated her. But she still didn't know why.

"Badges." Rage held out his hand impatiently. "Now!"

And he would have got them, too, if at that moment his office door hadn't swung open faster than a gate in a gale, slamming into his desk with a thunderous clatter as a burly spirit burst into the room.

"Wow! This must be the team of combat A.N.G.E.L.s who successfully tracked down Krot." The newcomer was grinning from ear to ear. "I hear reports that the mission was a great success. You must be a very proud man right now, Commander Rage. Very proud indeed."

Although Flhi had never met the potbellied spirit in person, she certainly recognized his face. Mayor Cheer was the only Evanescent in Evan City with a higher profile than Rage. There wasn't a day that passed when his face wasn't on the pathy-casts, and he usually attached himself to newsworthy stories like a barnacle to a boat.

Right now, Flhi Swift was big news, and Mayor Cheer wanted his face next to hers. Flhi and her team had just been reprieved.

Rage felt anger churning away inside him. There was nothing he'd have liked more than to grab the rotund politician by the scruff of his neck and hurl him out of the precinct with the rest of the departmental garbage. But Mayor Cheer called the shots; he was technically Rage's boss and never missed an opportunity to remind the precinct commander who was in charge. Barging into the office unannounced was the mayor's way of pulling rank, and all Rage could do was seethe in silence.

A sharp knock made everyone turn toward the open doorway. Pointing straight at them was the gaping lens of a huge pathy-camera. And above them, an overfed guinea pig appeared to be dangling from a long silver pole. It was the fluffy microphone belonging to a pathy-cast sound engineer and it was there to pick up every word the city's newest hero had to say.

The mayor had clearly been expecting them.

"Aah, at last! I thought you'd never get here. Inspector Swift, come over here. I want you on my left and Commander Rage on my right. Chop-chop, hurry up!" Cheer grabbed the two combat A.N.G.E.L.s by their elbows and dragged them into place. "These field crews cost a small fortune and the pathy-casters have promised me a lunchtime slot. It will give my election ratings a real boost, and that's got to be good for us all. Right, Commander Rage?"

Mayor Cheer was having fun. He loved being in front of the pathy-camera and knew how to spin a story. News of Krot's return had threatened to send his poll ratings crashing though the floor, but Flhi Swift was about to change all that. She was the city's hottest property; his team of PR spirits had guaranteed that. All he had to do now was show the citizens of Evan City that he was backing their hero and his ratings would soar through the roof. "I'll introduce our celebrity." He winked at Flhi before turning to her commander. "Then you can announce her promotion."

"Promotion?" Rage almost choked on the words.

"Of course. It's the least she deserves for flushing out Krot."

"But . . . she's only just become an inspector . . . and . . . she let him go. He's still at large."

The mayor disagreed. "Nonsense. As far as the public is concerned, the mission was a success—this pretty combat A.N.G.E.L. tackled Krot single-handed and defeated him. Next time she faces him, I'm sure he won't get away. Inspector Swift is a hero. Or perhaps I should say, Flieutenant Swift?"

"Never!"

"The public will expect it. Our heroes need rewarding."

Rage glared at Flhi and his eyes burned with murderous intent. "She's not a hero."

"Try telling that to the people of Evan City." The mayor put an arm around Flhi's shoulders and grinned. "Right now, she's the most high-profile combat A.N.G.E.L. we've got. Even more high-profile than you, Commander."

Rage froze. He knew the mayor had been looking for years for a way to retire him, but Rage's status as Krot's jailer had always made him untouchable. At least until now, because something in Cheer's voice made the commander realize things had changed.

Rage didn't like it one bit. Somehow he had to play the mayor at his own game, and to do that he had to think like a politician. That meant being sly, sneaky, and, on occasion, dishonest. Surprisingly, it all came rather naturally, and an insidious plan quickly began to unfold in his mind.

"Okay, she gets a promotion," Rage reluctantly agreed. "But it's only temporary."

Mayor Cheer looked at the commander suspiciously. "How temporary?"

"I have another special task for Inspector Swift. If she proves herself in the next twenty-four hours she'll become a real hero. And if she completes her next mission by this time tomorrow, it will be a pleasure to give her three white stripes."

Flhi gulped. An all-too-familiar feeling of dread wrapped itself around her. It was the same feeling she'd had when Rage explained her first mission. It was the feeling of a trap closing tightly around her.

"What kind of dog attacked you?" asked Marjorie Flint.

Wortley winced. The antiseptic burned his skin like a thousand bee stings but what really hurt was lying to his mother.

"A big one," he fibbed.

Alannah Malarra's live-in housekeeper stared at her son's largest wound. A freshly excavated canyon of open flesh traveled from the top of Wortley's thigh to the back of his knee. To her untrained eye, it looked as though her son had been wrestling with bears. And the bears had won.

"Where exactly were you when this big dog attacked you?"

Wortley was glad to be facedown on his bed. It meant his mother couldn't see his eyes. One look into them would uncover his deception.

"I was helping Alannah with her paper route."

"Hmmm, perhaps we should go into some other line of business," Marjorie mused. "Working for the Malarras seems to be getting a little too dangerous."

Horror welded Wortley to his bed. Did his mother actually know about last night? Or, worse still, had she discovered the truth about Alannah's business dealings?

Wortley had always wondered how much his mother knew. Marjorie Flint had been employed by the Malarras for longer than even she cared to remember. While Ben and Sadie had dashed around the country doing their "psychic thing," Marjorie spent her time vacuuming the carpets, dusting the shelves, cooking meals, and generally keeping the Malarra household running like clockwork. She'd answered the phones, too, sorted through the sacks of mail that arrived most weeks, and dealt with all manner of weird and unusual inquiries — mostly about ghosts. In fact, there wasn't much about the Malarras' lives that she hadn't known about. Did she know what Alannah really got up to, too?

Of course not. What was Wortley thinking? His mother would never spy on Alannah. Although it wouldn't be too difficult. All Marjorie would have had to do was pick the lock to her employer's study, where a few deft keystrokes on Alannah's precious laptop would reveal everything: dates, times, locations, fees, transactions, bank accounts, et cetera. It was all stored on the computer's hard drive, and on a few of those memory-stick gadgets that Alannah was so fond of leaving scattered across her dressing table. Wortley made a quick mental note about mentioning a security upgrade to Alannah.

"We could buy a little shop in a quiet village somewhere safe," muttered Marjorie. "I've been saving up."

"What about Alannah?" Wortley asked. The Flints were the closest thing Alannah had to a family. They all shared the same house, so what would she do if they abandoned her? There wasn't an orphanage in England that could cope with Alannah Malarra. And she'd go through foster parents at a frightening rate.

"What about me?" Alannah asked as she stepped through the open doorway into Wortley's small bedroom.

"Nothing, dear," Marjorie replied a little too quickly. "We were just . . ."

"I was just . . ." Wortley tried to help his mother.

"We were only . . . ," they said simultaneously.

"Oh, never mind," Alannah barked impatiently. "I'm not really interested anyway. I'm only here to remind Wortley that we have a physics lecture scheduled for ten thirty this morning. It's a satellite link with an eminent professor in Melbourne, and it's in my study."

She gave her business partner a knowing look. "Don't be late."

"I wish you two would go to normal school like other children," moaned Marjorie. She gently wrapped several layers of gauze around her son's injured leg. "You'd make so many new friends. And it might keep you both out of trouble."

"What can I learn at school that I can't learn online?" Alannah asked.

"People skills," Marjorie suggested quietly.

Wortley rolled off his bed with all the grace of an injured seal. He hated it when Alannah and his mother argued. There was only one way to stop them bickering.

"Come on, Alannah," he said, grabbing his friend's wrist as he limped gingerly out of the bedroom. "We don't want to keep the professor waiting, do we?"

Only when they were a safe distance from his bedroom did Wortley turn to his friend and whisper, "There is no physics lecture from Melbourne, is there?"

"Of course there isn't. We don't even study physics."

"So what's with all the urgency?"

Alannah stopped in her tracks and fixed her business partner with a look that could have melted steel. "After last night, you have to ask?"

"Oh, that," Wortley groaned. "I was hoping we could forget about last night."

"You want me to forget about the single most important event in my life so far? Last night changes everything for both of us. Forever!"

Why couldn't Alannah be happy to have escaped with her life? After a brush with death, most ordinary twelve-year-old girls would lock themselves away in their bedrooms for a month, Tweeting with friends, chatting on Facebook, and generally hiding away online. But Alannah Malarra wasn't ordinary.

"We've got unfinished business," she buzzed excitedly. "Just imagine the hoard of treasure that needs a whole gang of spirits to guard it."

"From what you told me, we walked in on a battle scene, not a treasure hunt," Wortley pointed out. "Perhaps we should leave them to it."

"Don't be naive, Wortley. If spirits and ghouls are fighting over it, the treasure must be priceless. This is the big one. I know it. Do this and we'll be set for life. We can retire!"

At last, Alannah had Wortley's full attention.

If they looked really carefully, anyone passing the row of well-kept Georgian town houses on Mahoney Terrace might have seen something that resembled a small patch of heat haze shimmering above the chimney of number 17. If they stopped on the pavement and stared at it for a few minutes, they might have even seen it move. But of course, nobody did. Fleshies were always far too busy to spot A.N.G.E.L.s at work.

"Do we really have to do this?" groaned Gloom as he

and Yell tottered like trainee tightrope walkers on the apex of the roof. "I have a really bad feeling."

"Focus on the mission, trooper," Flhi ordered sternly as she hovered beside them. "Get this wrong and we'll be issuing parking tickets for the rest of eternity."

She unfolded a plasma map and all three Evanescents studied it carefully. It showed an aerial view of Mahoney Terrace.

"Recon said the Fleshi girl lives in here." Flhi touched the map with her finger. Moments later, the view changed and a blueprint of number 17 replaced the row of houses.

"Oh, I love it when that happens," gushed Yell. "Those tech guys at recon are so clever."

"Time logs indicate she spends most of her day right here." Flhi prodded the room marked STUDY, and the plasma view rippled into a three-dimensional plan of the room. "I'll drop onto the ceiling. Yell, you get into position behind the wall on the right. Gloom, you cover the left. Don't move until you receive my command. Is that clear?"

The two troopers nodded nervously. The scars were still fresh from last night's encounter and they didn't relish the prospect of tangling with the Fleshi girl again. Right now, issuing parking tickets until the end of time seemed pretty appealing.

Although she'd never admit it to her troops, Flhi Swift

was every bit as apprehensive. She doubted there'd be any way even Mayor Cheer could save her career on this occasion. After all, no A.N.G.E.L. had ever apprehended a live Fleshi, yet that was what Commander Rage now expected her to do. And instead of a platoon of heavily armed sentinels backing her up, she had the help of Yell and Gloom. Hardly the firepower needed to overwhelm an alpha psychic like Alannah Malarra.

Fortunately, Flhi had a backup plan. She tapped her left hip pocket and felt a reassuring bulge through her ecto-suit. The astral net was still there. It had been decommissioned as a weapon shortly after a Gnarl bust several eons earlier and had been gathering dust in the precinct's impound warehouse ever since. Even the commander had forgotten it was there. But Flhi had spotted it during her induction and knew it would come in handy one day. Now, moments after leaving Rage's office, she had managed with a little bit of sweet talk and some fluttering of her long silver eyelashes to sneak it past the bored sergeant on the desk.

Having it meant that she could also add "possessing a contraband weapon" to her disciplinary rap sheet, but she didn't care. If using the astral net helped her bag the Fleshi girl, she'd return to Evan City a real hero — and she'd remain a flieutenant. Otherwise, her career was over anyway. She had nothing to lose.

"Okay boys, follow me." Flhi slowed her wings by just

a few beats a second but the effect was instantaneous. She dropped like a sycamore seed, corkscrewing down through the roof of the house in slow, tight spins.

The two combat A.N.G.E.L.s tugged on their flying strings and dropped through the roof like veteran bungee jumpers.

Flhi was first into position. She hovered facedown between the wooden joists of the first-floor ceiling, and when she was sure Yell and Gloom had reached their positions, she slowly lowered herself so that her nose nearly touched the plastered wooden surface below. There she listened carefully for sounds in the study beneath. Only when she heard nothing did she dip her face through the solid ceiling.

Her small nose popped through first, closely followed by a pair of bright turquoise eyes, which quickly surveyed the room. She had been right: The study was empty. But a steaming mug of hot chocolate and a whirring computer system told her its occupant wasn't long gone and would be back soon.

Flhi could see that this Fleshi room was an Aladdin's cave of technology and gadgets. In addition to the latest high-tech computer system and games console, an ultra-slim laptop was opened wide on the desk, quietly crunching its way through a database of numbers. Opposite the door, mounted on the wall, were four huge plasma televisions. The sound was muted on each but the bright screens were alive with images from the Discovery Channel, the National Geographic Channel, the History Channel, and CNN. An insurance claim for the roomful of technology would have run into five figures. Yet that was small change compared with the value of the room's antiques.

Flhi was wondering where it could all have come from when the door to the room burst open. Quickly, she pulled her face back up into the ceiling, leaving only two sparkling eyes visible through the plaster. She half closed her eyelids to stop them from shining. It was important that she retained the element of surprise.

"We have to get back there," said Alannah as she stared at a History Channel show about the Egyptian pyramids.

"I thought you hated Cairo?" Wortley asked.

"Not Egypt. I'm talking about the old manor house. We need to get back in there. Tonight."

"We can't," said Wortley, a little too cheerily. "I'm all out of horse tranquilizer."

"I know a zoo vet in London who owes me a favor. I let him have that lost Shakespeare poem on an eBay 'best offer.' I bet I could have got at least another five hundred for it. That's got to be worth a few shots of elephant sedative. I'll have him bike it up this evening."

Wortley groaned. "Horse tranquilizers didn't work the first time," he pointed out. "Who's to say elephant sedatives would work any better? Nope, count me out."

Alannah whirled around to glare at her business partner. "This is the big one. Everything we've ever done has led to this opportunity and you decide to go chicken all because of a few little scratches on your leg. I can't believe you're going to let me down."

"I saved your life, remember?" Wortley reproached his friend. "Isn't that worth a few days off?"

Alannah sighed, shook her head, and turned away. She was hard on him at times, she knew that, but it was only to bring the best out of him. He was just so good at what he did, and although she often hated to admit it, Alannah needed him, which is exactly why she always kept a box full of Gobstoppers tucked away in her desk drawer. Wortley couldn't resist them, often tucking two into his mouth at once, so that both his cheeks puffed out like a squirrel's. At times like this, when her friend was being as stubborn as a mule stuck in superglue, Alannah would resort to bribery.

She slid open the desk drawer, flipped the lid of a cardboard box, and stuck her hand deep inside, grabbing a handful of . . . nothing! The box was empty. Even after dragging it out of the drawer, tipping it upside down, and shaking it violently, the box was still empty. Somebody had stolen every last Everlasting Gobstopper, and the thief was still in the room.

Wortley looked sheepish.

"You took them all?" Alannah asked.

Wortley nodded.

"Aarrgghh!" Alannah screamed.

How was she going to persuade Wortley to help her now? Desperate for ideas, she gazed up into the corner of the ceiling hoping to find some inspiration, only to discover that she was staring straight into the brightest pair of eyes she'd ever seen. Turquoise eyes.

Alannah smiled. The strange entities were back. Only this time, she was their prey. Usually, she was the hunter, and now that the roles had been reversed she felt as excited as a toddler on Christmas morning.

"You might want to leave the room," Alannah whispered sharply to Wortley. "We're not alone."

The young burglar tensed immediately. He had heard Alannah's curt tone many times before and nothing good had ever followed. "Ghosts?" he asked. "Here?"

Alannah nodded. "The weird ones from last night: at least one, probably more. Just act normal. Head for the door as if nothing's wrong. I'll be out in a few minutes."

Wortley wasn't so sure. If the ghosts were pursuing them, that changed everything. The inside of his mouth dried to the texture of dehydrated mammoth hide and he suddenly felt very scared.

Alannah couldn't remember the last time she'd felt fear. Even the night before, when the huge scary specter had overpowered her, the young ghost hunter had felt only a grudging respect. But she'd also been left with a feeling of unfinished business and as she stared up at the two brightly colored eyes, Alannah realized their owner could probably help her resolve that particular issue.

Blast it! Flhi had lost the element of surprise. She needed to take the initiative. What could she do? There had to be something. These were children, not soldiers.

Bingo! The boy! He was frozen to the spot. His arms were shaking, his legs trembled like two saplings in an earthquake, and his face was flushed the color of a beet. Clearly, he was having some kind of panic attack.

The psychic's sidekick was vulnerable, and Flhi knew to target an opponent's weakness. All she needed was a few extra seconds.

"Yell. Gloom. Are you ready?"

"Well, seeing as you're asking, I always thought I could have done with a few extra eons of academy training," Gloom mumbled miserably. "But if you're asking if we're ready to execute our mission, then I suppose we are. It'll probably all end in tears, though."

Flhi made a mental note to register Gloom for the department's next seminar on Positive Thinking.

"The mission's changed. Ignore the psychic and focus on the boy. Use a pincer movement and douse him in quick-drying ectoplasm."

"What about the girl?" shrieked Yell.

"Just do your best to distract her," Flhi said calmly. "I've got something special up my sleeve."

The two troopers had been well hidden. One emerged quickly from behind a heavy oak bookcase, and the other seemed to leap out of a plasma TV screen. Neat trick! Alannah quickly fired up her fingertips and prepared to defend herself. Aiming a hand at each intruder, she waited for the first attack. But it was as if she didn't exist. By the time she realized what they were doing, it was too late.

"Wortley! Get out of here!"

Wortley never heard Alannah's desperate warning. With the first blast of ectoplasm, thick sticky gunk coated his skin completely, filling his ears and blocking out any sound. Within moments his head was encased inside a solid ball, and a rock-hard cocoon covered his body. Wortley toppled heavily to the ground.

Alannah was shocked. She'd been unable to defend her friend and now he was wrapped up tighter than an Egyptian mummy. Worse still, she was next.

The astral net was livelier than a freshly landed sword-fish. Flhi almost dropped it twice as she pulled it from her pocket and she struggled to hold it still. These weapons were manufactured to order by teams of specially trained sentinel scientists. Each one was uniquely woven from exactly a thousand enchanted ecto-strands. The model Flhi held was a single-entity version and part of a batch that had been developed specifically for sucking the souls out of Gnarls. They had all been recalled several eons ago following an unfortunate incident at an Evan City school, but the only child at risk right now was the alpha psychic shooting astral flares at her troopers.

Trying to anticipate the attackers' next moves, Alannah fanned her fingertips and fired a volley of arrows across the room. Ten streaks of fiery white light arched across her study, but the spirits were one step ahead of her again and her shots exploded against priceless canvases hanging on the walls. She'd need the services of a good restorer to get rid of the scorch marks. Her patience was exhausted. It was time to put these intruders in their place.

Spinning with a dancer's poise, she turned to face the spirits again. Only this time she didn't fire. She raised her hands toward the ceiling instead and concentrated her energies onto the center of her palms. At last, she was learning how to control her powers.

Two swirling globes of light appeared on each hand, growing larger and more menacing by the second. The two entities in front of her suddenly looked worried.

"Oh, don't fret, boys," Alannah growled icily. "I wouldn't waste these on you two." Her eyes darted up toward the corner of the room for less than half a second before she catapulted the first of her bombs up at the ceiling. "They're for her!"

The psychic's glance had given Flhi just enough time to get out of the way. She felt heat from the blast scorch the soles of her feet as her wings carried her to safety with barely a millisecond to spare. The second blast was close enough to singe her eyebrows.

The astral net sensed the urgency and Flhi realized it was time to act.

Cleverly, the sentinels had devised a mini containment unit that held the net at bay like a tiny force field while feeding off the net's own power. The more the device struggled to break free the stronger the force field became.

Only an authorized combat A.N.G.E.L. could release it, and to do that required a secret six-note musical code known only by the most trusted senior officers. Or any inspector smart enough to hack into the Evan City mainframe and use her commanding officer's access privileges to download the codes.

Evanescents adore music. Harps, flutes, bagpipes, you

name it, they play it. And combat A.N.G.E.L.s are no different. That's why the first piece of equipment issued to an academy recruit is a solid silver piccolo, which is used to communicate during field-training drills whenever telepathy is blocked, to open code-locked doors, or enter code-protected zones. So a good combat A.N.G.E.L. never goes anywhere without one. Flhi Swift was no exception, and she whipped her piccolo out of her pocket and blew air into it, the digits of both hands dancing across the instrument's tiny keys. The result was a beautiful six-note tune that Flhi played over and over again. On the fifth rendition the containment unit switched off and the astral net emerged with the grace of a stretching manta ray. Now Flhi would find out just how powerful the Fleshi girl really was.

What is this thing? Alannah thought as the astral net chased her relentlessly. Wherever she moved, it followed her, bouncing itself off the walls and ceiling to block her escape. Alannah quickly realized that there was no getting away from it. She was trapped.

"You can surrender whenever you want," a familiar voice called from above the ceiling. "We're not here to hurt you."

"You're the one who should be concerned about getting hurt!" jeered Alannah, firing a fistful of arrows in the direction of Flhi.

As though it had read Alannah's mind, the spinning

disk flipped like a tossed coin to intercept the blasts, absorbing their energy and snuffing out the attack.

Alannah stared closely at the spinning disk, studying it intently. With its flexible lines of interwoven light strands it did indeed look like a net, yet she doubted it was used for catching fish. This weapon was incredibly sophisticated and way out of her league.

"Call it off, or I'll destroy it." She was trying to sound confident, but it was a bluff.

Flhi smiled and descended until she was hovering just behind the net. "Brave words, little girl, but this is an astral net created by the sentinels to be indestructible. It'll simply feed off your energy and become stronger. But feel free to attack it if you really want to."

Astral nets. Sentinels. Who was this silver-haired spirit, and where did she come from? More important, what did she want from a twelve-year-old girl? Alannah mustered the courage to ask the question.

"Who are you, and what do you want?"

Flhi didn't like questions. Questions brought complications.

"I asked you who you are." Alannah released a fiery streak from her fingertip. This time, the net caught only some of the sparks and Flhi began to doubt its power. It might be the ultimate weapon against Malevolents, but this human was a threat of a different order. Perhaps she could just disclose their identity, and nothing more.

"We're combat A.N.G.E.L.s," she explained. "From the Higher Dimension."

Alannah looked surprised. "Angels? From . . ." She pointed toward the ceiling.

"No, definitely not those kind of angels."

The little Evanescent sighed; this was getting awkward, and dangerous, too. Dark Dimension folklore was littered with references to supernatural beings called angels, and Fleshies had been known to flock to places where these angels were thought to exist. Evans, if the young girl got the wrong idea it could lead to pandemonium.

"We're Evanescent soldiers," Flhi went on. "Part of the Attack-ready Network of Global Evanescent Law-enforcers. A.N.G.E.L.s, get it?"

Alannah attempted to decode the acronym, but lost patience and gave up after a few seconds. What had the little creature called itself? An Evanescent. Hmm, that seemed to make some sense. After all, they were practically invisible to most people. Alannah guessed that she could only see them because she was psychic.

"We protect our world against Ghouls, Gargoyles, and Gnarls," Flhi explained.

"Gnarls?" asked Alannah.

"That's the big creature with fangs that almost killed us both last night," Flhi said. "By the way, next time leave it alone. Or better still, run for your life."

"I'm doing nothing and going nowhere until you tell me what you want." Alannah sent a burst of astral light rippling across her fingertips, just to show she meant business.

Blast it! The Fleshi was giving Flhi no choice. She was going to have to break yet another A.N.G.E.L. Academy rule: Never reveal your mission.

There were eight rules hand-engraved into the solid gold walls surrounding the academy's vast and ancient atrium. Flhi could recite each one, word for word:

1. AIM FOR THE LARGEST TARGET — IT'S USUALLY THE MOST DANGEROUS.
2. YOU CAN BE OUTNUMBERED, BUT YOU SHOULD NOT BE OUTTHOUGHT.
3. NEVER REVEAL YOUR MISSION. EVER!
4. IF YOUR ENEMY CALLS SOMEWHERE HOME, MAKE IT YOUR HOME, TOO.
5. ALWAYS KEEP YOUR ECTO-BLASTER FULLY CHARGED.
6. STAY EVANESCENT. YOUR ENEMY CAN'T HURT WHAT IT CAN'T SEE.
7. TRUST IN YOUR TROOPERS — THERE'S NO "U" IN "TEAM."
8. IF ALL ELSE FAILS, RETREAT AND REGROUP.

Tutors revered them, students promised to respect and obey them, and everyone who had ever passed through the great doors of the A.N.G.E.L. Academy knew that to break a rule was as close to an act of treason as an Evanescent could ever get. Flhi had already broken Rule Eight, and now she was about to break another.

"I've been sent for you," she told Alannah.

Yell and Gloom both gasped in horror. Rule Three was the worst rule to break.

"By whom?" asked Alannah.

"A higher authority."

"You mean . . . ?" Alannah again pointed to the ceiling.

"Don't be silly," Flhi scoffed. "I've told you, we're not those kind of angels."

"And what if I refuse?" Alannah wiggled her glowing fingertips. The astral net acknowledged Alannah's aggression and hovered even closer, flexing menacingly. But it seemed to sense her powers and kept a safe distance.

"I'm afraid refusal isn't an option," Flhi said. "If you don't give us your full cooperation, you'll be taken by force."

That sounded a little too much like kidnapping, and Alannah wasn't about to play the happy victim to a trio of overzealous upstart entities — even if they were the smartest she'd ever encountered. She had to escape and that meant figuring out a way past that net, fast!

Flhi could see that her attempts to negotiate had fallen on deaf ears. The Fleshi girl was smart, had no intention of coming quietly, and was probably scheming right now, thinking of ways to give her the slip. Rage and Mayor Cheer both knew that even short inter-dimensional out-of-body trips could be dangerous, especially for Fleshies, so they probably wouldn't keep her in the Higher Dimension for long. But the girl didn't know that, and she was unlikely to believe any of Flhi's assurances. Things were about to get very nasty.

Bingo! An idea popped into Alannah's head. If she could just turn the astral net against the A.N.G.E.L., she might gain the upper hand. Now all she had to do was figure out a way to do it. Surely, that wouldn't be too difficult.

Alannah fired an arrow at each of the A.N.G.E.L.s. The astral net responded quickly, spinning like a turbo-boosted acrobat to intercept and absorb the first two arrows. But the third dart knocked Gloom off his feet.

He landed on the floor like a heap of dirty laundry. Dazed and disorientated, the trooper climbed to his feet and desperately tried to remember where he was. His head felt thick. Nothing looked familiar, and he was beginning to wonder whether Yell had taken him to yet another backstreet spirit bar when someone took hold of his ecto suit and hauled him into the air.

Alannah heard the buzz of the astral net only inches away. It sounded angry; was that possible? She whirled to face it, holding the stunned A.N.G.E.L. in front of her as a shield. The net recoiled and twisted away across the room, where it circled, waiting for an opportunity to strike. Alannah's hunch had been correct; it had clearly been programmed not to attack friendly spirits, and now all she had to do was hide behind the dazed spirit hanging from her left hand. At least, that's all she *thought* she had to do.

"A.N.G.E.L. down! A.N.G.E.L. down!" screamed Flhi as she raced into action. She knew Gloom was safe from the net, but she had no idea what the psychic might do to her captured trooper. This girl was a loose cannon.

"Cover me, Yell. I'm engaging the girl."

Yell wasn't sure what "cover me" meant and stood rooted to the spot as his commanding officer switched her wings to "combat ready." Immediately, they doubled in size, swelling across the back of her slender shoulders so Flhi could use them as weapons to beat the Fleshi girl around the head with as she tried to pull Gloom free.

Yell was watching the strangest tug-of-war competition he had ever seen, with his best friend being used as the rope. He had to do something. Taking a deep breath, he closed his eyes and blindly propelled himself across the room toward his commanding officer. Flhi wasn't going to like this, but what choice did he have? The trooper had to save his friend.

Yell slipped his hands around Flhi's waist, and his fingers gripped tight.

"At last," Flhi gasped. "Now pull on me as hard as you can. We've got to get Gloom away from this crazy Fleshi girl."

But Yell didn't pull. Instead, he dug his fingers into Flhi's waist even harder and gave them a wiggle. Flhi bucked and twisted as though Yell's fingers were charged with electricity.

"Not so hard," she squealed. "That tickles. Get off me, Yell. Get — oo — off!"

But this was all part of Yell's plan. The more Flhi struggled, the more he tickled. Until his commanding officer could stand it no longer and let go of Gloom.

As soon as Flhi released her grip, she was sent flying across the room. Yell was still holding on to her and they both jetted backward, only stopping when they crashed heavily against a solid wooden door frame.

Alannah and Gloom sprang away from them in the opposite direction, tumbling across the room. They were heading for the double-paned window at the far end and would have crashed straight through it had it not been for Wortley. He was directly in their path, and his cocoon of solid ectoplasm acted like a wall, stopping Alannah in her tracks. Gloom wasn't so lucky. He slipped from Alannah's grip and spun headfirst into the bank of screens on the wall. He'd always wanted to be on television, but that wasn't quite what he'd had in mind.

The net was on Alannah and Wortley in a flash, wrapping itself around them like an octopus and scooping one of the Fleshi souls into its unbreakable netted strands. It formed itself into a tightly sealed sack and bounced clear of its victim, leaving behind an empty body. Having paused for just a moment, as if to gloat, it then disappeared into a swirling gateway that had appeared to its right.

Flhi, Gloom, and Yell were powerless to resist the force. The homing portal had been automatically triggered as soon as the astral net had completed its mission, and now it sucked the three combat A.N.G.E.L.s back into their own dimension with the force of a mini black hole.

Flhi was last through, pulled feetfirst as the portal snapped shut around her. The final thing anyone would have seen was a flash of turquoise and the hint of a wide smile that said "mission accomplished."

Back in the old manor house, the automated Evanescent cleanup crew had already been and gone. Piles of valuable books had been restacked. Scorch marks had been expertly removed from the antique furniture. Even the carpets had been cleaned. To the untrained eye, the house looked remarkably unscathed. However, Klaut Horrad's eye was anything but untrained. The Hungarian psychic could clearly see the splatters of ectoplasm lingering in corners like bloodstains at a crime scene. Blast burns reached from one end of the ceiling to the other. And the acrid smell of recently melted plasma suits told him he was standing in the middle of a battle zone, one where a battalion of his best troops had suffered a painful defeat. Could a girl really be responsible for all this?

"Look! Right here, young man, this proves it!"

At fifty-two years of age, Horrad could hardly be called young. His pale, saggy skin made him look at least ten years older, and he moved with the labored gait of an arthritic retiree. But he appeared sprightly compared with the stooped and wizened old man who stood before him, jabbing a withered finger toward a teetering pile of books.

"Books?" Horrad said curiously.

"Yes, but look at them," the old man said angrily. "They're upside down."

"Ah, upside-down books. Now why didn't I spot that?"

The earl fixed Horrad with a stare that could have stripped varnish from wood. "Don't patronize me, Mr. Horrad. I might be eighty-seven years old, but my mind is still as sharp as a butcher's knife. This might look like an untidy mess to you, but each pile of books is carefully indexed and catalogued. Look closely and you'll see order."

Horrad meekly followed the earl as he slowly moved from one pile to the next.

"Sir Walter Raleigh's trading ledgers: originals, not copies. Captain Cook's sailing diaries: forgeries, I'm afraid. Wellington's wartime journals: not sure if they're the real thing. Father swore blind they were, but carbon dating has proved rather inconclusive. Strange, wouldn't you say?"

Horrad nodded, feigning interest and wondering where the earl's musings were leading.

"Take a close look and you'll see that the lettering on the spines all points downward. That's so that I can read them without cricking my neck. Now look again at the first pile I showed you."

The old man was right. When Horrad looked at the faded gold lettering, he found the words were upside down. And this was the only pile of books arranged in such a way.

"Ghosts!" the earl suddenly yelled.

"Where?" gasped Horrad.

"Here, you fool. Who else could be responsible? It's bloomin' ghosts, I'm telling you."

Decades of searching had finally led Horrad to the site of Pittingham Manor. Clues hidden deep within ancient medieval scrolls and decaying tomes from the Dark Ages described a location just like this one. Scores of ley lines all converged on this very spot and the area fizzed with psychic activity. There was nowhere on Earth quite like it, and Horrad was now certain that he had finally found the enchanted vortex. The Door of Souls was here.

Horrad hadn't expected Krot to fail. Running into a team of Evanescent combat troopers was an unfortunate coincidence, but one with which the Gnarl was more than capable of dealing. However, encountering a psychic youngster was another thing entirely. That changed everything.

"Tell me about the girl," Horrad said soothingly, his gentle tones working a form of hypnotic magic.

"The ghost hunter?" asked the earl dreamily.

Horrad nodded, increasing the strength of his hypnosis. "What's her name?"

"Alannah, I think."

Alarm bells instantly rang in Horrad's head. Surely not!

"Alannah Malarra?" he inquired timidly.

"Yes, that's her! Alannah Malarra. Found her on *goawayghosts.com*. Her name's got quite a nice ring to it, don't you think? Alannah Malarra, Alannah Malarra, Alannah Mal—"

"Quiet!" Horrad ordered, and the earl's lips were instantly sealed.

Malarra! Horrad knew that surname all too well. Ben and Sadie Malarra had been two of the most decorated ghost hunters of modern times. Warm, charming, and with made-for-TV good looks, they had seemed ideally cast to represent the psychic community to the public. As the glamour couple of the Ancient Order of Psychics, they were also poised to replace Klaut Horrad as Chief Ghost Hunter, when, just a few days before the AOP Elections, Ben and Sadie surprised everyone by answering a distress call. It came from a Scottish baron who claimed his castle was being overrun by ghosts. The Malarras vanished into thin air the following day, and the baron proved impossible to trace. In their absence Horrad retained the high office.

There'd been a police investigation and a more extensive inquiry by the AOP. Horrad told both that he knew nothing about the Malarras' mysterious disappearance and he'd been cleared of any involvement. People were suspicious, of course, but Horrad had grown more and more powerful, ruling the psychic circle with an iron fist and squashing anyone who dared to oppose him — not that many did.

Scores of once-prominent psychics quit the AOP in protest and left Britain to form the rival Psychic Council of Elders. Others were banished, or expressly forbidden from using their ghost-hunting powers, leaving Horrad's loyal supporters free to manage what was left of the Order. And that was just how Horrad liked it.

"Malarra," he growled. "I hate that name. It sounds so . . . feeble."

So, Ben and Sadie's child was psychic. Perhaps he should have expected it. After all, a union between two of Earth's most powerful ghost hunters was hardly likely to produce a descendant without abilities. But psychic skills were usually suppressed until adolescence and Horrad hadn't seen the young Alannah as a threat — at least not for the next few years. In fact, Horrad had quickly forgotten that the Malarras' child even existed. He now recognized that had been an uncharacteristic mistake. But how could he have known? Even by psychic standards, Alannah was a quick developer, with powers that were already incredibly advanced, and that was unheard of. It was also rather worrisome.

"Where can I find this girl?" Horrad asked.

The earl shook his head. "All I have is an email address."

"Fine." Horrad rubbed his hands together with glee. "Let's send little Miss Malarra an email, shall we?"

11

Flhi Swift dropped through the homing portal and landed heavily on the cold slate floor of Evan City precinct's impound warehouse. A minor sonic boom echoed off the walls as the portal snapped shut behind her and then the warehouse fell silent. Very silent.

She gingerly opened her eyelids. At first she could see nothing. The warehouse was rarely used and the backlighting had been switched off after the last round of departmental budget cuts. Flhi's eyes took a few seconds to adjust before objects began to take shape. Metal racks filled with seized goods climbed toward the ceiling. Stacked pallets were piled closer together than New York skyscrapers, and the hydraulic trolleys that were used to load and unload the racks sat in the shadows like petrified trolls.

On the floor, just a few feet from her, lay three

motionless figures. Flhi recognized two of them. Gloom and Yell were slumped in the exact spot where they had dropped out of the homing portal. In typical fashion they'd landed on their heads, which probably explained why they were still unconscious. They were both snoring more softly than snoozing babies and were clearly unhurt. Flhi hoped she could say the same about the third figure.

Still wrapped tightly inside the astral net, the captured soul was unable to move. Its breathing was short and erratic, suggesting it was conscious and scared. Flhi's academy training reminded her that those two attributes alone gave it a field ranking of "highly dangerous." The fact that it also possessed psychic powers blew its status right off the scale.

Flhi's wings twitched nervously as she pondered her next move. In theory it was simple: Deliver the prisoner to Commander Rage and it was mission accomplished. She'd collect her promotion, he'd claim the glory for himself, and they'd all live happily ever after. Only there was one itty-bitty thing standing in her way: the astral net.

She was in enough trouble already and knew she had to return the weapon to its secure vault before anyone noticed it was missing. But that would mean taking the restraints off her prisoner first, and Flhi had already witnessed the psychic's incredible power. If the girl could melt holes in a Gnarl like Krot, what would she do to an inexperienced A.N.G.E.L. like herself? Flhi was trying hard not to think about the answer when the inside of the warehouse exploded into a fireball of searing light.

Flhi fell to the floor clutching her hands to her face. The explosion had almost scorched her eyeballs and she gasped in agony. She was paralyzed. There was nothing she could do, even when she heard the rapid click of approaching footsteps and realized she was under attack. The stun grenade had done its job. Flhi was helpless.

"Grab her," barked a gruff voice she recognized instantly. "And put the cuffs on tight. Don't be fooled by the uniform; this one's unauthorized."

Unauthorized? When did that happen?

Flhi's arms were roughly tugged behind her back and the sting of cold steel tightened around both wrists. Strong hands hauled her to her feet.

"I was following your orders, Commander," she pointed out. "I apprehended the target and returned it to Evan City precinct. Just as instructed, sir."

"Did I instruct you to hack into the precinct's mainframe? Did I instruct you to download my personal access codes?" Rage's voice grew louder with each question. "Perhaps I instructed you to steal a decommissioned weapon, recklessly discharge that weapon in the

Earthly Dimension, and . . . oh yes . . . break the Third Rule of the A.N.G.E.L. Academy? That's a full house, Swift. You're finished!"

Flhi's best option was to remain silent. But when did Flhi Swift ever do what was sensible?

"You never actually instructed me not to."

"Technically, she could be right, sir," snickered the A.N.G.E.L. whose handcuffs were currently cutting off the plasma flow to Flhi's hands.

"One more word from you, Sergeant Stickler, and you'll be scanning tomorrow's 'Help Wanted' ads with *Inspector* Swift." The commander's eyes narrowed as he dared Flhi to challenge her sudden demotion from flieutenant.

"Actually, sir, I think you'll find there's a proper disciplinary process to go through before you can dismiss a trooper from the force," Stickler foolishly pointed out. "As the precinct's newly elected union representative, I think it's my duty to—"

"SHUUUUUT! UUUUP!"

A torrent of spittle spurted from Rage's mouth as he predictably erupted with anger. His roar echoed around the walls of the warehouse.

Then something happened that made Flhi realize she was in serious, serious trouble. She heard the unmistakable sound of a blaster being unholstered and the familiar whir of power that told her the safety catch was no longer on. All she could do was brace herself and hope the weapon was set to shock her, not send her to the Dark Dimension.

"How about you, In-spec-tor? Got any more big-mouth comments to make before I file your court-martial?"

Adrenaline had dulled the pain in Flhi's eyes just enough to let her tentatively raise her eyelids.

Rage pointed the twin barrels of his weapon straight at her. He really wanted to shoot. Flhi Swift was dangerous, and he had good reason to fear her. She had discovered his deepest and darkest secret. And it was a secret that could destroy him.

The information was buried deep within the pages of Flhi's final-year thesis. As Academy commander in chief, it was Rage's job to read all the fourth-year students' theses and award the final grades. He had the power to decide which students passed and which failed.

Flhi Swift could outshoot, outfly, and outwit every one of her fellow students with ease. The academy had had high hopes for her, and so had Rage. At least he had until the moment he'd read her thesis.

Flhi's work was worth an A-plus at least, and concentrated on the final throes of the last Great Spirit War. Its main focus was the commander's heroic and victorious battle with the Gnarl leader Krot. Even Rage had to admit that it was probably the definitive account of his finest hour, since it was his victory that had won the war for the Evanescents and made him a hero. No, more than that, a legend. But Flhi's work had been *too* good. Her research had been *too* thorough. And her conclusions had been *too* accurate. Somehow, she had rightly guessed that Rage had used more than his ecto-blaster and quick wits to defeat the evil Gnarl. Something darker and altogether more sinister was behind his success, and as soon as Rage spotted the accuracy of Flhi's observations his ectoplasm ran cold.

Rage's status within Evan City depended on certain information staying hidden forever. If it ever became public knowledge, he was finished. And he simply couldn't allow that.

His first step had been to quickly shred the thesis and claim it was lost. Next, he had broken into the star student's academy dormitory and fried the hard drive on her ecto-puter. He had also considered failing her, but that would have been a step too far, and could have attracted a few too many unwanted questions. Instead, he hacked into the academy's database and downgraded Flhi's confidential course work scores, instantly relegating her to the rank of an average student.

At the graduation ceremony, a few of the other students raised a quizzical eyebrow but nobody really cared. They were all just pleased to have passed. Flhi, though, was devastated. She had worked extra hard throughout the course and had set her heart on receiving the prestigious Golden Wings that were awarded to the Academy's Top of the Class. But as Rage had pointed out: "No thesis, no wings." And despite her nagging suspicion that somehow she'd been fleeced, Flhi had been happy to graduate.

Since then, the commander had waged a single-handed war against her. He'd watched her like a hawk, studied her every move, and waited for her to make a mistake big enough to get her completely discredited and destroyed. That would mean his secret would stay hidden forever.

"Do you know what will happen if Fugitive 1635 gets his hands on a weapon like the astral net?" The commander sounded surprisingly lucid. "He'll pour an army of Gargoyles through the net's homing portal faster than you can flap those pretty little wings of yours. And who are the residents of Evan City going to turn to then? You or me?"

"You?" Flhi didn't care who they turned to. She just wanted Rage to lower his blaster.

"Yes. Me. But I can't do that if I'm babysitting a rookie inspector who makes up the rules as she goes along. You're trouble, Swift, and there's no place for trouble in this precinct."

"I'm only following orders, sir." Flhi was relieved to see that Rage had finally holstered his blaster. "And right there is the cause of both our troubles."

She pointed at the motionless figure held prisoner by the astral net.

Rage sneered. "Wrong again, rookie. This is the *end* of all our troubles." He prodded the prisoner with his foot. "Right here is our only chance of defeating Krot."

Now it all made sense. Flhi finally understood the commander's cunning plan and his reason for wanting to capture the psychic. He didn't see her as a threat at all. He saw her as a weapon that he could use against the Malevolents. But it was a foolhardy ambition. The Higher Dimension and the Fleshi world had always remained separate. It was the First Vow of the Evanescent Code: Maintain and uphold the dimensional divide. If Fleshies ever had definitive proof that another dimension really existed, and that the energy of powerful psychics could be used to open a portal, it would throw both worlds into turmoil and anarchy.

"I know what you're thinking," Rage said calmly. "But these are dangerous times."

"You've broken the First Vow."

"No, Swift, YOU'VE broken the First Vow. And the Third Rule. They'll put you in Level Five for this, I'll see to it." Rage smiled smugly. "Personally, I can't think of a better place for you."

Flhi glanced desperately at Stickler, but he just shrugged apologetically. He was far too afraid of the precinct commander to defy him. The inspector was on her own. Then help came from an unexpected source. The prisoner tried to escape.

One moment the bundle was lying still, the next it was thrashing around wildly on the floor, desperately trying to break free from the astral net. Elbows, knees, feet, and fists all fought furiously to punch a hole through the tightly woven netting, and when that didn't work, the prisoner curled into a ball and started rolling across the floor.

Flhi was surprised by how quickly the Fleshi moved, tumbling faster than an Olympic gymnast toward the open doors of the warehouse at a rate of three rolls per second. Was the prisoner actually going to get away?

Rage knew better. He reached for a pouch on his utility belt and calmly pulled out his piccolo. He blew three shrill notes and the astral net responded immediately. In less than a second it had stopped the prisoner from rolling, and in the time it took for the piccolo tune to finish echoing off the warehouse walls, the Fleshi was pinned to the warehouse floor.

"Let me out!" screamed the prisoner.

Everybody froze. What they had just heard was impossible. And it changed everything.

"Somebody, help me!"

Oh dear, their prisoner wasn't female.

Alannah sat up and gazed around. Her study looked as though it had been attacked by a tropical storm. Shelves had been ripped from their walls, torn pages from books littered the floor like autumn leaves, and only one of her plasma televisions still worked. The repair bill would put a serious dent in her account and that hurt. But that was nothing compared with the pain that now began attacking her body. Every part of her body felt sore.

Gingerly, she climbed to her feet. It was time to assess the damage. Despite a large scorch mark that streaked like a splash of brown paint across the screen, and a couple of damaged keys, her laptop was still functioning.

It had been working twenty-four hours a day for the last year, constantly scouring the Internet for even the slightest trace of Ben and Sadie Malarra. So far it had drawn a blank, but Alannah refused to give up hope. She constantly reprogrammed her software to mine deeper routes into each commercial search engine. Recently, she'd added a stealth algorithm that could hack into every western government's military database. It had been burrowing away in MI5's electronic records for more than six days and was due to download its first report in less than seventeen hours. To suffer hardware failure now would be a disaster, and Alannah was relieved to find the computer was still in perfect working order. It was a shame the same couldn't be said of her backup tower. It had taken a direct hit from a stray ecto-blast and the smoldering memory chips told Alannah that months of archived data had just gone up in smoke.

"Wretched A.N.G.E.L.s!" she spat. "Why were they here?"

Hadn't they come for her? The female with wings and silver hair had certainly said so. She'd even threatened to take Alannah by force. But Alannah was still here. So what had been their actual target?

The answer had to be right there under her nose. The A.N.G.E.L.s had taken something valuable from her room, but what?

Alannah's head hurt too much to figure it out. A throbbing lump the size of a golf ball was threatening to burst through the top of her skull, and she needed a pill to dull the pain. Wortley always carried a capsule or two in his . . .

WORTLEY!

Fighting a scream, Alannah whirled around and desperately scanned the room. There he was, still lying motionless on the floor. A cocoon of dried ectoplasm had hardened over him, and Alannah had to claw it away with her fingers. It took a few moments to free him, but when she finally rolled him over and looked down at his face Alannah feared it was too late.

"Wake up," she pleaded, slapping his face hard. "Come on, Wortley, they've gone."

But Wortley didn't respond. He didn't hear Alannah's screams or feel her slaps. He couldn't. He wasn't there. Wortley's body was still and cold.

Alannah wailed. Wortley couldn't be dead! She refused to believe it. That would make these A.N.G.E.L.s as wicked as Gnarls.

She took a deep breath and tried to block everything else from her mind. *Focus*, she told herself. It wasn't easy.

Were they trying to start a war? No, if that's what they were after, they'd attack something more significant, like the Houses of Parliament, or the White House, or something really symbolic, such as a football stadium. The last place they'd come would be a twelve-year-old's bedroom. There had to be another explanation.

But Alannah didn't have the time to figure out what it was. Wortley's skin was growing paler by the second and his body temperature was dropping fast. She felt for a pulse, she listened for a heartbeat, but nothing. She opened his eyes in the hope that she'd find some glimmer of life and in the depths of his pupils she was amazed to see a faint flickering light. He wasn't dead! And then she realized what had happened: Wortley's soul had left his body. Or had been taken forcibly. Now she had to find a way to bring him back.

The sound of traffic passing by outside seemed unusually loud. And she could hear Marjorie Flint whistling cheerfully in another room. Unfortunately, Wortley's mother was tone-deaf. It didn't matter what tune she was aiming for, she always ended up sounding like a one-note sparrow on the wing. And today was no exception.

That was it! Alannah suddenly had her answer. She had to fly away.

It was so obvious she should have thought of it earlier. To rescue Wortley, Alannah had to follow him. She had to do what he had done and leave her body.

Only that was easier said than done. She'd managed it the day before when battling with the Gnarl, but she'd not had time to think about it then. How had she done it? According to her parents, it was like changing channels on a portable radio. "Tune your natural vibrations to a higher frequency," her father had urged. "Try to sense your own soul buzzing away deep inside your body. It's hard because all that heavy flesh and blood keeps it pinned down and under control, but you need to search for something that feels like a small ball of energy. Once you've found it, you can grow it. Make it big enough and strong enough and your soul should slip out of your body like a pea leaving its pod."

Ben had stuck his finger in his mouth and made a popping sound against his cheek.

"Try it, Lanni," Alannah's mother had cooed, using her daughter's nickname. "Show us how grown-up you are."

Her parents had made it sound so easy. So why couldn't Alannah do it when she wanted to? She hated failure. It made her feel as though there was something wrong with her.

But if Wortley was going to survive, all that had to change right now.

Alannah had never been so single-minded. Everything she had ever done, all her psychic achievements, counted for nothing. Saving her friend was the only thing that mattered now, and suddenly that steely determination gave her a burst of psychic power she'd never had before. Within seconds, every atom in her body was shaking. She'd found her soul's energy. Wow! And she could control it, too. Channeling her thoughts could make the buzzing grow or shrink. It was incredible. She made the vibrations increase, and the world around her seemed to slow and then dim, fading away until it was nothing but a hazy shadow. *I'm doing it,* she thought. *At last, I'm actually doing it!*

Alannah's elation was tempered by the kind of pain that nightmares are made of. Her bones seemed to rattle against one another. Muscles and ligaments stiffened as though rigor mortis was setting in. Her blood stung her veins like battery acid. But all that was nothing compared to what was happening to her skin. Suddenly, it no longer seemed to fit. It was shrinking, growing tighter and tighter until Alannah was sure it would crush every one of her internal organs. Her soul was being squeezed out of her body.

As her flesh and blood instinctively fought to hold on to her spirit, the higher frequencies were acting like a magnet, pulling at her with incredible force, and Alannah had no choice but to join in the struggle against her own body.

The fight didn't last long. The pull of the other world was far too strong. One second she was trapped inside her skin. And the next, her soul shot free.

Alannah looked around and was surprised to find that her bedroom no longer seemed real. What had once been solid furniture was now little more than a hazy image. She reached out to touch her bed and watched her hand pass straight through it. Fascinating!

Then she came across something that appeared to be even odder. There, in the corner of the room, was a tiny hole. And it appeared to be floating.

Tentatively, Alannah moved closer to examine it. The edges were ripped, as if something had torn an opening in midair. And the space in the middle was rippling like the surface of a silver pond. Stranger still, a small spinning thread appeared to stretch from a hazy figure on the floor and disappear into the opening.

Was this her friend's lifeline? Now that she'd spotted it, Alannah couldn't take her eyes off it. She seemed to be drawn toward it, too, and as she approached it, she could actually feel the slim cord fizzing with energy — exactly the same energy as hers.

Amazing! She and Wortley had more in common than she'd realized. They weren't related, even though elements of their separate life forces had been mixed together. But how? And then Alannah had a thought. By saving her life back at the manor house, could Wortley have transferred some of his own life force into Alannah's dying body? She'd read somewhere that people in a highly emotional state sometimes created unexpected psychic connections. That would explain why there was a sudden bond with her friend. But what would it mean for Wortley? Was he becoming psychic, too?

Alannah didn't have time to think about that now. Wortley needed saving and there was only one way she could do that—she had to follow his lifeline.

She thrust her glowing hands into the middle of the hole and pulled outward. Remarkably, the edges stretched. The more she pulled, the wider the opening became, until it was big enough for her to climb inside. She took a deep breath and followed Wortley's lifeline through the shimmering hole, and into the unknown.

The sight that greeted her on the other side of the portal was like something from a fairy tale. There were streets paved in polished marble; trees of living, flowing amber blossomed with petals of colored glass; and the buildings appeared to be carved from vast seams of strong ruby, sapphire, and diamond, each one climbing high into a breathtaking lilac sky.

The whole city looked as if it had been painted in gold and silver. Mailboxes, park benches, streetlamps, and signposts were all expertly crafted from chunks of polished precious metal. Even the quaint little trolley cars rode solid gold tracks as they wove their way gently through the streets. And out toward the horizon, past the city limits, Alannah could see plains of dazzling quartz.

There were no clouds in the sky, just two beautiful platinum suns that bathed everything in bright translucent light, and the atmosphere itself seemed to dance with energy.

It was a landscape of dreams, and Alannah could have gazed at it forever, but she was beginning to attract some unwanted attention. Strange creatures were everywhere; she supposed they were what the little silver A.N.G.E.L. had called Evanescents. And they were all staring at the trespasser.

Alannah gazed with interest at the Evanescents as they nervously crowded around her. They were small, yet each one appeared to be an adult. Their pearlescent skin shimmered in the silvery light, and pairs of brightly colored eyes sparkled up at her — some red, some green, and others various shades of blue. But the little silver A.N.G.E.L. had been beautiful, too, and if these Evanescents were anything like her, they'd be fast, cunning, and utterly ruthless. Alannah was immediately on her guard.

The crowd was growing, and the larger it became, the more threatening it felt. There was no time to follow Wortley's lifeline. She needed a Plan B, and fast! So she picked up the slender cord and gingerly coiled it around her wrist.

"Time to come back down to Earth, Wortley."

The thread felt softer than spider's silk, and just as delicate. Alannah was almost certain it would break if she pulled it, but what choice did she have? She closed her eyes, crossed her toes for luck, and then tugged really hard.

"Let me out!"

Wortley wriggled and squirmed, but whatever was holding him refused to let go. He was held flat against the floor beneath some kind of netting, and the harder he tried to move the tighter the net became. Getting in and out of tight spots had always been his specialty, but this was something new. Wortley sensed he was in serious trouble.

"Look, whatever you want, I haven't got it. You've got the wrong man. I mean, boy. Let me go now and we'll forget all about it. I promise not to call the police, honest."

He was still waiting for a reply when something hard prodded him in the back. It felt like the end of someone's boot.

"We *are* the police," an angry male voice said. "And by the way, you're wrong."

"About what?" Wortley asked timidly. Had Alannah's illegal activities attracted the attention of the authorities?

"You've got exactly what we want." The boot prodded Wortley again, only this time a little harder. "And you're going to give it to us."

"Commander, what are you doing?" a female voice asked. She sounded alarmed.

"I'm doing something they don't teach in the academy, Inspector; it's called 'using my initiative.' It comes with years of experience, which is something I'm glad to say you'll never acquire. Now get the boy to his feet."

Wortley was unnerved. Being abducted by the police and held against his will was surely against his human rights. Could they really get away with this?

He was about to demand to see a lawyer when what sounded like a cell phone ringtone filled the air with noise. The netting around him immediately loosened, but before he could make a bolt for freedom he felt strong hands grab his arms and haul him to his feet. At least now he would see his captors. He wanted to be able to identify them when his case came before the Police Complaints Authority. Boy, was he going to make them pay!

"Urgh! I'd forgotten Fleshi children were so ugly. Now I know why so many of them wear hoods."

Wortley stared in disbelief. The police officer's

bright gold uniform resembled a wardrobe mistake from a 1970s sci-fi movie, but that wasn't what had widened Wortley's eyes to the size of saucers. The officer had wings. Huge white wings that seemed to be attached at his shoulders and folded neatly down his back. And he wasn't the only one.

"Y-you're not the p-p-police," Wortley stammered. "Y-you're n-not even hu-hu-hu . . ."

"Human? Certainly not," snarled Rage. "But we *are* the police and right now you're under our jurisdiction. So, unless you want to be separated from your body forever, you'll do exactly as I say."

Nothing was making sense. Wortley couldn't decide whether he was dreaming or whether he'd been the victim of alien abduction. He pinched himself. No, he hadn't woken up, so the alien abduction theory must be right. At least that explained the wings.

"What do you want with me?" he asked, desperately hoping they wouldn't say anything else about separating him from his body.

"You? We don't want you. My soon-to-be-ex-inspector and her team of incompetents snatched you by mistake. We wanted the psychic."

"Alannah? Why would aliens want Alannah?"

Rage seemed to inflate like a balloon before suddenly exploding with laughter. "ALIENS!" he boomed. "He thinks we're aliens. Fleshi children aren't just ugly;

they're stupid, too! Tell him who we are, Inspector. I haven't got the time. Or the patience."

Flhi leaned forward and whispered into Wortley's ear, "We're not aliens. We're Evanescent combat A.N.G.E.L.s."

Wortley gasped. "Angels?"

Flhi sighed deeply; hadn't she already covered this with the girl? "We're not *that* kind of angel. We're part of the Attack-ready Network of Global Evanescent Law-enforcers."

"Angels," Wortley whispered to himself dreamily. "So that must mean that this is . . ."

"No, it's bloomin' not," snapped Rage. "This is the Higher Dimension, not someplace where you can come and float around on clouds. You shouldn't even be here, so just be quiet while I figure out how best to use you."

Use him? Wortley didn't like the sound of that at all. In the old black-and-white movies he liked to watch with his mother, the phrase "use him" often meant being held hostage, or made to work for a criminal master-mind before facing a horrible death, perhaps tied in a sack and dumped into the sea. He sniffed heavily, to see if he could smell salt water.

"What on Evan is the boy doing now?" spat Rage. He checked his armpits. "Do we smell?"

Wortley was about to tell them that actually they smelled lovely—especially the little one with silver pigtails who seemed to be wearing the most adorable perfume—when he felt a sharp tug on his back. At first it was a little jolt that dragged him back a few feet. But then the tugging got harder and, before he knew it, Wortley was skimming over the polished warehouse floor faster than a motor-powered Frisbee. The A.N.G.E.L.s were getting smaller and smaller as he was propelled backward through the air.

"STOP HIM!" bellowed Rage. "He's trying to escape."

Flhi wasn't sure what to do. Kidnapping the young boy had been wrong and she was going to pay for that mistake with her career, but was using him as bait to lure the psychic really the right thing to do? Instinct told her it wasn't. But even a half-second delay was long enough to alert Rage to her doubts, and in his opinion that qualified as mutiny. He drew his ecto-blaster and pressed both barrels against Flhi's temple.

"It's you or the boy," he said coldly. "Personally, I'd prefer to shoot you."

As Alannah went on tugging at Wortley's lifeline, she could feel her friend wriggling wildly at the other end and she had to strain every muscle in her tired arms to reel him in. Loops of the cord were now coiled behind her, like a mountain of freshly cooked spaghetti, and Alannah wondered how much more there could be before Wortley finally appeared. Then she had a terrible thought. Could Wortley's lifeline simply be stretching? And if so, could it eventually snap and leave his soul stranded? Would all her effort do nothing more than kill her best friend?

But she had no choice. Back on Earth, Wortley was as good as dead anyway. His lifeless body was an empty shell, so doing nothing simply wasn't an option. She pulled the lifeline even harder.

Around her, the Evanescents were still staring, as if they were waiting to see what she did next before they attacked. But trouble was on its way. Alannah could sense it.

"Hurry, hurry, hurry!"

Something *was* happening. Alannah could hear a growing murmur of disgruntled Evanescents in the distance. The noise was coming from somewhere deep in the city. Whatever was causing it was on its way toward her. And it was traveling fast.

Alannah yanked harder, willing the cord to travel even quicker. But as its speed increased, so did the murmur. And then she saw why. A figure was being dragged toward her through the streets of Evan City. Shocked residents toppled like bowling pins as the form bounced against golden telephone booths, ricocheted off silver mailboxes, and crashed into them. Others dived for cover inside trolley car stops, and Alannah was tempted to seek refuge behind a thick-trunked amber tree until she recognized who it was: Wortley.

"Stop!" she cried, mostly in hope, before instinctively bracing herself for impact; this was going to hurt.

Nothing happened. The collision she expected never came, and Alannah was still crouched in a defensive ball when she heard a familiar voice.

"Alannah?"

Wortley was hanging in midair, not even an inch away from her. He was suspended off the ground like an astronaut in zero gravity and appeared to be floating at the end of his lifeline.

Alannah laughed; she couldn't stop herself. He looked ridiculous.

"I'm glad one of us finds this funny," growled Wortley. "But then, you're not the one who was just kidnapped by a gang of angels."

"They're not those kind of angels, Worts," Alannah explained. Now, what was it the silver-haired female had told her? "They're part of an Attack-ready Network of—"

"—Global Evanescent Law-enforcers," Wortley finished. "The little one already told me. I pretended not to be listening but sometimes it pays to keep alert. Anyway, why am I here?"

"I don't know," Alannah admitted. "Perhaps they want you for your sparkling wit."

Wortley pulled his best annoyed face. "I'm being serious. I don't think I'm supposed to be here. I think they thought I was you."

Alannah couldn't help giggling again.

"I'm sorry, Worts," she said, "but just look at you. You're floating in midair at the end of a cord."

"What's happened to me?" he asked. "Where the heck are we?"

"It's hard to explain," Alannah admitted. "And I haven't got the time right now."

"Haven't got the time?" spluttered Wortley. "In case you haven't noticed, I'm having some crazy out-of-body experience here. I'd appreciate a little explanation."

Alannah pointed back toward the glittering city. "I'd love to tell you everything I know, Wortley, I really would, but I don't think *they* are going to let me."

Wortley glanced over his shoulder and felt a wave of panic sweep over him. Two familiar figures were rushing toward them at the speed of hunting cheetahs. Each one carried what looked like a large gun in its hand and, if he wasn't already in deep trouble, there was every chance he soon would be.

Flhi had never seen the commander so focused. It was a scary sight. His face was set in steely concentration. More frightening still was the way his lips had curled away from his teeth in a strange rabid snarl of a smile. He was clearly happy, but his expression was the kind of look she'd seen on the Gnarls and Ghouls. She wondered if Rage had ever considered anger management.

"Blasters to STUN, sir?" Flhi inquired.

"Negative, Inspector. EVAN-SENT. And make sure you only aim for the boy; he's dispensable. Leave the girl to me."

"But . . ."

"Are you questioning another order?"

Reluctantly, Flhi shook her head. "No, sir."

She wasn't happy. Fully charged weapons were only permissible during times of war, and Flhi knew that

Rage was overstepping his authority. Throughout history no combat A.N.G.E.L. had ever banished a Fleshi to the Dark Dimension. The inspector had no intention of taking the rap for something so wicked. Defying Rage, she set her blaster to STUN.

But the Fleshies had seen them, which was bad news. The element of surprise was lost and it was only a matter of seconds before they escaped back into their own dimension.

Rage fired off a warning shot that fizzed past the girl's left ear.

"Stop right there or I'll shoot again," he bellowed. "And I assure you, the next one won't miss."

Alannah aimed her finger at the approaching A.N.G.E.L.s and smiled. This seemed too easy. "Freeze!"

Nothing happened. Alannah's magical powers didn't work on the A.N.G.E.L.s and the two marauding entities closed in on their prey.

"I said, FREEZE!" she yelled, only this time thrusting both palms toward the A.N.G.E.L.s. Still nothing happened. Alannah's magic had deserted her.

Actually, that wasn't strictly true. Alannah's magic was no more or less powerful than it had always been. It was just that Rage had chosen that precise moment to test the latest upgrade to his commander-level utility belt. Like all troopers' belts, his was packed with state-of-the-art tech equipment, but in addition to the usual array of gadgets and gizmos (flying string, ecto-grenades and landing cloud, ammo pouches, ecto-holster, and telepathic communicator), Rage had a few customized extras. For starters, there were two hidden ecto-pouches for storing emergency weapons or a handful of ballistic dust. An inter-dimensional astral ladder was also provided, just in case he ever needed to bridge dimensions in a hurry.

However, the addition that excited him the most was a prototype astral shield. He had volunteered to test it himself and he couldn't believe that he had a chance to deploy it in action so soon.

It had been designed to shield combat A.N.G.E.L.s from the dark powers of a Gnarl. But Rage was still taking one heck of a risk. The Fleshi girl had a kind of astral magic that no Evanescent had ever seen and there was no guarantee that the shield would work. So when he'd pressed the little yellow button positioned just behind his ecto-holster, he'd also closed his eyes and crossed his fingers.

It worked! A bubble of positive energy had instantly sealed the two combat A.N.G.E.L.s inside an invisible shield, deflecting the Fleshi's assault harmlessly away. Rage and Flhi kept on walking.

"Do something!" pleaded Wortley. "These guys are nasty."

Alannah didn't need reminding. She'd already seen the silver-haired female in action and knew exactly what she was capable of. The second A.N.G.E.L. was a mystery. Obviously a male, he was larger, aggressive, and there was a cruel look on his face that suggested he had a mean streak a mile wide. He also had what resembled a huge double-barreled pistol aimed straight at Alannah, who had no desire to stick around and find out how much damage the weapon could inflict.

"Let's get out of here," she told Wortley, pushing him toward the shimmering hole. "I get the feeling we're not welcome."

Rage was not about to let them escape so easily. With military precision, the two A.N.G.E.L.s split apart and circled the Fleshies from opposite directions. The commander was first to reach the portal and, before the two Fleshies could jump through it, he triggered his astral shield once again.

Wortley felt Alannah's hand shove him in the back and he needed no further encouragement. He took two steps forward, then threw himself headfirst toward the hole. He was wondering what it would feel like to plunge from one dimension into another when he hit something that felt remarkably like the skin of a balloon and bounced backward. He sprang to his feet and tried again, but the same thing happened. Some kind of invisible force field was shielding the opening and, no matter how hard he tried, Wortley couldn't break through it. They were trapped.

"You might as well stop wasting your energy," Rage told Alannah. "There's a force field protecting me and the portal. You'll never break through it."

There seemed to be nothing Alannah could do. Her magic didn't work, her attacks were harmless, and she couldn't get to their only means of escape. Frustrated, she put her hands on her hips and glared at the two spirits.

Rage watched in amusement as the young Fleshi studied him in detail. He doubted she had any military training, but she did have a clever mind and he knew she was looking for an advantage to exploit. Of course, he had nothing to fear. The astral shield had proven itself, but he remembered what the tech team had told him: Don't shoot from inside the shield! It kept things out, but it also kept things in, so a bolt or two from an ecto-blaster would bounce off the inside wall and hit whoever was in the bubble. The Fleshi couldn't harm him, but he couldn't harm her, either. It was stalemate.

"We don't belong here," Alannah finally said. She was still trying to spot a weakness. Talking to the A.N.G.E.L. was a way of buying more time. "You kidnapped my friend and all I've done is rescue him. I'm not here to do anything else. I don't want to hurt any of you, so why don't you just let us both go home?"

"It's a little more complicated than that," Rage told her. "And I'm afraid I'm going to have to ask you to stick around for a while."

Alannah didn't like the sound of that. Remaining outside her body for too much longer would probably kill both her and Wortley. The sooner they returned to Earth, the better.

"Staying here will harm us," she pointed out. "Surely I'm worth more to you alive, aren't I?"

Rage sighed. This wasn't easy.

"Krot, the creature you fought at the manor house, is an escaped fugitive known as a Gnarl: dangerous, ruthless, and extremely powerful. We also have reason to believe that he's building an army to attack our dimension. If he does, there's no guarantee that we will defeat him. We got lucky last time, but if he's victorious our world *and* your world will change forever. We protect Earth from the Gnarls, Ghouls, and Gargoyles. Without us, your dimension would be destroyed."

"So what's that got to do with me?" Alannah asked, shrugging.

"Apparently, you possess the power to defeat Krot. Since Inspector Swift first encountered you, our tech boys have been monitoring your movements. They've also been carrying out a little background research on you."

"Tech who?" asked Alannah, astounded. "Researching what?"

"Well, it appears that the anger and frustration of losing your parents probably enhanced your psychic abilities. We've never seen anything quite like it, ever. You're a freak. But if you can defeat the Gnarl, you can stop his army's assault in its tracks. You could save both our worlds."

Alannah was no longer listening, and frankly didn't care. She had finally spotted a weakness and was already planning to exploit it. In seconds, Alannah and Wortley would be back at home.

Buoyed by the presence of Rage, a growing number of Evanescents had crept close to the confrontation zone. They sensed that the two Fleshies were dangerous, particularly the female, but with their heroic commander to protect them, they were convinced they would come to no harm. How wrong they were.

Alannah knew she had only one shot at success and struck with speed. By the time her victim had thought to react, Alannah had secured the little creature in the kind of grip a club bouncer would have been proud of. She fired up her finger and pointed the glowing digit at the side of the startled entity's head.

"Talking's over, flyboy," she hissed at Rage. "Open the portal or I'll start firing."

"You wouldn't dare," Rage gasped.

Wortley and Flhi spoke at the same time. "Oh yes, she would!"

To prove the point, Alannah ran her fiery finger across her hostage's head, burning the innocent hostage's hair.

"STOP!" pleaded Rage.

Blast it! The Fleshi was going to escape and there was nothing he could do to stop her.

"Commander?" Flhi probed. She couldn't believe that Rage was considering his options. As far as she was concerned, he didn't have any.

"All right! All right!" Rage snapped. "Just give me a moment."

He turned to Alannah and glowered at her. It was time to play his trump card. "You should be begging to stay."

Alannah wasn't impressed. "You should be begging me to be merciful." She waved her finger again and this time scorched the hostage's clothing. The little creature howled.

Rage swore under his breath before quickly pressing the little yellow button on his combat belt. The powerful astral shield popped as it disengaged. Now he was just as vulnerable as the poor civilian. Reluctantly, he ordered Flhi to follow him and move away from the open portal.

Holding the terrified hostage in front of them, Alannah and Wortley shuffled toward their escape route. Both were still wary of the A.N.G.E.L.s' firepower, and Alannah kept one eye trained on the impressive-looking weapons. They weren't safe yet.

"We can help each other," said Rage. "I've got something you need."

Alannah was tempted to listen. After all, it wasn't every day she had the chance to negotiate with A.N.G.E.L.s, and she had a sneaky feeling that she could make them give up the location of every piece of hidden treasure in England. Maybe next time.

The portal rippled gently, like the surface of a pond in a breeze. It was beautiful and Alannah could have stared at it for hours, but she didn't even have seconds. As soon as they were close enough, she bundled Wortley through the hole.

"You're going to regret leaving," Rage insisted.

"I don't believe in regrets," Alannah replied.

"Oh, really?" Rage sounded surprised. "Don't you regret growing up without your parents?"

Alannah froze. Suddenly, she was nervous. The A.N.G.E.L.s seemed to know everything about her.

Rage smirked. It always paid to do a little research. The report from the boys in the tech team had told him all he needed to know about the young Fleshi.

"Leave my mum and dad out of this," she snapped. "This has got nothing to do with them."

"It has everything to do with them. I know you've been searching for them." Rage tried to appear sympathetic, unsuccessfully. "But you don't have to do it alone any-more. I can help you. We can help you. Only you'll have to help us first."

Alannah didn't get the chance to respond. Twisting violently, her hostage chose that exact moment to squeeze out of her grip and, with a parting kick, it dashed forward into the safe arms of Inspector Flhi Swift.

The kick sent Alannah stumbling backward. She flapped her arms wildly, desperately trying to keep her balance, but it was no use. With Rage's offer still ringing in her ears, she toppled through the portal and fell back to Earth.

"Aarrgghh! I'm not drinking that." **Wortley bobbed** and wove his head with the skill of a veteran boxer. "It's disgusting."

Marjorie Flint was undeterred. She poked the plastic spoon toward her son's mouth and tried to force the swamp green liquid between his tightly drawn lips.

"Just one teensy spoonful," she insisted. "It will get rid of your flu by the end of the day."

Wortley ducked beneath another spoon lunge. "I've already told you, I don't have the flu."

"Your bones ache, your muscles feel sore, you can't stop shivering, and your temperature is sky-high," Marjorie reminded her son. "That's the flu! Now stop acting like a baby and take your medicine."

There was absolutely no way Wortley was going to let a single drop of his mother's foul concoction into his mouth. The disgusting acrid odor of it had started creeping up from the kitchen early that morning, and since the first whiff had reached his nostrils, he had known what was coming: the Flint family flu remedy.

"What do you put in that stuff?" he asked, eyeing the medicine suspiciously. "There's no way anything smelling that bad could possibly do me any good."

Marjorie proudly ticked off the ingredients. "Cabbage, red onion, garlic, ginger, echinacea . . ."

"Wing of bat, eye of toad, tongue of newt?"

"You can scoff, Wortley Flint," his mother scolded. "But this recipe saved your great-grandfather's life during the last flu epidemic. In fact, if it wasn't for this medicine neither of us would be here today."

According to his mother, half the human race was alive as a result of taking the remedy. But Wortley wasn't convinced.

"Has Alannah taken any?"

"Do I look that stupid?"

Alannah had slipped quietly into Wortley's bedroom and now shuffled stiffly around the end of his bed. She headed for a comfy armchair and gingerly lowered herself onto soft cushions. She was clearly in pain and it was a few seconds before she was able to relax.

"I'd prefer to have flu for a month than drink that potion," she muttered, then sniffed the air and recoiled in disgust. "Did you extract it from the stomach of a dead animal?"

Marjorie Flint glared at her young employer from behind the thick lenses of her spectacles. "Your mother and father swore by this remedy, young lady. And if they were here today . . ."

Wortley cringed and slipped weakly beneath the bedcovers. His mother had touched a nerve and he had no intention of being caught in the cross fire. He held his breath and waited for the first explosion.

It didn't come. Alannah was in far too much pain to pick a fight. In fact, she could barely summon enough energy to build a trickle of tears. Besides, she knew that Marjorie Flint was right: Her parents had always preferred their housekeeper's potions to modern medicines. The real reason Alannah hated the flu remedy was because it reminded her just how much she missed her mum and dad. And that made her think of the A.N.G.E.L.s' offer.

"I'm sorry, dear," Marjorie said meekly. "I shouldn't have said that."

"It's okay, Mrs. F, I know you miss them, too."

Alannah gazed into Marjorie's friendly brown eyes and knew she was looking at a kind soul. The warmhearted housekeeper had been a part of Alannah's life since she was very young, and her memory held as many images of Marjorie as it did of her own parents.

Wortley couldn't believe it. Was Alannah really being kind to his mother? He poked his head out from beneath the covers to see if it was true.

Marjorie Flint watched Alannah's eyes fill with tears and realized how vulnerable and alone her young employer was. She suddenly felt racked with guilt. How could she have contemplated leaving her job? Ben and Sadie Malarra hadn't just been her employers; they had been her best friends, too. And, wherever they were, whatever they were doing, they would expect Marjorie to take care of their precious little girl—even if Alannah did behave like a self-important chief executive most of the time.

"Perhaps a bowl of hot chicken soup would do you some good."

Alannah nodded. "That would be nice," she said sweetly.

Marjorie smiled, then headed out of the bedroom and shuffled off toward the kitchen.

"You hate chicken soup," Wortley said as soon as his mother had left the bedroom.

"I needed to get rid of her," Alannah confessed. She used her sleeve to wipe away the tears. It was back to business. "We need to talk about what's been happening to you."

"I know exactly what's been happening to me, thanks very much," Wortley snapped. "I've just slept for thirty-five hours solid. My muscles are so weak that I can't get out of bed. Oh, and in case you've somehow forgotten, we've both had more than our fair share of brushes with death."

"I'm not talking about that," Alannah said. She seemed to be searching for the right words. "Haven't you felt strange lately? You know, different somehow?"

"Um, yeah," Wortley mocked her. "It's not every day I get whisked out of my body."

"No, no, no." Alannah shook her head, clearly frustrated. "I don't know how to say this. . . . Do you feel closer to me?"

D'oh! Wrong words. All Alannah had done was make herself sound soppy and stupid.

"Are you asking me if I fancy you?"

"NO!" Alannah blushed. "Don't be so stupid, Worts. Look, forget I ever said anything."

Wortley fiddled with the bedcover and looked a little embarrassed. Now he felt stupid, too.

Eager to change the subject, Alannah pulled her laptop from beneath the thick folds of her bathrobe and opened it up. It beeped as the screen glowed into life.

"Hmm, we've just received a very interesting email."

Wortley was glad the subject had changed. "Unless it's from Triggs' candy store telling me I've won a lifetime supply of Everlasting Gobstoppers, I couldn't care less."

"It's from the Earl of Pittingham. He insists the manor

house is still haunted and will pay us whatever we want to make the problem go away."

Wortley buried his head in his hands. "Oh, well, how can we refuse? After all, it's not as if we BARELY ESCAPED WITH OUR LIVES the last time we were there, is it?"

"He's talking big money, Wortley." Alannah held up two fingers. "And I still think there are treasures hidden somewhere in that house."

"Yeah, but the house is also full of angry beasties and winged thingies with guns," Wortley reminded her. "Only someone completely demented would even think about going back there."

"I have no choice, Wortley. Those A.N.G.E.L.s know where my mother and father are, and if I ever want to find them, I have to go back. Besides, you've seen how powerful my abilities are now. Why should I be scared of an ugly old Gnarl?"

Because one of them almost killed you! Wortley wanted to scream. But he didn't waste his breath. He could tell she wouldn't listen to a word he had to say. His friend had an all-too-familiar look in her eyes. Alannah was going to the old manor house, and that was that.

Wortley had absolutely no intention of joining her. He had known from the very beginning that setting foot on the Pittingham estate was a bad decision, and everything that had happened since had proved him right. There was no way he was going to make the same mistake twice. He pulled the bedcovers tightly across his chest and anchored himself to the mattress.

Alannah recognized the stubborn look on her friend's face and sighed. "You're not coming, are you?"

Wortley shook his head. "Nope!"

Alannah fumed. Her freckled cheeks flushed the color of ripened tomatoes and she clenched her fists so tight that her own fingernails drew blood. How could Wortley let her down? How could he be such a coward?

"If you're not at the gates to Pittingham Manor at six o'clock tonight," she growled, "you can consider yourself unemployed."

"You can't fire me!" Wortley yelled. "I resign. Now get out!"

At half past six, when Wortley woke, it was dark outside. He checked his watch and realized he had missed the rendezvous with Alannah. Strangely, he felt relieved. Perhaps now he could return to the life of a normal boy. A life without haunted houses and ghosts. A life without Alannah?

Slowly, he sat up. It took a few seconds for his eyes to adjust and a few seconds more to realize that he wasn't alone. His room was crawling with spirits.

"I think the boy can see us," fretted Gloom. "He just looked straight at me."

"Don't be ridiculous," whispered Flhi. "Only the girl can see us."

"He can definitely hear us!" Yell roared. "See, he looked at you when you spoke. Should we retreat?"

Flhi Swift shared her troopers' suspicions but didn't want to admit it. "He's just a Fleshi boy," she said, trying to give herself a bit of reassurance. "He has no powers whatsoever. Stay in your positions. We'll just wait here until the girl shows up."

There was a sinking feeling in the pit of Wortley's stomach and he felt sick. He wasn't supposed to see ghosts and ghouls on Earth. That was Alannah's job. Oh boy, was this what Alannah had been trying to tell him? Did she know this was going to happen?

He rubbed his eyes, hoping the visions would disappear, but when he took his hands away the entities were still there. And they were all staring right at him.

"This isn't good," observed Gloom. "He's acting very strangely."

"Well, how would you act if you could suddenly see ghosts?" Wortley snapped.

"TOLD YOU!" screamed Yell.

"RETREAT!" bellowed Gloom.

"Stay right where you are," Flhi ordered. "He's harmless."

The inspector hoped she was right.

"You can see us?" she asked.

Wortley nodded reluctantly. He didn't want to believe it. This changed everything.

"Have you always been able to see us?" Flhi probed.

As she expected, this time Wortley shook his head.

Psychismic Transformation! Flhi had studied the phenomenon briefly at the academy. There were only ever a few recorded cases each year, and they always involved Fleshies who had survived what Earthly Dimensional doctors called a "near-death experience." By abducting the boy's soul and taking it back to their own dimension, the A.N.G.E.L.s might have inadvertently triggered the part of Wortley's brain responsible for psychic powers.

Or, of course, the Fleshi girl might have transferred some of her abilities, infusing him with enough psychic energy to see beyond his own dimension.

Whatever the reason, the boy's new powers were minimal, probably limited to seeing a few stranded ghosts, and there was every chance that they were temporary, too.

Wortley was amazed at how real and vibrant the spirits looked now that he was back on Earth. Dressed in what looked like military-style jumpsuits, they clearly packed some serious firepower. As if that wasn't frightening enough, he recognized one of them: The silver-haired female had been one of his kidnappers. Jeepers! Was she was back to finish the job?

Flhi saw the panic on the boy's face and realized what he was thinking. If she didn't do something fast, this could get messy. Quickly, she unholstered her ecto-blaster and pointed it straight at Wortley's chest.

"This is for your own good," she said apologetically, before pulling the trigger.

An ugly goblin's face stared at Alannah from a carved stone pillar supporting one of a pair of vast wrought-iron gates. Alannah stared into its unblinking eyes for a moment, then reached out and prodded its stubby nose.

Seconds later, an intercom crackled to life.

"Yes?" inquired an aloof voice.

"I have an appointment with the earl," said Alannah impatiently. "My name is Alannah Malarra."

"We've been expecting you. Come to the front door. And don't mind Antony and Cleopatra, they've already been fed."

The iron gates slowly swung open and she crunched her way up the wide gravel driveway toward the house. The old building grew higher and more imposing with every step. Suddenly, the manor house seemed like a very unfriendly place.

Antony and Cleopatra, the earl's pet hyenas, tracked Alannah's progress up the drive. Their eyes burned with recognition and, as she gingerly stepped past their ken-nel, both animals lunged forward. Alannah jumped back in fright, and was relieved when thick chains caught the beasts in midleap. She paused to let her racing heart slow down a few beats, and then kicked gravel toward the glowering hyenas.

"Try eating that," she suggested.

Five granite steps, each mottled with lichen, led to two ornately carved wooden doors. Alannah was about to put her foot on the first step when the doors swung open and a well-dressed gentleman stepped forward to greet her.

"So glad you could come." The man's tone was very formal. "I'm Samson, the earl's footman. I'll take you through to the library. The earl is looking forward to meeting you. Frightfully strange goings-on here recently; we hope you can help."

As Alannah followed Samson down a beautifully furnished hallway she noticed that something about the house had changed since she was there before. Although the lights were on and the rooms were brightly lit, an unnerving darkness lingered in every corner. It seemed to sit like puddles of dense oil wherever there were shadows, and Alannah was sure that these patches of darkness were moving. The hairs on the back of her neck instinctively stood to attention as her senses became alert.

"This way please, Miss Malarra." The footman opened a door and beckoned Alannah inside.

The icy blast was sharp enough to make her gasp and

turned her breath into a tiny cloud of condensation. She stepped into the library doorway and scanned the room for signs of danger.

"Sorry about the temperature," called a frail male voice. "I've turned the thermostat up as far as it will go, but it seems to make no difference. Must be on the blink again."

The Earl of Pittingham was smaller than Alannah had imagined, and thinner, too. As he shuffled across the polished floorboards to greet her, his balding head and large hooked nose reminded her of a vulture.

"Perhaps I should ask Samson to put another log on the fire," he said, giving the flames that raged in the huge hearth a wistful look. "Can't seem to get any heat from that, either. Maybe it's my age?"

Alannah didn't think so. In any other house a fire like that would make the room hotter than a blast furnace, yet the library remained icy. She doubted whether an entire forest of logs would make much of a difference.

"How long has it been this cold?" she asked.

"Oh, a couple of days now," the earl replied. "It seemed to start right after you emailed to say you'd solved my little problem. Are you quite sure you got rid of all the ghosts?"

Quite obviously she hadn't. There was only one explanation for such a concentrated drop in temperature, and Alannah knew only too well what it was. What really concerned her, though, was the level of spectral presence needed to keep a room so cold. There had to be an entire army of apparitions lurking close by.

"Is this the only room that's so cold?" Alannah asked as she carefully lowered herself onto a rather uncomfortable-looking armchair. Every part of her body still ached and she was beginning to realize that Wortley might have been right after all: Perhaps she should have stayed at home.

"The old wine cellar is even colder," the earl told her. "But you'd expect that, really, wouldn't you? We don't use it any longer, but years ago it used to keep the French stuff at the right temperature. Oh, and the west-wing bedrooms are frightfully cold, too. I'm afraid it all seems to be getting a bit out of hand, my dear. Which is why I was so glad when a colleague of yours offered to lend a hand."

"A colleague?" Alannah was confused. Since when had Wortley started working freelance?

"Actually, I'm not sure that *colleague* is the right word." The deep Eastern European voice slithered out from beside an antique long-cased clock. "*Fellow professional* might be a more appropriate way of describing me."

When an unusually tall, lean man stepped out of the shadows, the first thing Alannah noticed about him was his suit. It was obviously vintage, probably from the Victorian era, yet it looked immaculate, almost as if the man had recently bought it new. The second thing she noticed was the tiny ember that danced across the tip of his right-hand index finger. Like her, the stranger was psychic.

"You look so much like your mother," the man said as he approached Alannah. He smiled and offered her his hand. "My name is Klaut Horrad. I knew your parents well."

"That's funny," Alannah said. "My mother and father never mentioned you."

"Oh, we knew each other on a purely professional basis," Horrad said calmly. His expression betrayed nothing. "It's no surprise to hear that Ben and Sadie didn't take their work home with them."

"Mr. Horrad kindly offered to help me—" the earl began, but the psychic silenced the old man with a single look.

Alannah saw fear flash across the old man's eyes before they suddenly dulled and he fell silent. A vacant expression settled upon his wrinkled face as he slowly turned to study the fire. It was as though he had just been sedated.

"Your work here was very good," Horrad congratulated Alannah. "Some of the best I've seen in a while."

Alannah was cautious. How much did Horrad know? "I just helped an old man get rid of some unwelcome squatters."

The Hungarian laughed. "That's certainly one way of putting it, young lady. But from what I've been told, you demonstrated some remarkable abilities. It's probably a product of all your pent-up anger. A girl of your age should never have to cope with being abandoned by her parents."

"Mum and Dad didn't abandon me," Alannah growled furiously. "Something has happened to them, and I'm going to find out what."

Horrad smiled horribly. "Learn to harness your anger, Alannah, and you'll be able to do amazing things. You'll become stronger and more powerful than you could possibly imagine. If you'll let me, I could teach you. We could work together. I could certainly use a girl with unique talents like yours."

"How could I possibly help you?" she asked suspiciously.

Horrad ignored her question and fired back with one of his own instead. "Does that mean you're prepared to work with me?"

"I'm not sure that you could afford my fee."

Horrad laughed again. His piercing green eyes locked on to Alannah's. "Work with me and I'll reward you with something far more valuable than treasure."

"What could be more valuable than treasure?"

Horrad grinned. "The love of family."

Wortley was paralyzed. His muscles were frozen solid and he couldn't even blink. He was beginning to wish he'd gone with Alannah.

"I'm sorry I had to do that," said the silver-haired A.N.G.E.L. She re-holstered her weapon and slowly glided to the foot of Wortley's bed. "Fleshies have a tendency to panic when they first encounter combat A.N.G.E.L.s and I didn't want you to do anything that might cause you an injury. I've only stunned you; the effects will begin to wear off in a few moments. Please stay calm."

Stay calm? Wortley's heart was beating faster than a rock band's snare drum. He had never envied any of Alannah's special talents. So why was it that he could now see ghosts?

The other two A.N.G.E.L.s floated into view, joining their colleague at the foot of the bed. They stared at Wortley with curiosity.

"What do we do now?" asked Gloom. "I thought we were only supposed to observe."

"I had no idea he'd be able to see us," Flhi snapped. "I suppose we'll just have to abort the mission and return to Evan City."

"And what will you tell the commander?" Yell's bellowed question left a ringing in his inspector's ear.

"I wish you'd master the art of whispering," Flhi moaned, rubbing her lobes. "Your voice could wake a comatose troll."

She really didn't want to answer Yell's question. She'd have to admit that they'd come to the Fleshi dimension without permission. It was better if Yell and Gloom didn't know. At least that way they could plead genuine ignorance.

"Let's freeze him, just for a few hours," suggested Gloom, altering the setting on his own blaster. "I'm sure the girl will turn up before the sedation wears off, and we can gather information before he blows our cover."

Flhi was horrified by Gloom's suggestion. Traveling unauthorized was one thing, but freezing a Fleshi was simply out of the question. The effects were notoriously unpredictable and it sometimes took weeks for the victim to come around. Having to summon an emergency recovery team was the last thing she wanted to do right now.

"Put your weapon away," she ordered firmly. "We're not freezing anyone. We'll just have to abort the mission. At least we won't be late for litter patrol." Flhi checked the time implant embedded into her palm. "Our first shift starts in seven hours."

Flhi saw the look on their faces and knew that her troopers were disappointed. She also felt a strong sense of guilt. After all, it was her fault that they were all facing a career in waste management. Tracking the girl in their spare time had seemed like a good idea. Covertly monitoring Alannah's movements would provide an opportunity to feed valuable intelligence into the precinct's database. Okay, she knew it wouldn't resurrect her career but it might help secure a better future for Yell and Gloom. Only now her plans were in tatters.

Wortley could wiggle his toes. The effects of the A.N.G.E.L.'s stun blast were beginning to wear off and his body no longer felt numb. Soon he'd be able to move his arms and legs and then he could think about escaping. All he had to do was come up with a plan.

"The girl should be here," Flhi was talking to herself. Her frustrations were obvious. "After leaving her body, she should be in no fit state to do anything but lie in bed for days. I thought this was going to be easy."

"Let's hope she hasn't gone looking for ghosts," Gloom said mournfully.

Yell shook his head and sucked on his teeth. "No, no, no, no. I wouldn't like to be in her shoes if she has."

All thoughts of escape fled from Wortley's mind. There was something much bigger at stake.

"Fot yoo yoo ween?" Wortley's lips were still numb. Even he didn't understand the sounds that had come out of his mouth.

"What did he just say?" asked Gloom. He rested his hand on the butt of his blaster. He was ready to draw it if the Fleshi made any sudden movement.

"Don't know," confessed Yell. "Sounded like gobbledy-gook to me."

Flhi shushed them both. "I think he's trying to ask us something. Give him some space, guys. You'll scare the poor boy."

It was hard to speak with a thick tongue and lips that felt fatter than fried sausages, but Wortley tried again.

"What yoo yoo mean?" He sounded clearer. "Awout whosts?"

Amazingly, Flhi understood him. And from the terrified look on his face, she knew this was serious.

"Your friend hasn't gone ghost-hunting, has she?"

Wortley nodded slightly.

"Back to the old house?" Now Flhi was really worried.

Wortley nodded again.

"Then she's in serious danger," warned Flhi. "We have to stop her before she gets there. What time did she leave?"

The clock opposite Wortley's bed told him it was almost seven o'clock. Alannah had already been at the manor house for nearly an hour. He groaned.

"It's woo wate!"

16

"Let me get this clear," said Alannah, covertly checking the room for easy exit points. She was unnerved to see that the library's three doors were each firmly closed. "Are you telling me that you know where my parents are?"

Horrad smiled thinly and shook his head. "I wish I did. But if we work together I'll make sure that every resource available to the Ancient Order is focused on finding them." He steepled his fingers together, and rested his chin against them. "Frankly, Alannah, I'm surprised you didn't ask for our help earlier."

The words leapt out of Alannah's mouth before she could even think about stopping them. "Oh yeah? Well, I'm surprised you didn't offer help earlier. Like three years earlier!"

Horrad's green eyes darkened in anger and he

narrowed his gaze. For a brief moment his pupils seemed to swim with evil intent, but quickly his sympathetic smile returned.

"I promise you, we have been looking," he assured Alannah. "Ben and Sadie were . . . are . . . valued members of our psychic community. We want to find them just as much as you do."

I doubt that! Alannah wanted to scream at him. Behind Klaut Horrad's charm and smiles, Alannah could sense something deeply sinister.

"I'm sure your mother and father would want us to work together to find them," Horrad continued. "Maybe we can help each other in different ways at the same time."

"Now you're confusing me, Mr. Horrad. You keep saying that you need my help, but I really can't imagine why the leader of the Ancient Order of Psychics would require the assistance of a young girl. What have I got that you could possibly want?"

Horrad took a few moments to reply. He seemed to be choosing his words very carefully. "You appear to have friends in very powerful places. All I want is the opportunity to meet them."

Alannah still didn't understand. Her only friend in the world was Wortley Flint and right now she wasn't even on speaking terms with him. What could Klaut Horrad possibly want with a juvenile burglar? And why did her eyes suddenly feel so tired?

"I have no friends," she replied truthfully, blinking heavily. "Certainly none in high places."

Horrad was rapidly losing patience. In different circumstances, Alannah Malarra would be a dispensable irritant: somebody he could destroy with a single click of his fingers. But right now he badly needed her help, and that annoyed him. Horrad hated needing anything from anyone, especially the daughter of his bitter rivals, but he appeared to have little choice. Alannah had already made contact with beings from the Higher Dimension and that made her a vital part of his warmongering plans. And that wasn't all. He could sense an energy running through the youngster that wasn't entirely human. Perhaps she'd absorbed something magical from the Higher Dimension, or perhaps her powers had simply mutated to a level that had never been seen on Earth before. Either way, Alannah was clearly special. She was also a potent weapon that Horrad desperately wanted to harness for himself. If she could persuade or trick the A.N.G.E.L.s into opening a portal to the Higher Dimension, Horrad could pour his army of Gargoyles and Gnarls straight through and quickly take control of Evan City. He'd catch the enemy by surprise and launch a decisive attack that would wipe out the A.N.G.E.L.s once and for all. With those interfering do-gooders out of the way, there would be nothing to stop him turning Earth into his own psychic realm. And that day couldn't come soon enough.

He was tired of ordinary little people being in charge. The gray-suited politicians of the world didn't deserve their privileged positions, and they certainly had no right to wield power over alpha beings like himself. Centuries ago, psychics were regarded with awe. Kings and queens bowed to their incredible abilities. They were the medieval wizards, soothsayers, and alchemists; some even saw them as walking, talking deities. Horrad yearned to return the Earth to those more enlightened times. He was planning to create a second Dark Age, and with the help of Krot's murderous army of Gargoyles, he would terrorize the world until every citizen bowed to his will. Or died.

He wasn't prepared to stop there, either. Krot had already told him about the energy and riches that were just waiting to be harvested in the Higher Dimension. And Horrad was hungry to discover them for himself. Why settle for ruling one world, when he could rule two? He'd be twice as rich, twice as strong, and it would feel twice as good.

It was such a simple plan. All he needed was Alannah's cooperation. And he had hypnotic ways of getting exactly what he wanted.

"I'm talking about your friends with wings," Horrad explained.

He looked directly into Alannah's eyes and held her gaze. At first, he sensed resistance as she fought hard to turn her eyes away from his, but he soon felt the girl weaken and succumb. "You know the friends I mean—the ones with the shiny suits and guns. I'm sure they could help us find your missing parents."

Could he be right? The A.N.G.E.L. had said something like that before Alannah and Wortley escaped back to Earth. Everything she'd sensed told Alannah that Horrad should not be trusted. Yet his words were persuasive. If she hadn't known any better, she would have sworn he was influencing her thoughts, but such a notion was clearly laughable. After all, she was a powerful psychic and a psychic's will cannot be controlled. Can it?

"But you mustn't trust the A.N.G.E.L.s," Horrad told her. He could feel his hypnotic hold over her getting stronger and stronger. "They have been waging war on mankind for longer than history has been recorded. Why else would they arm themselves to the teeth and interfere with our lives? People like you and I have a responsibility to protect Earth from their constant incursions. That's why we have been blessed with such incredible powers. It's time you took your place in the psychic community and helped us drive out these invaders once and for all."

Why hadn't Alannah realized the truth earlier? A.N.G.E.L.s were the enemy. She could see it now. Flhi and her troopers had broken into her home. They had attacked her without provocation, kidnapping her best friend's soul in the process. They'd even tried to bribe her with the location of her mother and father. Surely only the worst kind of entities would employ such underhand tactics?

"Do you really think they *might* know where my mum and dad are?" she asked hopefully.

Hypnosis was such fun, and so effective, too. Horrad allowed himself a brief moment of triumph. He finally had the girl exactly where he wanted her.

"I'm absolutely convinced they do." He reached out and placed a reassuring hand on top of Alannah's. "Why don't we find out together?"

A sinister and ghostly chuckle brought Alannah back to her senses. To anybody else it would have been inaudible but, unfortunately for Klaut Horrad, she wasn't just anybody else. She could hear a ghost breathe from one hundred paces and a Gnarl's laugh was like a foghorn. It was as if a spell had suddenly been broken and Alannah's mind was her own once again. What had just happened?

She looked carefully at a peculiar shadow in the corner of the room, certain she'd just seen it move. "Who else is in this room?" she demanded to know. "Or should I say, *what* else?"

Horrad realized he now had little choice but to switch to Plan B. And Plan B meant brute force.

"I think it's time you met my associate." He slapped his palm theatrically against his forehead. "Oh silly me, how could I forget? You two already know each other."

The shadow instantly began to boil. Bubbles of darkness erupted from the floor, bursting and re-forming as something hideous began to take shape. Limbs quickly appeared. They were thick and heavily muscled, with spines riveted to the skin. A powerful torso followed, densely armored with a jigsaw of thick black plates. Last to form was the creature's head. Huge horns curled off an overhanging forehead and an all-too-familiar set of razor-sharp fangs fell from its wide jaw. Krot was back, and when he stood upright he was almost ten feet tall.

Krot could feel the Fleshi's vulnerability. He prowled toward Alannah, sniffing the air around her. Something seemed to please him and his lips peeled away from sharpened teeth in a very unfriendly smile.

"She's weak," he snarled. "Very weak. I could destroys her now."

Horrad held up his hand.

"Not yet, Krot. She has extraordinary powers and could still be of use to us. All we have to do is persuade her to help."

Alannah didn't like the sound of that. What did Horrad have in mind? Torture?

Krot sniffed the air again and his smile grew wide. "Now she's scared," he gloated. "Very scared."

"No harm will come to you, provided you agree to work with me," promised Horrad. "All I want you to do is take me to the A.N.G.E.L.s."

"The A.N.G.E.L.s are my enemy," Alannah told him truthfully. "They ambushed me in my own home and kidnapped my best friend. The last thing they'll want is to have any contact with me."

"Do they still have your friend?" asked Horrad.

"No, I managed to rescue him."

Horrad looked at her with suspicion. "Where did they take him?"

Alannah paused. She sensed her next answer would do her no good at all, but she didn't know what else to say.

"They took him with them," she said finally. "To their own dimension."

Now it was Horrad's turn to stay silent for a moment. This was so much more than he had expected. He rubbed his chin thoughtfully.

"If they took your friend with them, it would be impossible for you to rescue him. Unless, of course, you managed to . . ."

"She followed them," Krot barked. "The girl knows how to reach the A.N.G.E.L.s. She must have the power to open the Door of Souls."

"Shut up!" ordered Horrad. He stepped forward and grabbed Alannah by the shoulders. His eyes gripped hers. "Is that true? Did you follow them to the Higher Dimension?"

Alannah tried to shake herself free but Horrad was too strong. His fingers gripped her slender shoulders like the steel claws of a building-site crane.

"Let me go!" she cried.

Horrad's grip tightened further. "Answer my question, girl. Did you follow the A.N.G.E.L.s?"

Alannah nodded gingerly.

Horrad released his grip as though a thousand volts had surged through his hands. He stepped back and looked at Alannah in awe.

"Even I can't access the Higher Dimension. In fact, I've never met a psychic who can. If you can really do that, it would make you—"

"Even more powerfuls than you," interrupted Krot.

Horrad didn't speak. Instead, he raised his left hand and fired a huge astral bolt straight at Krot. It struck the Gnarl in the middle of his two vast chest plates, knocking him off his feet and propelling him across the room. A bookcase caught him and dumped him onto the floor.

"—a very powerful psychic," Horrad finished his sentence. "And if that's the case I must absolutely insist that you remain here with me. You cannot be allowed to fall into the hands of the enemy."

"Wait, I've already told you . . . ," Alannah began, but Horrad ignored her.

"Krot, get off the floor and make our guest comfortable." He walked across the library toward a large open fireplace. A huge antique mirror hung above the marble hearth and he stared into the reflection of the room, smiling as he watched one of Krot's gnarled hands seize Alannah by her hair. "I think there's something the young lady can help us with."

"Are you absolutely sure this is the right house?"
Wortley asked the A.N.G.E.L.s. "It looks so different in daylight."

They were standing in front of the two huge wrought-iron gates.

Flhi flapped her wings and glided effortlessly toward them, stopping when she reached the goblin-shaped metal intercom. For a moment she studied the bulbous nose, then reached into a small pouch that hung loosely from her combat belt and pulled out a handful of purple dust.

"This should tell us whether the girl is here." She sprinkled the dust onto the goblin.

At first nothing happened. Then the dust seemed to react with chemicals on the metal and the intercom began to glow. They all watched as it turned green, then red, and finally a beautiful shade of autumn orange.

"Check your recog chart, boys." Flhi sounded confident. "Tell me what it says."

Yell was first to pull what looked like a small plastic card from his chest pocket and hold it up to the goblin. It was his standard-issue entity recognition chart, or recog chart for short. Containing more color swatches than a paint chart, the recog chart could identify the presence of more than a million different beings and entities. The latest models could also give a date and time match. Yell's was already busy whizzing through its spectrum of colors.

"Found it!" Yell screamed excitedly as the card stopped its search.

"Read out what it says," ordered Flhi.

Yell peered at a line of tiny words sitting next to the orange swatch. "Fleshi female, adolescent. Warm trace, less than two hours old."

"Bingo!" Flhi nodded. "Alannah is here. And from what I know about her, she's probably in deep trouble."

"She can look after herself," said Gloom. "Remember what she did to Krot? If there's any trouble in that house, ma'am, the girl's probably causing it."

Flhi looked concerned. "At any other time I'd say you were correct, but right now she'll still be feeling the effects of astral flight. It takes your average Fleshi a week to fully recover. If she tries to use her powers she could be in for a shock."

"What kind of shock?" Now it was Wortley's turn to look worried.

Flhi sighed. "Her body is in no state to produce psychic energy. If she encounters a Gnarl and tries to engage it, she'll definitely come off second best. And if Krot has returned . . ."

"Who's Krot?" asked Wortley.

Flhi winced. "Let's hope you never find out." She turned to Yell and Gloom. "It's time we went to work. Yell, secure the perimeter. If anything moves, shoot first and ask questions later. Set your blaster to STUN. Gloom, do a silent sweep of the house. Start in the cellar and slowly work your way up. Be careful; we need to retain the element of surprise. As soon as you see anything, retreat to safety and use your telepathic communicator to contact me."

"I'll stay here and cover the gates, shall I?" Wortley asked hopefully.

Flhi pulled her ecto-blaster from its holster and flicked the setting from STUN to EVAN-SENT. She pointed her weapon at the goblin-shaped intercom and fired. It exploded in a shower of sparks and molten microchips and there was an audible *click* as the lock disengaged.

Flhi gave the iron gates a vicious kick. As they swung open she grabbed Wortley's hand. "You're coming with me."

Wortley resisted, pulling the A.N.G.E.L. back toward him. "Have you ever heard of hyenas?"

"If you're talking about those two little puppy dogs," Flhi teased, "we've got nothing to worry about. Now follow me, and stay behind the trees."

Crikey, this was worse than being with Alannah.

Wortley crept carefully along the line of horse chestnut trees that flanked the gravel driveway. He ducked behind the thick gnarly trunks, desperately hoping he couldn't be seen from the house or sensed by the hyenas.

Flhi was thinking about the hyenas, too, but for completely different reasons. Highly trained combat A.N.G.E.L.s can always find a way to turn a hazard into an advantage, and making use of two pairs of bone-crushing jaws, four rows of flesh-ripping teeth, and two hundred pounds of solid muscle seemed like an opportunity too good to miss. All she had to do was stop the animals from eating Wortley.

They reached the final tree and Flhi held up her hand, silently indicating that they should stop.

Wortley's military training consisted of little more than reruns of *The A-Team*, so it was hardly surprising that he completely ignored Flhi's instruction. In fact, he was still wondering why she'd stopped and who the heck she was waving at when he peered around the A.N.G.E.L.'s wings and found himself face-to-face with a twin set of snarling muzzles. Hyenas!

His first instinct was to run. His second was to run

even faster. And he would have, too, if Flhi hadn't quickly attached a snap hook to his belt loop and halted his retreat.

"Let me go." Wortley tugged and pulled, but didn't have the strength to break free. "Are you crazy? Those things are deadly."

"That's what I'm hoping." Flhi aimed her blaster at the thick steel chains holding the hyenas in place and calmly pulled the trigger twice.

The next few seconds seemed to happen in slow motion. Pulses of energy sailed toward the animals, singeing the fur on their muscled shoulders before slicing through the metal restraints. If there was ever any doubt that hyenas were dumb, the next moment proved it beyond doubt. Without metal chains to hold them in place, they tumbled forward, sprawling face-first onto the gravel. Yet instead of leaping to their feet and pouncing on a potential meal they remained prostrate on the ground, still unaware that they were free. And that was exactly the kind of delayed reaction Flhi had been hoping for. The poor beasts didn't stand a chance.

Flhi's wings flapped furiously, bashing Wortley about the ears as she flew toward the hyenas, dragging him behind her like a kite tail. One of the hyenas looked up as she approached and peered at her quizzically.

"Sit!" Flhi tweaked the animal's nose and fired a jet of astral gas from a concealed vent in the sleeve of her combat suit. The gas shot straight up the hyena's nostrils. Wortley was amazed to see the creature sneeze once, then fall back onto its haunches with the obedience of a household pet.

"Your turn now," she said to the second animal, administering an identical dose of gas. "Sit!"

The second hyena sneezed, too, and then did exactly as it was told.

Wortley was impressed. "How did you do that?"

"Easy," Flhi said nonchalantly. "We can control most low-sentient creatures such as reptiles and mammals. Elephants and whales can sometimes be quite difficult, especially the young ones, and dolphins simply refuse to cooperate. The bottlenose variety is a particular problem; they're sometimes even more aggressive than Fleshies."

"Fleshies?"

"It's the name we give to human beings like you," explained Flhi. "On account of the disgustingly sloppy and cumbersome shell that surrounds your souls. Ugh, I don't know how you can bear it." She gave a little shiver of revulsion.

Wortley looked down at his body and shrugged. He'd never thought of it quite like that.

"Here, take these." Flhi handed two lengths of thick metal chain to Wortley. At the end of each one sat a docile hyena. "Bring them with us; I think they'll be quite useful."

"But . . . they're . . ."

"Hyenas, I know. Don't worry. They're in a deep trance and they couldn't hurt an ant right now." She gave Wortley a look that told him he'd better be on his best behavior. "Well, not unless I tell them to."

Yep, this was definitely worse than being with Alannah.

Gloom didn't like cellars at the best of times, but the one belonging to the old manor house was particularly grim. He had been hoping for a nice, dry, well-lit wine cellar, packed floor to ceiling with vintage vino. Instead, he got a cold damp hole in the ground. The walls oozed with slime, the ceiling dripped mucus, and the floor was crawling with things that wriggled and squirmed.

He had dropped into it through a raised wooden trapdoor at the side of the house, situated next to what had looked like the old servants' entrance. A set of slippery stone stairs led up to the house from inside the damp room, and Gloom was eager to climb them. But first he had to follow orders, and that meant a thorough search of the area.

It was dark down there. The only light source came from slim cracks in the wooden trapdoor and those weak shafts of daylight were quickly swallowed by the room's foggy blackness. Even Gloom's astral glow struggled to make much of an impact, so he tapped the console on the side of his halo and switched to ecto-vision.

The effects were similar to night vision goggles, only twice as potent. He could now see from corner to corner as clear as day, only what he saw made him really wish he couldn't.

The walls, the floor, even the ceiling were all covered in a thick coat of brightly glowing ectoplasm. It was fresh, too, still quivering like splats of jelly, and that was what worried Gloom the most. It would take an army of Malevolents to produce this much gunk, and if it was as fresh as it looked, that army had to be somewhere nearby.

"Inspector Swift," he whispered feebly. "Are you there? Come in, Inspector Flhi."

"Oh, listen to the poor wikkle A.N.G.E.L.," a voice mocked from above him. "I fink he's calling for his mama."

Gloom looked up toward the ceiling, anxiously searching for the owner of the voice, hoping that perhaps Yell was playing a trick on him. But when he saw a dozen pairs of green eyes staring down at him like spotlights, he realized it was something far more sinister. He was surrounded by Ghouls.

Part of him was relieved that they weren't Gargoyles, but that was only a very small part. Ghouls might not be as big or strong as Gargoyles, but they were just as cruel. Gloom had read a few ecto-pedias from the academy library and knew that history had been unkind to these creatures, but he had little sympathy. He was far too busy being scared.

As the original inhabitants of the Dark Dimension, Ghouls had prospered long before the Gargoyles ever existed. They ruled their demonic dimension unchallenged, but eventually they grew bored of their natural habitat. So when a curious Ghoul stumbled across the natural portals linking their hostile realm with the much brighter and far more comfortable Earthly Dimension, they poured across the divide, causing as much mischief and mayhem as they could, teasing earthbound ghosts and terrifying the simple cave-dwelling folk who roamed Earth at the time. But then Gargoyles entered the Dark Dimension and the Ghouls' world was turned on its head. After a brutal war, the surviving Ghouls had been cast into slavery, forced to tend to their Gargoyle masters' every whim, and had turned even nastier. Some were conscripted into the Gargoyle army, often sent to certain death on the battlefield. A squadron of these Ghouls now lurked in the bowels of Pittingham Manor, and they were itching for a fight.

"Isn't Mama wistening?"

A huge blob of oil seemed to drip from the ceiling as the owner of the voice landed at Gloom's feet. The Ghoul boiled into the shape of a gremlin and grinned up at the lone combat A.N.G.E.L. "We covered the walls in spit, see. The big boss said it would block your twans-missions. Clever, ain't it?"

"You won't be needing that." A scaly hand grabbed Gloom's ecto-blaster and pulled it from its holster. A second ugly Ghoul examined the weapon closely. "Oo-oo, nice toy."

More Ghouls fell from the ceiling. The floor writhed as they all took shape, filling the cellar with a swarm of unpleasantness. Gloom stopped counting at twenty. This was serious.

"Come in, Inspector Swift," he pleaded. "Backup required. Combat A.N.G.E.L. under attack. Send help. Please send—"

"Shurrup!" A heavy hand cuffed Gloom around the head, knocking his halo to the ground. It severed the telepathic link immediately and took away his ecto-vision. Suddenly, the room was plunged into darkness again, and Gloom was virtually blind. The only things he could see were green eyes all around him.

"Shall we take him up to the big boss?" a small Ghoul asked excitedly. "I weckon he'll be dead pleased."

"Not yet," said the group's leader. Somewhere in the darkness a switch was flicked, and a whir that Gloom recognized all too well echoed off the cellar walls. A Ghoul had powered up his ecto-blaster. "Wet's have some fun first, boys, eh?"

Flhi tapped her communicator again and spoke urgently. "Yell! Are you receiving? Come in, Yell."

"Blimey, Inspector," responded Yell. "There's no need to shout."

"Gloom's in trouble. I think the enemy are back."

"And Krot?" Yell sounded nervous.

"Let's hope not." Flhi hoped she sounded convincing. "Meet me at the entrance to the cellar. And draw your blaster. I think you're going to need it."

"What about me?" asked Wortley. "And what's all this about an enemy?"

"You'll find out soon enough." Flhi clambered onto the back of one of the docile hyenas. "Now hop onto yours. I knew these things would come in handy."

Yell had been first to arrive at the entrance to the cellar and now couldn't quite believe what he was seeing. Flhi and the Fleshi boy had just emerged from the darkness, riding bareback on what looked like a couple of pygmy bears.

"What the . . . ?" Yell spluttered.

"I'll explain later," shouted Flhi as she approached. "Stand back, Yell, we've only got one shot at this."

She kicked her heels against the side of her mount, and the hyena's trot turned into a sprint. Flhi clung on to the ridge of fur that grew across the animal's shoulders. "I hope that blaster's fully charged, Yell. Now follow me in!"

Yell stepped aside just in time. Flhi and her hyena thundered past, closely followed by Wortley and his. At first, it seemed that they would crash straight into the stone wall of the house. But, at the last minute, Flhi pushed her animal's muscled neck forward and pointed its snout toward the rotting wooden trapdoors. There was no time for the hyena to alter course or even slow down. It simply crashed onto the doors, shattering the weak wood into tiny fragments, and disappeared into the darkness below.

Wortley hung on as his hyena followed Flhi's and plunged headfirst into the dingy cellar. Yell shook his head in bewilderment and tentatively peered into the dark hole in the floor. He could hear the sound of a struggle below.

He edged closer to the hole, straining to see into the blackness. "Inspector, are you all right?"

A gnarled green claw reached out of the cellar and grabbed Yell by his collar. "Don't be shy, wikkle A.N.G.E.L. Come and join the party."

Alannah knew she was in serious trouble. The Gnarl had her pinned against the library wall and she could do nothing about it. No matter how hard she struggled, she simply couldn't break free. And when she attempted to use her psychic energy, she found she could do little more than dribble harmless ectoplasm onto the floor.

"You've a lot to learn, young lady," Horrad snickered. "Astral travel isn't something you should undertake lightly. It drains your body of energy and leaves you weak. The first time I tried it, it took me a week to recover. And it's no use trying to use your astral powers, because you won't have any for days."

"You're defenseless," sneered Krot, tightening his grip on Alannah's chest. "Do you wants to beg for mercy?"

"You can't do this," Alannah said unconvincingly. "People know I'm here. When I don't return home they'll come looking for me. And they'll probably bring the police."

"By the time anyone realizes you're missing it will be far too late. We'll be long gone and you'll be . . . well . . . dead. Now hold her still, Krot."

The demon growled into his prisoner's ear and gleefully tightened his grip, forcing the air out of Alannah's lungs in a surge. She gasped weakly, struggling to breathe, and then squirmed as Horrad stepped toward her. He came close, too close, and their noses almost touched. She could feel his foul breath on her cheek. Even his oily skin had a stale, unpleasant odor that reminded Alannah of decaying wood.

When he placed his hands on her cheeks she whimpered helplessly. For the first time in years she cried out for her daddy.

"Ben can't help you now," Horrad sneered. "Nobody can."

His thick thumbs dug painfully into Alannah's skin as he held her head still. He was staring into her eyes, but it was no ordinary stare. It was as if he was searching for something that existed behind her eyes, and he kept turning his head from side to side, trying to get a better view. Finally, his eyes widened and a smile twisted across his lips. Horrad had found whatever he was looking for.

"She's so weak," he told Krot. "The light is barely visible but I think I can see it. This shouldn't take long."

Excitement was urging Horrad to rush, but the old psychic took a deep breath and calmed his dancing nerves. In just a few seconds' time he might finally be able to unlock the secret door to the vortex that lay between his world and the next.

Victorious Evanescent sentinels had used powerful astral enchantments to slam the door shut after the first Great Spirit War, supposedly forever. But Horrad had always suspected that a force existed somewhere on Earth that was powerful enough to overcome the sentinels' magic. And he wasn't the only one. According to a set of mystic scrolls, thought to once belong to King Arthur's psychic, Merlin, the key to the Door of Souls was a family possession — passed from one generation to the next. Horrad had spent the best part of half a century desperately trying to find it, frantically scouring the world's museums, searching the heirlooms of aristocratic households and buying private antiquity collections in his attempt to track it down.

He'd failed of course, because he'd been looking in all the wrong places. He now suspected that the key wasn't a physical talisman at all. It was probably something genetic: an enchanted piece of DNA perhaps, carried in the blood of a single family and passed down from one female to the next. And if his suspicions were accurate, there was every chance he was holding the precious key in his hands right now. He'd just never expected it to be in the form of a freckle-splattered twelve-year-old girl.

"Aarrgghh!" Alannah couldn't stop herself from screaming. Horrad's fingertips felt like burning matches against her cheeks. Needles of heat penetrated her skin, heading toward her skull. The pain twisted and turned as if it had a mind of its own. Sometimes it burrowed straight ahead, other times it turned and doubled back. It seemed to be deliberately searching for something, and every movement took it deeper and deeper into Alannah's body.

"It's no use resisting." Horrad was breathless. "You can't repel me. But I can ease the agony. Surrender and this will all be over quickly. Don't you want the pain to go away?"

Just like a vampire, he was ready to drain his victim.

The psychic tubes at the ends of his fingers were all firmly embedded into Alannah's flesh, but it wasn't her blood that he wanted. For his plans to work he needed to slowly siphon every last drop of Alannah's psychic energy from her body into his own. Gently, dribble by dribble, the transfer began.

Alannah was terrified. She could feel her power being drained away. She shook like a rag doll in a toddler's hand as she put up a desperate struggle. Then, after one final convulsion, she surrendered.

Energy suddenly flooded into Horrad's body and he pulsed with so much force that at one point he thought he might explode. His body struggled to contain the incredible surge of power, and, one by one, shards of blinding light began to burst through the pores of his skin. Flames of energy were licking across his limbs, devouring him, but he didn't stop. Now that he finally possessed a weapon that could defeat the A.N.G.E.L.s, Horrad felt invincible.

"Is she the key?" Krot asked hopefully. Shards of light from Alannah's energy were burning pinprick holes in his ecto-shell and he cowered behind a solid wood bookcase. "Can you uses her energy to unlocks the Door of Souls?"

"I don't need to," Horrad gasped triumphantly. "Look!"

He nodded toward the huge mirror hanging above the open fire. What had once been a wide pane of reflective glass was now a swirling mass of blinding white energy. Twisting clouds of air and dust were being sucked toward it, corkscrewing their way across the room before vanishing into the vortex. Finally, the astral enchantments had been removed.

"I think it's time we assembled our army. In twenty-four hours' time, the Higher Dimension will be ours!"

"Where are they, soldier?"

Stickler didn't know what to say. Flhi and her troops had been due to report for litter duty more than thirty minutes ago but they still hadn't shown up. Rage had come down to street level expecting to gloat. Watching Flhi Swift being humiliated was one of his favorite spectator sports and he had been in unusually buoyant spirits. And in particular he wanted to let her know that she would be missing out on the biggest mission in eons — to resecure the Door of Souls. He couldn't wait to see her face when he gave her that little piece of information.

Yet as the seconds had ticked by, his mood had grown darker and darker. That blackness was now matched only by his temper.

"There had better be a good reason for this," he

snapped as he impatiently checked the timepiece sewn into the cuff of his combat jacket.

"We could always track them," suggested a nervous Stickler. "That way we'd know exactly where Inspector Flhi and her crew are."

Rage was impressed. Few combat A.N.G.E.L.s knew that the precinct's sophisticated tracking system existed, and fewer still would dare to suggest it was used to find a member of their own team. Not only would that be illegal, it would also violate every one of the missing A.N.G.E.L.s' rights. Tracking was always a last resort and was usually reserved for Evan City's worst rule-breakers. Stickler clearly had leadership potential.

Rage was the only Evan City officer authorized to use the system. That way, he could stop suspicious combat A.N.G.E.L.s from tracking their wives, or prevent paranoid parents from snooping on their children. And as a result, the system was rarely utilized and Mayor Cheer had recently threatened to shut it down and use the savings to fund an extension to his palatial office.

"Breathe a word of this, Stickler, and I'll have you cleaning the city's sewers for the rest of eternity," Rage hissed. "If anyone asks, we were running a scheduled system test."

Rage reached into his combat suit and pulled a small console from a concealed pocket. He pressed his thumb against an ID sensor and seconds later the gadget burst into life. A fountain of blue light spewed from a tiny screen, constructing a three-dimensional hologram of Evan City. Tiny red dots crawled around the holographic streets like an army of ants, each one representing a single resident. There were thousands of them.

"Locate Inspector Flhi Swift!" he ordered.

The console whirred as it trawled the red dots searching for Flhi. Names flashed up over each dot as the powerful processor scanned every single inhabitant. Moments later, the console beeped loudly and displayed its search result:

NEGATIVE SEARCH — INSPECTOR FLHI SWIFT NOT FOUND

"That's impossible," Rage growled. "Search again. Locate Inspector Flhi Swift."

The console whirred again. Seconds later it beeped.

NEGATIVE SEARCH — INSPECTOR FLHI SWIFT NOT FOUND

How could this be happening? The tracking system was foolproof. Any A.N.G.E.L. could be located in seconds, and that included Flhi Swift.

"Locate Trooper Yell!" Rage snapped.

NEGATIVE SEARCH — TROOPER YELL NOT FOUND

"Locate Trooper Gloom!"

NEGATIVE SEARCH — TROOPER GLOOM NOT FOUND

Rage couldn't believe it. Either the system was malfunctioning or Flhi Swift had found a way to block it. And Rage doubted that even she was that clever. He had one last test.

"Find Commander Rage!"

The console whirred again. This time it gave two beeps.

POSITIVE SEARCH — COMMANDER RAGE

LOCATED IN SECTOR 9

Sections of the three-dimensional map melted away until only a small corner of Evan City remained. In the middle, a red dot pulsed like a throbbing spot and the commander's name hovered above it. Beside it was a second dot, and in smaller letters was the name of Sergeant Stickler. The tracking system was working. And that could only mean one thing.

"She's not in the city," Rage said in disbelief. "There's only one place she can be."

He tapped the keypad on his console and a new, much larger map appeared in the air. This time it was in the shape of a sphere, and billions of tiny green dots swarmed all over it. There were no names above these dots. They belonged to anonymous Fleshies and the tracking system had no idea who they were. Elsewhere, large swathes of the sphere were colored in ocean blue. Rage gave the order. "Sweep the Earthly Dimension for Inspector Flhi Swift."

Technically, he needed the mayor's permission to perform an out-of-jurisdiction search, but Commander Rage paid little attention to technicalities.

The console whirred for what seemed like a decade.

Finding a pin in a mountain of needles would have been an easier task but, just as Rage was beginning to fear the machine wasn't up to the job, the console beeped twice. It was the result he had been hoping for.

POSITIVE SEARCH — INSPECTOR FLHI SWIFT LOCATED IN ED SECTOR 8, REGION 1

The sphere turned in midair, coming to a stop when it reached a funny-looking island off the coast of a large continent. As before, the rest of the image melted away until only a small strip of land remained. At the top a little red dot pulsed away angrily. Above it was a familiar name: Inspector Flhi Swift.

"Got her!" Rage punched the air. "She'd better not sabotage our mission in Pittingham Manor. Charge your blaster, Stickler. We've got a fugitive to apprehend."

Flhi Swift was surrounded by Ghouls. They howled and cackled excitedly as they circled like a gang of playground bullies. The only thing that stopped them from attacking was the snapping jaws of the fretting hyenas. And from the determined look on the Ghouls' ugly faces, that was unlikely to keep them at bay for long.

"Nice doggies," sneered one of the hideous creatures. "Do they beg?"

A scaled claw reached out from the crowd, uncurled a long talon, and jabbed Wortley's hyena on the leg. A chorus of amused snickers rang out as the animal whirled and snapped at thin air, almost jettisoning its frightened rider in the process.

"I know, wet's get the pretty wikkle Evanescent to show them how to," the largest Ghoul suggested cruelly.

An ecto-blast tore a strip of light through the darkened cellar, narrowly missing Flhi's shoulder before it exploded against the soggy wall behind her. Oh boy! These Ghouls had weapons.

"Go on, A.N.G.E.L., beg us not to hurt you."

A second blast grazed her left knee pad. Flhi knew not to panic. Unfortunately, the same couldn't be said of her hyena. The ecto-blast had singed its hind leg and the smell of the creature's own frazzled fur was making it crazy. The last place anyone wants to be when a hyena goes loco is in an enclosed space. Like a cellar.

Ghouls crashed against the damp walls as the hyena bolted blindly around the room. It snapped and snarled, sinking its powerful jaws into anything it could find, and it had no trouble finding Ghouls. The small room was packed solid with them. Their sticky ecto-shells were no protection against one of the animal kingdom's strongest bites, and before long the cellar was awash with dismembered body parts.

Soon the Ghouls were doing the hyena's job for it. Panic spread among them and in their desperate rush to escape through the walls they began to fight one another. Talons clashed like dueling sabers—chopping, cutting, slicing, and hacking.

And it didn't stop there. Wortley's hyena had no intention of missing out on all the fun and happily bit chunks out of any passing Ghoul it could get its teeth into.

When it was all over, the inside of the cellar looked worse than a medieval battle scene. Flhi had never seen so much ectoplasm, and that troubled her.

"I knew it; the Door of Souls *is* open," she said out loud. "I've never seen so many Ghouls together in one place before. It's as if someone has gathered a demon army. And if that's the case . . ."

"We need to get out of here," urged Gloom. "I've never been good with armies. It's kind of like an instinctive fear of being outnumbered."

"Me too!" bellowed Yell. "I get this urge to run. It's really strange; I just can't control my legs."

"Pull yourselves together; we're not going anywhere yet." Flhi gently patted her hyena. "Those Ghouls seemed to be allergic to hyenas, so as long as we've got these two, I think we'll be safe. Anyway, Alannah's here somewhere and I get the feeling that when we find her we'll also find out why this place is crawling with enemy troops."

"Oh dear." Gloom rolled his eyes. "I was afraid you were going to say something like that."

This was the moment Horrad had dreamt of. Nothing could stop him now, and in less than twenty-four hours' time he would be master of the Dark Dimension, the Higher Dimension, and every dimension in between. Power and glories beyond even his ego-fueled dreams lay ahead and it would all begin with the death of the only being capable of standing in his way: twelve-year-old Alannah Malarra.

"Stop this," Alannah pleaded weakly. She could feel her life slipping away. "Please."

"I can't," he told her. "You're too dangerous."

"I don't want to die," she sobbed.

"Nobody ever does," Horrad laughed. "But you must. There's no other way."

"Let me kills her," begged Krot, excited by the prospect of a sacrifice. The threatening horns on his head stood to attention.

"You?" Horrad laughed. "Even now, so close to death, this girl would be too powerful for you. Look . . ."

He swung around and poured Alannah's energy toward the Gnarl. Krot's ecto-shell instantly began to bubble and pop.

The Gnarl stumbled backward, retreating from the unbearable heat. Horrad smirked as he turned away. It never hurt to show who was in charge.

Krot nursed his fresh wounds. "So how *do* we kills her?"

"We don't," Horrad told him. "The vortex will do it for us. Right now, it's absorbing her powers. With each strand of her energy, it becomes stronger and larger. Eventually, there will be nothing left of Alannah Malarra; she will *become* the vortex, and when that happens there won't be an entity alive with enough power to close it. At that moment, nothing will stand in our way. Then you can have your revenge."

A small figure stirred in the corner of the room.

"What have you done to my mirror?" The earl pointed toward the vortex. "Do you know how much that's worth? It's been in the family for generations!"

"Sleep!" But this time Horrad's hypnosis didn't work. Channeling Alannah's energy had weakened him.

Defiantly, the earl pushed himself up from the chair, his legs buckling slightly as he stood.

"Sleep? Certainly not! I think I've had quite enough shut-eye for one day." He looked quizzically at Horrad. "What on Earth are you doing to that poor girl?"

"Help me, please." Alannah's desperate plea was little more than a whisper. "He's trying to kill me."

The earl struggled to make sense of what he was seeing. Horrad appeared to be burning. He shone with a blinding glow that chased away even the room's darkest shadows. And the flames seemed to be coming from the girl.

"Put her down at once," he ordered.

"I said SLEEP!"

"And I said no! Now stop whatever it is that you're doing right now, young man." He took a determined step toward Horrad. "Or I'm afraid I'll have to ask Samson to call the authorities. Or at least bring a fire extinguisher."

Krot stepped between the two Fleshies, snorting with disdain. "Do you wants me to put him to sleeps permanently?"

Horrad didn't answer. He was still trying to figure out what had happened to his hypnotic powers. Surely, his abilities should have been stronger, not weaker.

"Have you been in some horrific accident, sir?" The earl gazed up in curious disbelief at the huge Gnarl. "Or are you modeling this season's latest Halloween costume?"

Krot flexed his talons and growled menacingly. "I'm really going to enjoys this, old fool. And as soon as I've killed you, I'm going to kills you again."

The earl finally sensed that he might be in a spot of trouble and retreated from the huge Gnarl. His look of curious amusement was quickly replaced by a frown of fear.

"There's no escape, old man. Looks behind you." The Gnarl pointed toward the mirror. The boiling light was alive with green-skinned figures. Krot's army of hideous Gargoyles was already beginning to stream through the vortex. "It's time to die."

Gulp! A swarm of fangs and horns and claws and vicious spines was surging forward, threatening to spill into his library at any second. It had to be stopped!

"I might be old," said the earl, circling away from Krot and his demons. "But I'm not ready to die just yet."

Before Krot could stop him, the earl lunged toward a frayed rope that dangled from the wall. He pulled it frantically. Then pulled it again. But nothing seemed to happen.

"Oh dear," Krot hissed sarcastically. "Looks like it's broken."

The earl smiled and shook his head. "On the contrary, my good sir. I've just had the entire communication system serviced. It's never worked better."

Elsewhere in the manor house, twenty polished copper bells rang out louder than screeching seagulls. Connected by over a mile of thin copper wire, most of them were in the bowels of the house, where a small army of servants had once lived and worked. Unlike his ancestors, the current Earl of Pittingham had neither the money nor the need to employ staff on such a grand scale. Instead, he had learned to rely on the services of his trusted footman, Samson. Employee and employer had long since agreed that the bells were only ever to be rung in a dire emergency. So when an explosion of sound filled the back rooms of the house, Samson jumped with fright. This meant trouble.

He leapt to his feet and snatched up the weapon he kept in the servants' quarters, safely out of the earl's way. There was no shortcut to the library. It was two hundred paces away, up a steep flight of stairs, and he'd have to sprint along three long corridors to reach it. At full speed, he could be there in forty-five seconds. He hoped that would be quick enough.

Samson wasn't the only one to hear the bells. They rang out in the cellar, too. Despite its damp and dark appearance, the subterranean room had once been used to store a rather impressive selection of wines. Though the bottles had all been drunk now, the bells still worked perfectly well and, when the earl tugged on the frayed rope in the library, Flhi Swift heard his call for help.

"That's got to be Alannah," she said. "And it sounds like she's in trouble." She pointed up at the rattling bell that hung from the wall. "Yell, Gloom, follow that wire. My guess is that it will lead you straight to her. Take a shortcut through the walls and send me a signal as soon you get there."

"What will you be doing?" asked Gloom.

Flhi patted her hyena. "Wortley and I will be bringing help."

Wortley watched the two troopers glance nervously at each other before they stepped toward the nearest cellar wall and disappeared, slipping effortlessly behind the slimy brickwork. Neat trick.

"What if it's not Alannah?" he asked.

"Then she'll be close by, I'll stake my wings on it." Flhi's reply was confident. "You can stay here if you want."

It was a tempting offer. But he knew that Alannah would never leave him stranded, and loyalty forced him to be brave.

"No chance." He shook his head. "She's my friend."

Flhi admired his spirit; perhaps Fleshies weren't quite as bad as they seemed. "Hold on tight, then."

She kicked her heels sharply against the hindquarters of her hyena, slapping the backside of Wortley's animal at the same time. Both creatures lurched forward and sprung up the wooden steps that led into the house. A bolt from Flhi's blaster disabled the rusted lock and the sole of her boot sent the cellar door swinging outward.

As she had expected, they emerged into a large and deserted kitchen. A single bell was bouncing furiously in the corner of the room beside a number of other identical brass bells. The others were all still, and above each bell was a tiny plaque with a single word painted upon it. The word above the ringing bell was LIBRARY.

"Look." Flhi pointed up at the panel. "That's where she is."

"This house is huge," Wortley said. "How will we find it?"

Footsteps suddenly hammered out a rhythm on the floorboards outside. Somebody was running along the corridor toward the kitchen. They were moments away from being discovered, and there was nowhere to hide. Flhi gripped her blaster reluctantly. Would she really have to shoot a Fleshi?

The running feet reached the entrance to the kitchen but didn't stop. They continued on up the corridor, carrying their well-dressed owner with them.

"That's how we find the library," said Flhi, spotting an opportunity. "Follow that Fleshi!"

"Any last wishes, old-timer?" Krot snickered.

"My elephant gun," the earl croaked. Then he heard the footsteps.

Krot heard them, too, and smiled, unsheathing his large fangs. "Looks like you won'ts be the only person I get to kills today."

The library door swung open and crashed against the wall, squashing a stray Ghoul against the antique wallpaper. Samson didn't see that. Nor did he see the huge Gnarl that was holding his employer three feet above the ground. All he saw was the Earl of Pittingham floating in midair.

"Shoot it!" urged the earl. "Shoot it now!"

Krot dropped the old man. A Fleshi with a gun was much more of a challenge and, as the newcomer waved the barrel in the air, Krot calmly closed in for the kill.

"Freeze, demon! You're under arrest!"

Flhi's hyena bounded into the library and crashed straight into the back of Samson. The hunting gun went off with a bang, spraying the ceiling with hundreds of tiny pellets, and the footman stumbled forward, falling next to the cowering body of his employer.

"Good thinking," the earl congratulated his employee, patting him weakly on the back. "You brought reinforcements."

The impact was too much for Flhi, who lost her grip on the hyena. She tumbled off its back and bounced onto the floor, rolling head over heels across the carpet. When she finally came to a halt she was at Krot's feet and her fully charged ecto-blaster was no longer in her hand.

Krot was about to bring his clenched fist down onto the A.N.G.E.L.'s skull when a second hyena leapt into the room. The creature stared him straight in the eye and showed no fear. The same couldn't be said of the Fleshi boy clinging desperately to its back.

Wortley stared in horror at the army of Gargoyles dripping through a burning hole in the wall, and at the huge creature that seemed to be staring directly at him.

After a few deep breaths, Wortley realized the creature was actually looking past him, at the object flying toward him through the air. He reached out and grabbed Flhi's ecto-blaster as it came close. It felt like a toy gun and easily slotted into his small palm, but the heat that pulsed from the insulated handle told Wortley he was handling something with frightening power.

"Throw me the blaster," yelled Flhi. "Quickly!"

"Not so fast!" Krot reached down and dragged Flhi off the floor.

His razor-sharp talons easily penetrated the ecto-armor in her combat suit, and Flhi gasped in shock as she felt her skin being sliced open.

Krot used the fallen A.N.G.E.L. as a shield. "Shoots and she dies. Don't shoots and she still dies. It's up to you."

"Run, Wortley. Run!" a weak voice suddenly urged. "Save yourself!"

Alannah? Wortley scoured the room until he spotted his friend slumped in the arms of a man Wortley didn't recognize. She looked barely alive.

"You shouldn't have come . . . too dangerous," Alannah croaked. "Go home . . . while you still can."

"That's good advice, little boy," Horrad agreed. "But it's too late for that now. I'm afraid you'll have to stay right here, with your friend."

Wortley pointed Flhi's weapon at Horrad.

The old psychic smiled coldly. "You can't hurt someone as powerful as me with that puny A.N.G.E.L. weapon. Go on, try it."

Wortley needed no second invitation. His finger gleefully squeezed the trigger and the ecto-blaster spat two fiery bolts from its short barrels. It took a millisecond for them to reach their target, but Wortley was horrified to see them deflect past the strange man and explode harmlessly against the wall behind. He tried again, but the second round was just as useless.

"There's nothing you can do to hurt me," Horrad smugly told him. "And there's nothing you can do to save Alannah."

19

Stickler could hardly believe what the tracking system was showing him. Either the hardware was malfunctioning or there was a bug in the complex software.

"Where's my reconnaissance report, Stickler?" barked Rage. He didn't like to be kept waiting and, if he was going to apprehend the fugitives, every second would count.

"Just give me a minute, sir," Stickler requested as he tapped in the coordinates for a third time. "I'm having a spot of trouble getting an accurate readout."

"You've got ten seconds." Rage meant it. If the inspector and her team slipped through his fingers this time, he'd make sure Stickler paid the price.

Ten . . . nine . . . eight . . . seven . . . Stickler counted down the seconds in his head as he waited for the tracking system to produce its report. He hoped that this time it would be glitch-free. The hologram finally appeared on the count of *two*. And it was identical to the last one.

"I'm afraid it's malfunctioning," Stickler said miserably. "We'll have to go in blind."

"Malfunctioning?" snapped Rage. "That system swallows an eighth of my departmental budget every single year. The last upgrade cost more than our entire staff salary. Something that expensive simply doesn't malfunction. Whatever it says, it's right. Now read the report!"

It couldn't be right. It was impossible.

"Three A.N.G.E.L.s. Five Fleshies. Two large nonsentient creatures, probably dogs. And . . ." Stickler paused. He refused to accept what he was seeing.

"And what?"

". . . and seventy-four Malevolent entities. Make that seventy-five . . . seventy-six . . . seventy—"

"NONSENSE!" Rage exploded. "You're misinterpreting the data. Look again."

Stickler did as he was ordered and found that his commanding officer was indeed right: Now there were even more entities.

"Eighty-nine, sir. Ninety. Ninety-one . . ."

Rage shoved Stickler out of the way and stared at the tracking holograph. What he saw horrified him. An army of Malevolents really did appear to be gathering in the library of the manor house, and all that was standing in its way was a rookie inspector and a couple of incompetent troopers.

"It can't be true," Rage whispered to himself.

But there could be no doubt. The Malevolents now numbered more than one hundred, and the count was increasing with every passing second. After several eons of peace, the Door of Souls had been opened once again and the second war between Evanescents and Malevolents had already begun.

"Return to the precinct and raise the alarm," Rage calmly instructed Stickler. "Get every available combat A.N.G.E.L. armed and ready for battle within the hour. Then contact the mayor and tell him to summon the sentinels. It looks like our mission needs to be brought forward twenty-four hours."

"Sentinels, sir?"

Rage nodded sagely. It was going to take far more than a battalion of combat A.N.G.E.L.s to protect Evan City this time. The Higher Dimension was about to be hit by a tsunami of pure malevolence, and only the Ancient Powers could protect them, as they had once before. Even then, it might not be enough. If the enemy had somehow recruited Alannah Malarra, her power would make them too strong to repel.

"We need all the help we can get," Rage admitted. "And perhaps a little luck, too."

Wortley wasn't about to watch his friend die. He had saved Alannah before and he would save her again. Only this time, it would take a lot more than a few whacks to her chest. He hoped that the hyenas would provide him with a little cover. Their snarling jaws were ripping through the hapless Gargoyles as easily as in the cellar but, as one creature fell, three more dropped out of the vortex to replace their fallen comrade. The library was rapidly filling up with Gargoyles and the hyenas would soon be overwhelmed.

Yell and Gloom were doing their best to help. They had followed Flhi's instructions and traced the vibrating copper wire back to the library. What they found when they arrived made them want to beat a hasty retreat back to Evan City, but even they knew that this was no time for cowardice. Something cataclysmic was on the verge of happening and they were the Higher Dimension's only line of defense.

The appearance of the two A.N.G.E.L.s had bought Wortley some time. Horrad was distracted, even Krot was ducking to avoid the flying ecto-bolts, and nobody seemed to notice as Wortley edged his way toward Alannah. Now, all he had to do was figure out how to rescue her. Surely, there had to be a way.

Flhi knew what Wortley had to do. But did he have the strength? And was he brave enough? Somehow he had to sever the tie between Horrad and Alannah.

It was the only way to save his friend. But time was running out.

"Break the bond," she urged. "He's draining her like a vampire!"

Vampire? Wortley didn't like the sound of that. Suddenly, he wished he'd let his mother add extra garlic to last night's chili con carne.

"I don't suppose you've got any silver bullets, have you?" he asked. He already knew the answer, but he was desperate for a little help. Anything at all!

Then he spotted something that he knew vampires hated: A large golden crucifix was hanging on the library wall. And it was just above his head. Quickly, he snatched it off its brass hanger and thrust it toward Horrad.

"Get off her, or I'll melt you."

Horrad looked down at the young boy holding the crucifix. It was a beautiful trinket, but unless it was made from radioactive plutonium, it was hardly a threat. The boy was clearly an idiot.

The first wave of Krot's Malevolent army was an impressive sight. As they poured through the Door of Souls, green demons jostled for position, snapping and snarling at their neighbors, and some of the larger Gargoyles rattled razor-sharp fangs in a crude display of dominance. The hyenas were overwhelmed.

Horrad had waited decades for this moment, and it was made all the sweeter by the knowledge that Alannah Malarra was dying to make it happen. What would Ben and Sadie think of that? Their beloved daughter murdered by the very man they had sought to destroy. His only regret was that his enemies weren't there to see it.

The heat had gone from Alannah. Her body lay cold and spent in Horrad's hands and the last wisps of energy were being sucked toward the vortex. In seconds she would be empty. Nothing could stop Horrad now. Absolutely nothing!

Or so he thought. Because the last thing he expected was a bang to the side of the head from a solid gold crucifix.

The golden cross struck with a reassuring *thud*.

Horrad staggered, released Alannah, and collapsed onto the floor in a heap.

Wortley spotted his chance. He dived across the floor and grabbed hold of Alannah. Frantically, he dragged his friend back across the room. He retreated behind an upturned desk and breathed a sigh of relief. They were safe!

Horrad had other ideas. He shook his head and sat up, wondering what had hit him. Something warm and sticky dripped from a gash above his temple and when he spotted the bloodstained crucifix he realized what had happened. The small boy had actually attacked him. Now somebody else would have to die.

"Krot, find the girl," Horrad ordered. "And kill the meddling boy!"

"I wouldn't do that if I were you!" warned a sinister voice. It seemed to come from behind the library walls. "Unless, of course, you want to give me the perfect excuse to find out what the Evan-sent setting on my ecto-blaster can really do."

Commander Rage stepped effortlessly through the walls and trained his supercharged ecto-blaster straight at Krot. His other hand held Stickler's smaller weapon, which he waved as a warning to any Malevolent that dared to attack. Both trigger fingers spasmed excitedly; he had waited a long time for this moment.

"Rage," hissed Krot. "I hads hoped you'd retireds."

"Retired?" Rage responded in surprise. His huge wings were set to battle-ready, and he could feel the incredible power surging against his shoulders. "There's no way I'd miss out on the chance to put Fugitive 1635 behind bars."

"Those sentinels of yours couldn't holds me. What makes you thinks you can do any better?"

"The sentinels were careless," admitted Rage bitterly. "But I'm not! Now why don't you put my inspector down and try your luck with somebody who can fight back?"

"Gots a soft spot for her, haves you?" Krot ignored Rage's threat and lifted Flhi up into the air. He gently stroked a talon through one of the A.N.G.E.L.'s silver pigtails and sniffed her hungrily. "I likes her. If you hands over those little peashooters of yours, I mights even let her live."

"You know what, Krot?" Rage asked, smiling. "That's exactly what I hoped you'd say."

He moved with the speed of a hunting leopard. Both wings snapped open, filling half the room and decapitating a gaggle of screeching Gargoyles in the process. "Here Flhi, catch!"

Stickler's ecto-blaster left Rage's hand and shot through the air. It was far too high for Flhi to catch but it was never intended for her anyway. The weapon was bait for Krot and the huge Gnarl eagerly snapped it up!

Instinct made Krot let go of Flhi and he reached out for the spinning ecto-blaster, only realizing his mistake when it was too late.

Flhi dropped to the floor. She was free. Quickly, she rolled away from the Gnarl and sprang to her feet.

Krot tossed the useless blaster aside and snarled gleefully. There was only one way to deal with Rage, and he had hoped all along that it would come down to this: hand-to-claw combat.

Flhi needed a weapon, but Krot still stood between her

and the one he'd dropped. "Hey, Fleshi!" she shouted. "Throw me my blaster!"

Wortley ignored her. He was holding Alannah in his arms and appeared to be sobbing. For Evan's sake, young Fleshies were so weak.

Flhi was by Wortley's side in two brisk flaps of her wings. A trio of drooling Gargoyles had spotted her maneuver and excitedly closed in for the kill. Flhi wasn't worried. She let them get near, then batted them away with a flick from her wings.

She tapped the boy on the shoulder. "Where's my weapon?"

"What has he done to her?" Wortley looked up at Flhi through watery eyes. "She's dying."

Flhi didn't have time for this. Couldn't the boy see that she had a battle to fight?

"Just give me the blaster!"

"She won't move," Wortley ignored Flhi. "We need a doctor."

Flhi sighed. She had once attended a lecture on basic Fleshi bio-structures. She thought hard, trying to remember the things she had learned.

"Check her eyes?" Flhi asked. "Look for a light."

Wortley peeled back Alannah's eyelids and checked her pupils. The flicker of light he'd seen the last time he'd saved her was visible again but fainter, much fainter.

"It's there." He glanced up at Flhi. "But just barely."

"Then she'll live." It was a guess but it seemed to placate the boy. "Now, can I please have my blaster?"

Wortley pulled the A.N.G.E.L. weapon from his pocket and passed it to Flhi. He had been hoping to keep it as a souvenir. Now he just wanted to get Alannah out of the manor house alive.

"I have to take her home," he told Flhi. "My mum will know what to do."

"Good! Great!" replied Flhi, ducking a stray ecto-bolt fired from the barrel of Gloom's blaster. "Ask her if she's got any tips on fighting Gnarls, will you?"

Flhi didn't expect a reply, but nor did she expect what happened next. Strong hands gripped her by the wings and hauled her off the floor. She struggled to break free but it was useless.

"Look at this," said a male Fleshi's voice. "I've always wanted my own little A.N.G.E.L."

Horrad held Flhi in the air and studied her curiously. He seemed more excited than a child with its first-ever carnival prize.

"You're pretty, too." He grinned. "I'll share you with Krot. Perhaps we'll keep you as a house pet."

It was happening again. Rage could feel the all-*too*-
familiar quickening in the pit of his stomach and, just
like the last time, two patches on either side of his head
were fiery hot. He knew exactly what it meant, and that
was what scared him the most; the foulness was back to
reclaim him.

Nobody in Evan City ever mentioned the foulness — at
least not anymore. Hundreds of eons had passed since
the scourge had first threatened the Higher Dimension.
Thousands of Evanescents had fallen prey to the disease, and its symptoms had always been the same.

First, the bad moods took hold. Next, the aura began
to fade. And finally, hideous horns sprouted from either
side of the victim's head. Hours later the foulness would
mutate. According to the few records that remained, it
was a painful and horrific process. Ecto-skin bubbled

like melting plastic, hands hooked agonizingly before eventually turning into scaly green claws. Then, worst of all, the brain would shrink to the size of a grape. When it was over, every trace of the Evanescent had gone, to be replaced by a vicious, snarling Gargoyle.

There was no cure. The process was irreversible. And the Gargoyles were summarily banished, forced to live out their lives in the depths of the Dark Dimension. Good news for Evanescents, bad news for Ghouls.

And then, just when it looked as if the disease would destroy the whole of Evan City, it simply disappeared. The last recorded case had occurred centuries before the first Great Spirit War. It had been so long ago that now only the dusty history books and unread ledgers in Evan City's Hall of Records contained any mention of the outbreak. Even the healers, the Higher Dimension's oldest and wisest entities, had no knowledge of it. But one Evanescent did. One Evan City resident was a living, breathing expert. And that being was Commander Rage. Because he was infected.

Rage had always been angry. His mother used to complain that he'd kicked her black and blue in the womb, and from the moment he was born, Rage had been fuming. Few things ever made him happy and keeping his temper in check had always been a daily battle.

Of course, he blamed his parents. And their parents. And their parents before them. Clearly, they'd all been carriers of the wretched disease, and each generation had passed it to the next. Until it reached Rage. And that's when it got busy.

Like a parasite, the foulness fed on the commander's anger. Whenever Rage became annoyed, it grew in strength. And whenever he really, really lost his temper, the disease threatened to possess him completely.

But Rage was clever. He had quickly discovered that by remaining in a state of perpetual moodiness, he could harness the disease, and as its symbiotic host he could weave the blackest dark magic.

It was this that had enabled him to defeat Krot at the end of the first Great Spirit War. With ultimate irony, the foulness had returned to save the inhabitants of Evan City but there had been a terrible price to pay for its help. Rage was finally at its mercy.

The disease had continued its struggle to possess him every day since. Rage knew that using the dark magic just one more time would be like committing astral hara-kiri. The foulness would overwhelm him. Sadly for Rage, that moment had finally arrived.

Howling Malevolents bounced against his winged shield like small green demolition balls. Some exploded in a shower of putrid mist while others simply catapulted backward, landing on the ground in dazed bewilderment. None of them got through. Rage's wings were far too strong.

"Leaves him to me, you idiots!" ordered Krot. "I tolds you I wanted the commander all to myself."

The Malevolents wheeled away, looking for new prey.

"Why should they haves all the fun?" Krot went on. "I'm going to really enjoys ripping your wings off." He smiled meanly. "You has it, don't you? You've gots the foulness!"

Rage didn't answer. He shook his head instead, hoping it would be enough to deter Krot. It wasn't.

"That's why you weres able to use dark magic," the Gnarl continued. "Ha! You're turnings into one of us!"

"I'm turning into your worst nightmare," snarled Rage. The foulness was infesting his body now and it felt surprisingly good. It also felt incredibly powerful.

"There's nothing you cans do that I haven't seens before," Krot said confidently. "We haves the same powers."

"There's nothing about you and me that's the same," said Rage angrily.

"Maybe not right now," admitted Krot. "But if those horns of yours gets any bigger, I thinks that'll change."

Rage touched his hands to his head. Krot was right. What felt like the horns of a baby goat were poking out of his head. They were still covered by his wiry white hair, but if they grew any larger they'd be impossible to hide.

"So," said Krot. "You're not an Evanescent anymore. And if you're not one of them, you're one of us. They'll wants to kill you just like you wants to kill us. We can fights them together!"

"Never!" roared Rage. The foulness fed on his anger, swelling the horns on his head until they twisted and curled like a ram's. "I'll never fight my own kind. I'd rather die before I ever help you."

Krot was losing patience. "Death it is, then!"

Krot's blackest spells swarmed all over Rage, covering the A.N.G.E.L.'s wings like an oily second skin and biting into the feathery shield with thousands of razor-sharp fangs. Yet the commander was still alive and even seemed to be resisting. Amused, Krot boiled a couple more spells with his huge claws. But Rage was ready. Battle-ready. He dropped his wings and prepared to face his attacker.

For a second, Krot's spells recoiled. They hung in the air like a couple of black bedsheets caught in the wind. Then they lunged forward, faster than hungry pythons, only to stop inches from Rage's throat. Two claws, each the size of farmyard shovels, held them at bay. Yikes! They were his claws.

First horns, then claws. What was coming next, bat's wings?

"If you're not prepared to joins us, where will you go?" asked Krot.

"Perhaps I'll set up my own inter-dimensional consultancy," Rage growled. "I could specialize in ridding the world of Gnarls. Starting right away."

Now he was going to cast some dark magic of his own. Black energy began to boil between his claws. It was a physical force, alive with nastiness, and the more he fed it with hate, the stronger it became.

One direct hit was all it would take and Rage felt as though he couldn't miss. Pulling back his arms, he prepared to throw. Then a voice spoke and everything changed.

"I think it's time you two boys learned to play nicely," suggested Horrad. "Or my nice new pet will have to die."

Snarling, Rage whirled to face a tall male Fleshi whose dark hooded eyes glared back at him with menace. It was as if the man had absolutely nothing to fear.

Horrad bowed. "Allow me to introduce myself. My name is Klaut Horrad and, if you'll excuse a little presumption, I'm about to conquer your world."

Rage growled but said nothing. He was concentrating on the wiggling creature that dangled from Horrad's left hand. It was Flhi.

"Ah, so you've seen my little pet." Horrad raised his arm and showed off his possession proudly. "One of yours, I presume?"

"Release her," ordered Rage. "Or—"

"Or what, exactly?" Horrad interrupted. He seemed amused. "In case you haven't noticed, Commander Rage, you're surrounded by an army of Ghouls, you have no backup, and you're turning into the kind of creature your own kind would happily shoot on sight. I hardly think you're in a position to be calling the shots."

"Maybe not," agreed Rage. "But I am in a position to do this!"

Two black spells erupted from Rage's palms like gushes of crude oil and made a beeline for Horrad. The old psychic made no attempt to get out of their way, merely raising his free hand and calmly drawing a shield of silver light across his body. The spells struck the shield and rebounded away.

Horrad snorted. "Do you really think I can be stopped? By you?"

"Maybe." Rage shrugged. "Maybe not. But what have I got to lose by trying?"

"How about this?" Horrad waved Flhi in the air. "And millions like her."

Flhi made no attempt to escape or fight the Fleshi off; she was too stunned by the appearance of her commander. Rage was barely recognizable. The hero of Evan City had become a monster.

Rage looked at his captured inspector with the usual amount of contempt. She seemed terrified. Rage stared hard into her eyes and acknowledged her existence with an almost imperceptible nod, before snarling back at Horrad.

"You're not going to spare the Evanescents if I agree to join you."

"I will if they don't resist us," lied Horrad. "You could help negotiate their surrender. They'll listen to you."

"You're overestimating my level of influence," laughed Rage. "I'm a soldier, not a politician. Besides, they'll never agree to it. Start a war with the Higher Dimension and it will be a fight to the death. Your death, hopefully."

Horrad sighed. "That's such a shame. Inter-dimensional domination would be so much easier if everyone would just cooperate. Ah well, nobody can say I didn't try."

He turned to Krot and casually tossed Flhi across the room. "Why don't you begin by killing this?"

Rage reacted instantly. "Now, Flhi. Fire!"

Flhi had been coiled tight, every muscle ready and waiting for action. Rage's nod had alerted her. It was such a strange thing for him to do. He never nodded at her, ever. That had to be a cry for help. She sprayed the room with incinerator-charged bolts of energy that banished Malevolents ten at a time. She managed to unleash half a dozen rounds before she saw Krot's huge claws reach out to pluck her from the air. At the last second, she twitched her wings into life.

The library was still in chaos. Ghouls screeched, hyenas yelped, and ecto-blasts were exploding like deafening grenades. But there was one sound that was louder than all the others: Horrad's laughter.

It was booming and manic, the kind of laugh that makes psychopaths and lunatics sound sane. And it was making Rage nervous.

The foulness was surging through his body now, but he had to stay Rage for just a little while longer or he might as well hand the keys of Evan City to Krot.

"Look around you," Horrad said. "There are hundreds of Gargoyles here already, and thousands more waiting to join them. I could attack your dimension right now and wipe it out. All I have to do is reverse the vortex and it will lead us straight there."

That was it! Rage suddenly knew what he had to do. The Door of Souls held all the answers.

Twin tracks of gas spewed from his palms. His spells headed straight for the vortex and crashed into its swirling heart with the force of two giant ramrods. Scores of invading Gargoyles were melted on the spot, dissolving faster than ice cubes in a furnace. Those lucky enough to survive suddenly found themselves dragged off their feet, hurled backward, and sucked violently toward the swirling hole.

Horrad's army was vanishing fast. The Door of Souls was feeding off his own power, drawing more and more dark energy from his fingertips and growing stronger by the second.

Krot was desperately clutching a heavy wooden table leg, hoping to avoid the same fate as the rest of them, but the pull was too strong. One by one, his fingers uncurled from around the table leg, and when the last finger could hang on no longer he was catapulted out of the library and back into his own dimension.

The Malevolents were gone, or torn apart, and Horrad was alone. "Looks like it's over, Fleshi," gloated Rage. "Your army seems to have gone AWOL."

Horrad didn't reply. A cyclone of swirling light quickly reached out into the room and swooped down onto Horrad, swallowing him headfirst. There was no escape, and the Fleshi's muffled screams faded from hearing as the cyclone recoiled back into the vortex, pulling its prey into the Dark Dimension.

"That's the last we'll see of him!" whooped Rage, punching the air triumphantly.

Flhi wasn't feeling quite as elated. Something very precious to her was missing from the room. "Has anyone seen Yell or Gloom?"

21

"**Whatever were you thinking, young lady?**" asked Marjorie Flint as she pressed a freshly soaked cold compress against Alannah's burning forehead. "Outside is no place for a girl with flu. You should have been tucked up in bed with a hot-water bottle, not out playing hide-and-seek with Wortley. I'm surprised you didn't catch your death."

Alannah and Wortley exchanged knowing glances; if Mrs. Flint ever found out how close Alannah had come to death, she would never allow either of the children to leave the Malarra residence again.

It had been less than twenty-four hours since the battle at the manor house, and Alannah had only just regained consciousness. Even now, she slipped in and out of sleep every few minutes and the Flints fussed around her with growing concern.

"I think we should call the doctor," Marjorie insisted.

"Perhaps you could give her one of your potions, Mum," suggested Wortley. He was afraid of what a doctor might detect if his friend was examined. "There must be something you could try first."

The housekeeper gave her son a stern glare. "You know I don't like it when you use the *p* word, Wortley. They're remedies, not potions. And yes, as a matter of fact, there is something I can try but I'll need to go out into the garden to pick some herbs. And I don't want to leave Alannah alone."

"I can stay with her," said Wortley.

Mrs. Flint lifted up the cold flannel and felt Alannah's head with her palm. "I don't know. She's still awfully hot. What was her temperature last time we checked?"

Wortley glanced at the figures his mother had jotted down on a scrap of paper. "One hundred three point one. Crikey, Alannah, you're as hot as Dubai!"

"I'll be fine," insisted Alannah with a weak smile. "I just need to rest."

"That's the first sensible thing I've heard you say in weeks, Alannah," observed the housekeeper. "Now, is there anything I can get you, my dear?"

Alannah thought for a moment and then remembered something her mother used to do for her whenever she felt unwell. "Maybe tomorrow, if I'm feeling a little bit better, you could run me a hot bubble bath?"

Mrs. Flint nodded sagely and fought the urge to give her employer a great big hug. There were times when even Alannah Malarra needed to be cuddled, and now was definitely one of them.

The housekeeper sniffed into a rolled-up tissue that she'd pulled from the pocket of her apron. As she blinked away tears she said, "Wortley, keep an eye on Alannah's temperature, will you? If it gets any higher, come and find me straightaway."

Wortley looked up.

"I'll be out picking those herbs." Marjorie smiled. "Apparently, the remedy tastes foul, but it gives your immune system a kick start. Whatever you've got, Alannah, it won't stand a chance." She slipped into the hallway and marched off toward the garden.

"A hot bubble bath?" Wortley asked, once his mother's footsteps had faded to a whisper. "I'm beginning to wonder whether that's really you in there. Perhaps I brought somebody else back from the dead. Maybe the real Alannah is still floating around with the clouds."

Alannah shivered. "Nope, it's definitely me, Worts. It's just that last night was too much. It's all getting a bit too scary. Why don't we take a break? You know, do normal stuff like go to school."

"I thought you always said school was for geeks."

"Yeah, I did," admitted Alannah. She reached out and placed her hand on Wortley's arm. It felt odd, but strangely comforting; so she left it there. "But just think how easy it would be. I could hack into the school mainframe and download all the test papers. We'd be top of the class in weeks."

"And everyone would hate us," warned Wortley. "Why can't we just go to school and learn things? You know, like everyone else."

That was the problem. Alannah wasn't like everyone else, and she didn't want to be, either. She loved being different. Knowing she could do things other children couldn't do gave her the kind of buzz that makes adrenaline junkies leap off cliffs armed with just a folded cotton sheet and blind hope.

"Perhaps we could find one of those schools for talented children," she suggested. "You know, the kind of place where extraordinary abilities would be respected."

Wortley raised his left eyebrow. "What, a school for psychics and burglars?"

Alannah's face lit with excitement. "Do you think there is anywhere like that?"

"Yeah," her friend snickered. "It's right next to Hogwarts."

"I'm serious, Wortley," Alannah barked. "You said you

wanted to retire, so let's retire. I can't do this anymore. Mum and Dad have been missing for three years. The police can't find them and I'm no nearer to tracking them down than I was a year ago. It's hopeless. And now it's dangerous, too. I mean, we almost died, Worts. What do you say? Do you want to try being a normal kid?"

"I don't know," Wortley said. "Are you sure it's over?"

There was a feeling in the pit of Alannah's stomach that she had been trying to ignore. It was a chilling knot that was filling her with dread. She squeezed Wortley's arm. "You said they'd all died. You said you saw them killed."

"I never said they died," Wortley said, shaking his head. "I said they all got sucked into a great big swirly thing. That little A.N.G.E.L. friend of yours said the Gargoyles had gone back to some place called a Dark Dimension."

"She's no friend of mine, Wortley Flint," Alannah corrected him sharply. "And I think the Dark Dimension is where the Gargoyles originally came from."

Suddenly, there was a strange rustling noise in the room. It seemed to be coming from inside Alannah's wardrobe. Then the wardrobe spoke.

"That's very perceptive of you, young Fleshi." The voice was deep and ever so slightly pompous.

Alannah moaned and pulled the bedcovers over her head. It wasn't over. They were back!

"Go away!" she pleaded. "We're retired."

The wardrobe door swung open and an officious-looking, portly Evanescent stepped out from between a couple of winter coats. A thick golden chain of office was hung around his shoulders. It looked like something borrowed from an overdressed rap star.

"If only it was that simple," said Mayor Cheer. "But I'm afraid we require your special talents once more. Evan City needs your help!"

Alannah could hardly believe what she was seeing. The big fat Evanescent had been followed into the bedroom by what looked like a fully staffed television crew. There was a soundman, a cameraman, and even a bossy producer who buzzed around barking orders and scribbling notes onto a clipboard. The portly one seemed oblivious to the media crew, but when Inspector Flhi Swift stepped out of the wardrobe, the little A.N.G.E.L. made no attempt to hide her contempt. After aiming an awkward nod of recognition in Alannah's direction, she skulked off into a corner to sit in moody silence.

Wortley closed and locked the bedroom door. The last thing he wanted was his mother stumbling into a room full of Evanescents, even if she wouldn't be able to see any of them.

"You're probably wondering who I am?" the porky entity said.

Alannah stayed half buried under the covers. "I couldn't care less who you are," she snapped. "I just want to know when you're leaving."

"I'm Mayor Cheer of Evan City," he continued. "Think of me as being like your prime minister, but a lot more popular. You can bow if you like."

He smiled cheesily as the cameraman lunged forward for a close-up.

"Fantastic, Mayor, you're looking very regal," the bossy producer gushed.

"So you're in charge up there?" asked Wortley in disbelief.

"Sort of," admitted Cheer, a little reluctantly. "But give it a few eons and a couple more landslide election victories and the elders will have to give me more authority."

"Can you believe this guy?" muttered Flhi a little too loudly.

"Did you say something, Inspector?" asked the mayor.

"I said it's certainly worth a try, Mayor Cheer." She flicked her thumbs up and grinned falsely, then stuck her tongue out as soon as the mayor looked away.

"I'm not interested," Alannah groaned. "Whenever I have anything to do with A.N.G.E.L.s, things go horribly wrong. I've nearly died twice and I've no intention of trying for my hat trick. So if you don't mind, I'd like you to climb back into the wardrobe and get lost."

The producer made a square with her fingers and gazed at Alannah through the hole. "Quick, move in for a shot of the grumpy Fleshi. The viewers love a bit of wildlife."

"I said GET LOST!" Alannah yelled. She quickly pulled a hand out from beneath the covers and fired a weak bolt of energy that meandered through the air and only just reached its target. The camera frazzled and melted like a tortured Wellington boot.

"Hey!" objected the cameraman as he stared at his ruined hardware. "Do you know how much that thing cost?"

"You're confusing me with someone who cares," hissed Alannah. "Now if you lot don't get out of here in five seconds flat, I'm going to start melting A.N.G.E.L.s."

"Feel free to shoot if you like," said Flhi in a bored voice. "But that last shot of yours looked pretty weak to me and I reckon you're running out of ammo. What have you got left? Enough energy for one, maybe two more shots? And unlike cameras, we can move." She pulled out her ecto-blaster and waved it in the air with menace.

Alannah glared at her old adversary. The silver-haired A.N.G.E.L. was smart, and there was something about her that Alannah begrudgingly liked. Perhaps it was because they were so much alike.

"Girls, girls!" interrupted Mayor Cheer. "We're all friends here. There's no need to fight." He sighed heavily and, when he next spoke, he actually sounded sincere. "We came in peace, Alannah. We've got enough enemies already without making new ones. In fact, it's because of those enemies that we're here right now. Like I've already told you, we need your help."

"What can I do to help you?" asked Alannah. "I've already met your enemies, and look what they did to me. Ask her," she pointed at Flhi. "There was nothing I could do."

"We don't want you to fight Krot or the male Fleshi," Flhi explained. "All you need to do is close a door for us."

"A door?" asked Alannah. "What's wrong, don't they have handles in Evan City?"

"It's the Door of Souls," snapped Flhi. "We need you to close the vortex at the manor house."

Alannah scowled. "If I'm that stupid, flygirl, why don't you close it yourself?"

Flhi scowled back. "Because I'm not the one who opened it, am I?"

Alannah had no retort. The feisty little A.N.G.E.L. was right: Technically, Alannah had been the one who had opened the door to the vortex, even if Horrad had forced her do it.

"Why do you need Alannah?" asked Wortley. "That

weird-looking commander of yours destroyed the . . . what did you call it?"

"Door of Souls," the mayor said helpfully. "And what do you mean, weird-looking commander?"

Wortley was puzzled. How else could he describe an A.N.G.E.L. with horns, fangs, and green skin? "Weird" seemed to sum the look up perfectly.

"She saw him!" he said, pointing at Flhi. "One minute he was an ordinary A.N.G.E.L., and then the next minute he changed into a—"

Flhi interrupted and quickly changed the subject. "Name your price. We'll pay whatever it costs to keep the vortex shut away." She looked at Alannah. "What's it going to take? Do we have to beg?"

Something didn't seem right. The little A.N.G.E.L. was acting strangely and Alannah was curious to know why.

"Where's your commander?" Alannah asked.

The look of panic on Flhi's face told her that her instinct had been spot on. Something *was* wrong.

Mayor Cheer sighed heavily. He seemed to have tears in his eyes. "We don't know. He's MIA."

"MIA?" Alannah and Wortley asked together.

"**M**issing **I**n **A**ction," explained Flhi. "So are Yell and Gloom. None of us have seen them since Rage reversed the vortex. They vanished at about the same time as the Fleshi."

"You don't think they got sucked through the door of whatchamacallits, do you?" suggested Wortley.

"We hope not," said the mayor. "We're not sure how he did it, but Commander Rage somehow managed to reverse the polarity of the vortex. So instead of being a gateway leading out from the Dark Dimension, it became a conduit that led straight back in. That's why it sucked all the Gargoyles out of the library. It appears to have latched onto everything evil and dragged it back to where it belonged. Gloom, Yell, and the commander are all A.N.G.E.L.s, which should have made them immune to the pull of the vortex. They can't have been sucked in."

"It took Horrad," Alannah pointed out. "He wasn't a Gargoyle."

"Perhaps not," agreed the mayor. "But he was evil. I'm guessing the Door of Souls sensed that and made sure he went anyway."

"What if one of the Gargoyles dragged your troopers in?" suggested Wortley.

Mayor Cheer nodded slowly. "That's what we're afraid of."

"I still don't understand why you need me," said Alannah. "Your A.N.G.E.L. magic seems to work perfectly well on the Door of Souls. If the Gargoyles come back, just do whatever your commander did."

"I wish it were that simple," the mayor said. "Believe me, I'd rather not be here. But the thing is, we don't know how Commander Rage did it. None of us has the power to reverse a vortex like that, not even our sentinels. There's only so much we can do to keep it closed and there are already signs that the Gargoyles are trying to open it again. All they need is someone with enough power to . . ."

Alannah knew what was coming next. ". . . reopen the door. And that means me, right?"

The Evanescents nodded solemnly.

"They need your power to get to us," Flhi explained. "We could assign a team of sentinels to protect you but even that wouldn't guarantee your safety, especially if the Fleshi has survived."

Now it was Alannah's turn to be fretful. "Horrad? I thought he was dead."

Flhi shook her head. "His body will be unrecognizable by now, but his soul is now probably more alive than ever. And if it is, I'm not sure we could stop him."

I'm the only one who can stop Horrad, Alannah thought.

She looked Mayor Cheer straight in the eye and smiled. "You don't just need me to close the Door of Souls. You need me to save your world."

She turned and winked at Wortley. "That's got to be worth a huge reward."

Wortley groaned. So much for normal!

"Do we have a deal?" the mayor asked.

Alannah checked her notepad and ticked off each demand one by one: four chests of sunken Spanish gold; one lost manuscript by Charles Dickens; a double-sided Monet; da Vinci's real *Mona Lisa* painting (the version hanging on the wall in the Louvre was apparently a poor copy); three missing Dead Sea scrolls; King Arthur's solid-gold Round Table; and, finally, the original studio tape of a John Lennon album that even Yoko Ono didn't know existed. She was going to have more money than Bill Gates.

Alannah stuck out her hand. "Yes!"

Mayor Cheer pumped Alannah's hand with a mixture of relief and exhilaration. She had been Evan City's last and only hope. The entire future of the Higher Dimension had rested on the mayor's negotiating skills, and a few trinkets was all it had taken to secure the psychic girl's help. The elders would be overjoyed to secure Alannah's services so cheaply, and the residents of Evan City would probably vote him mayor for life!

"Oh, I almost forgot. You'll be low on astral power," Cheer pointed out. "So I'll arrange for a sentinel to give you an ecto-surge."

Alarm raced across Alannah's face, and she looked toward Flhi for a little reassurance, only agreeing when the little A.N.G.E.L. gave her a reassuring nod.

"So much for retiring," Wortley lamented. "I was looking forward to cashing in my pension plan."

"This *is* your pension plan," Alannah pointed out, tapping the page on her notebook excitedly. "We're going to be multibillionaires."

"What's the point in having money if you're dead?" asked Wortley.

"No one's going to die," insisted Alannah. "You heard them; all they want me to do is close the Door of Souls. No Gargoyles, no Gnarls, and no Horrad. What's the problem?"

"Nothing's ever that simple, Alannah," warned Wortley. "Something bad will happen, it always does. Why don't you just walk away? You don't need to do this."

"Of course I need to do this," said Alannah. "They promised to help me find Mum and Dad, didn't they?"

"Rage promised to help you," Wortley reminded her. "And he's MFI."

"MIA," Alannah corrected him. "But I'm going to find him. And, when I do, he's going to give me that information."

Mayor Cheer clapped his hands. "Good, good, good. I'm so glad we all agree. You close the Door, you find Rage, Rage finds your parents, and everyone lives happily ever after. Isn't it great when a plan comes together?"

"You just keep your end of the bargain," Alannah growled. "Because I can always open the Door of Souls again if you don't cough up."

The mayor looked hurt. "My dear, I'm an Evanescent. We never lie."

Flhi coughed nervously in the corner of the room. Luckily, no one heard her.

"There's a first time for everything," Wortley said under his breath.

The mayor straightened his halo, brushed back his wavy white hair, and fixed Flhi with an authoritative glare.

"Inspector, take it from here. I've got a press conference booked and I'm already late."

He breezed across the bedroom toward the wardrobe, and the media crew scuttled after him. As he was about to step into the jungle of dresses and coats, Cheer paused and turned to look sternly at Alannah.

"You've just made a promise to us and we expect you to keep it. Evanescents make great friends, but we make even greater enemies. I'll see you at the manor house this time tomorrow. Don't let us down!"

Cheer switched his attention to Flhi. "She's all yours for the next twenty-four Fleshi hours, Inspector. Make sure our savior gets some sleep. And if anything happens to her, don't bother coming home."

He walked through Alannah's clothes and disappeared, closely followed by his entourage.

When she was sure they had all gone, Flhi flew to the bottom of Alannah's bed. She landed gently on top of the duvet and fixed Alannah with a worried glare.

"There's something you need to know," she whispered. "And it changes everything."

"I thought that fat mayor of yours said your kind don't lie," snapped Wortley. "Yet now you're telling us Rage isn't missing at all. He's in hiding."

"Sounds pretty untruthy to me, too," agreed Alannah. "You'd better explain what's going on, or the deal's off."

Flhi folded her wings and took a long deep breath. Things were going to get messy.

"Rage has no choice but to hide," she began. "He's holed up behind a wall in the manor house cellar. The place is crawling with sentinels and if one of them sees him he's finished."

"Why?" asked Alannah. "He's their commander."

"You saw him." Flhi realized she'd have to explain everything. "He's got the foulness. It's a disease that turns us Evanescents into Gargoyles. Apparently, Rage is a carrier and as soon as he used dark magic to fight Krot and Horrad, the disease must have taken over. There's nothing he can do to reverse the effects. Right now, he's half Gargoyle and half Evanescent and that's just about the worst thing you can be. The A.N.G.E.L.s fear him and the Gargoyles hate him. You're either one or the other. But not both."

"But Rage is both," Alannah said. "You just said so."

Flhi nodded. "He is right now, but he's only just clinging on to his Evanescent self. If he's not careful, he'll become a fully fledged Gargoyle, and he doesn't want that to happen. He'd rather stay a hybrid than end up in the Dark Dimension. That's why he needs your help to rescue Yell and Gloom."

"And what do I get out of it?" Alannah inquired.

Commander Rage pried a juicy black slug from the gooey mud that sat behind the damp cellar walls. It was fatter than a freshly stuffed cannoli, and thick slime oozed from its belly like warm jelly. Rage thought it looked scrumptious and eagerly sank his huge fangs into the pulsing flesh. *Delish!* It was his second slug in as many minutes and as he chewed on it hungrily his eyes were already scanning the walls for more creatures just like it.

Urgh!! He shook his head. *What was he thinking?* He spat what was left in his mouth on to the floor.

Right now, his mind was the battleground for a war between two rival identities. A.N.G.E.L. was fighting Gargoyle in a titanic struggle to control his body and spirit.

Where is she? his A.N.G.E.L. side wondered. Flhi had promised to get back to the manor house as soon as she could, but that had been hours ago. Gargoyles aren't smart enough to hide, and the foulness wanted to make some mischief; Rage could sense it. He could sense something else as well. And it was coming closer.

A dangerous entity was lurking nearby. As a Gargoyle, he had been unaware of the being's presence. But as an A.N.G.E.L., his feelings were acute and he knew at once that a sentinel was lurking behind the cellar door.

He could feel the extraordinary power. It surged into the cellar, sweeping away all traces of fear and dread with pulse after pulse of positive energy. The dark, dank room suddenly felt warmer and more welcoming. Evil simply couldn't survive. The Gargoyle in Rage couldn't bear it. It howled and retreated into the back of his mind, cowering from the excruciating sense of positivity. His Evanescent self had never felt stronger.

Yet he knew that self had to remain hidden. He looked like a Gargoyle. He acted like a Gargoyle. He even smelled like a Gargoyle. All he could do was burrow deeper and deeper into the muddy foundations of the cellar. It was his only chance of survival.

Thankfully, the doorbell saved him. It rang once and the sentinel left to investigate. Relieved, Rage was squeezing himself out of his muddy hiding place when a voice almost made him jump out of his green skin.

"That's a great new image, Commander," Flhi snickered. She'd felt surprisingly liberated since Rage had "turned." She realized he now needed her. She was in charge. And she was enjoying it. "You look like a teenage Fleshi at a rock festival."

Rage scowled but said nothing. He had never been so happy to see Flhi.

"Sentinels keeping you on your toes?" Flhi asked.

"They're relentless," growled Rage. "One almost caught me a second ago. If somebody hadn't rung the doorbell, I'd have been history."

Flhi smiled. "Then I guess Alannah Malarra just saved your life."

"She came?" Rage sounded surprised.

"I had to promise her something first, though," Flhi admitted.

"Not . . ."

"Yes."

"Why?" Rage groaned.

"Because it's the only way I could get her to help," Flhi pointed out. "Besides, you already told her you could help."

Rage shook his head. "I lied. I don't know where her parents are, nobody does. I asked our tech team to run a global scan shortly after Alannah's *visit* to Evan City, but there's no trace of them anywhere."

"So why did you tell her you could find them?" asked Flhi, hardly able to believe her former commander's deceit.

"Standard military strategy," he explained. "Find your enemy's weakness and exploit it. It was a textbook move. Perhaps if you'd paid more attention at the academy, you'd already know that."

Flhi ignored the insult. "Then you'd better employ another textbook maneuver, *ex*-Commander, and think about covering your back. Because when this girl finds out you've lied, she'll make you wish you'd been fried by a sentinel."

"It won't matter," Rage confessed. "As long as she keeps her end of the bargain I won't care. My life is worth sacrificing just to keep Evan City safe. And I'd rather be dead than live a life like this."

"But she might be able to turn you back," Flhi pointed out. "She has the power."

Rage snorted. "When she finds out I lied, that's the last thing she'll want to do." He shrugged. "Forget about me. Concentrate on saving Evan City. Everything else will take care of itself. What do the Fleshies call it . . . fate?"

Flhi knew that they also called it luck, and Rage was going to need plenty of that if he was going to survive Alannah's wrath.

The doorbell was still ringing loudly when one of the large front doors was snatched open. A disheveled-looking Samson stared out at the two children on the doorstep. Sharp gray whiskers covered the footman's chin like tiny cactus thorns and his short white hair desperately needed combing. Two bloodshot eyes suggested he hadn't slept in some time. He looked disappointed to see Alannah and Wortley.

"Oh, it's you," he said gloomily. "I was hoping it would be the doctor. Never mind, I suppose you'll have to do. Come in! Come in!"

He ushered them into the hallway and peeled off their coats.

"Why do you need a doctor?" asked Wortley

"It's the earl," explained the footman. "He seems to be going a bit gaga. He claims he can see angels."

Alannah smiled to herself. Perhaps the old earl wasn't as loopy as his footman thought. "Can we see him?"

"He's in the sitting room. Fourth door down, on your left." Samson pointed down a long corridor. "The library's out of bounds, I'm afraid. Still haven't gotten around to cleaning it up. I want to make sure it's safe first."

Samson looked hopefully at Alannah, who got the hint.

"Would you like me to take a look inside?" she asked.

The footman nodded sheepishly. "Never did believe in ghosts," he said. "But after the other night . . ."

"I understand," said Alannah. "They take some

getting used to." She winked at Wortley. "Especially the ones around here."

Wortley didn't reply. He was too busy gawking at the peculiar figure that had just stepped out from the wall behind them. Slowly, as if he were in a trance, Wortley lifted his arm and pointed over his shoulder.

"Um, Alannah!" he muttered. "There's something you should see."

Alannah felt the entity before she saw it. Her heart was suddenly filled with intense positivity and optimism. Her newfound confidence was so strong that the excitement literally pulled the breath from her lungs. But that was tempered by a sudden sense of apprehension. Whatever this new entity was, it was very powerful!

"What is it?" asked Wortley. "And why do I feel so happy to see it?"

"Oh no!" groaned Samson. "Not you two as well. Am I the only sane person left on this planet?"

Alannah ignored him. Standing in front of them was the most amazing entity she had ever seen. It was huge, towering above her like a ten-foot-tall pillar of glowing white neon. Its halo danced across the ceiling when it moved and positive energy radiated from it in pulses, washing the room in waves. In seconds, the aches and pains had disappeared from her body; it was incredible.

"Wow!" she said. "I never thought they would look like this."

"Like what?" asked a puzzled Samson. "There's nothing there."

It was no longer just a pillar of blinding light. Alannah's eyes had adjusted to the glare and she could make out huge silver wings, a flowing ivory gown, and a golden halo. The triple-barreled ecto-rifle looked a bit out of place, but she was prepared to overlook that.

"Can you feel that power?" she whispered. "It's unbelievable."

Samson shrugged. "You're just as crazy as the old man—you should have a chat to him. Go on. I'll bring tea and treats."

The footman went to perform his duties, leaving the two houseguests alone. Well, kind of.

"All I can feel is excitement," said Wortley. "It's weird, but I really feel as though I could do anything right now. Maybe I should try out for Major League Soccer."

"That's just it," Alannah said excitedly. "What we're feeling is pure positivity. There isn't a negative atom anywhere in this room. If your soccer tryout was held here, you'd probably have your pick of teams. There's only one being I can think of with a supernatural power like that."

"Santa Claus?" Wortley asked hopefully.

Alannah shook her head. "A sentinel. Flhi mentioned them, and so did Rage," Alannah told him. "This entity can recharge my astral powers. What did Cheer call it?"

"An ecto-surge?" Wortley said, remembering.

The powerful sentinel looked down at Alannah, studying the young Fleshi carefully. Could this puny female really be the potential savior of Evan City?

"Stop!" he ordered. His voice dripped like honey into the children's ears and they obeyed instantly.

"Autohypnosis," whispered Alannah, clearly impressed. "These sentinels are good."

"Good?" said Wortley. "They're bloomin' amazing. I want to be just like them when I grow up."

Alannah made a mental note about managing Wortley's expectations before turning her attention back to the sentinel. She didn't like the way that all three barrels of his weapon were less than three inches from her nose. The Dark Dimension beckoned. "Cheer sent me," she said firmly. "You know, the fat little mayor."

The sentinel made a noise that was between a snicker and a cough, then lowered his huge rifle. "Ah, we've been expecting you."

"You could have been a little more welcoming," Alannah said sarcastically.

"I'm trained to defend Evan City, not be polite," the sentinel snapped. "Now stand still."

Positive energy poured into her body like helium filling a balloon. It raced up her arms and across her chest, churned her stomach, and then rushed down both legs until she was ready to burst. The inside of her head seemed to be alive with the beat of a thousand tiny wings. It was an indescribable feeling and she didn't want it to stop. Ever.

Wortley was horrified. The sentinel appeared to have his friend in some kind of fiendish death grip.

"Get off her," he pleaded. "You're hurting her."

The sentinel took no notice. A swell of silver light rolled across his shoulders, twisting high toward the ceiling like a thick curl of smoke before gathering into a rolling cloud of energy. Wortley just had time to gasp as the cloud ripped open and a lightning fork of power crashed through the top of Alannah's skull.

Alannah exploded! Needles of glowing energy burst through her skin, turning her into a pincushion of light. Her whole body throbbed and convulsed until it became too much to bear and she folded heavily on the floor.

Wortley rushed to her side. "Alannah! Alannah! Are you okay?"

His friend blinked, raised her head, and looked up at Wortley. "Okay?" she gasped. "I feel amazing!"

Wortley looked shocked. "It looked like that thing was killing you."

Alannah climbed to her feet. She flexed the muscles in her arms and shoulders, loving the feeling of renewed strength. When she fired up her fingertips, they burned brighter than lightbulbs. She waved them at Wortley. "Look, I've got more power than a fireworks factory."

★ ★ ★

The earl was beside an open fire, perched on the edge of a worn leather reading chair. A flimsy pair of half-moon spectacles balanced unevenly across the bridge of his nose and his hands were busily polishing the biggest gun Alannah or Wortley had ever seen.

"Ah, children." The earl seemed happy to see them. "I was hoping you'd come." He put the gun down and shuffled toward Alannah. "Are you well, my dear? The last time I saw you, you looked distinctly under the weather."

"I'm fine," Alannah reassured him. "In fact, I've never felt better."

A knowing grin spread across the earl's wrinkled lips. "I take it, then, that you've already bumped into one of my new houseguests."

"One of them? How many are here?" Alannah asked.

"I think there are a least a dozen of them patrolling the house. It's very reassuring, and the health benefits are incredible. I feel like a twenty-one-year-old again." The earl danced a little jig, then took Alannah and Wortley by the hand. "Come and see for yourself," he urged. "I can usually find most of them in the library."

Bright light exploded from the room as soon as the library door was opened. Alannah's retinas felt as though they'd been washed in acid and it was at least a minute before she dared to take her hands away from her eyes. Gradually, she adjusted to the glare and followed the earl into the room.

Wortley wasn't so brave. As soon as the light attacked his eyes, he yelped in pain and ducked back into the corridor, where he decided to stay and wait for Samson. The prospect of tea and cake was far more appealing than entering another room of giant entities, even if they were supposed to be the good guys.

"Oops," said the earl, who had conveniently slipped a pair of sunglasses over his eyes a second before opening the door. "The light can be a bit of a shock if you're not prepared. Should have warned you. Sorry about that, young lady."

Alannah wasn't listening. Instead, she was gazing into a room that seemed to be heaving with glowing entities. There had to be at least enough sentinels to make a soccer team, including the substitutes, and more were emerging from behind the walls every few seconds. Some took up defensive positions in front of the large bookcases, but many joined a scrum directly opposite the fireplace. They faced the mirror that had not so long ago been a swirling vortex, and together they fired a continuous stream of radiant energy directly at the reflective glass. Amazingly, the light didn't bounce back into the room. The mirror seemed to absorb it.

"Oh!" gasped the earl in surprise. "They appear to have brought some friends."

"I think it's an army," said Alannah. "And I'm glad we're not the enemy."

"What do you think they're doing?" the earl asked, edging closer to the mirror.

Alannah grabbed the old man by the shoulders and pulled him away. "Look!"

She pointed up at the mirror. A gaggle of ugly green monsters had appeared behind the glass. They looked as though they were swimming against a strong current and just when it seemed as if they would pop out through the mirror, their faces slammed against an invisible force field.

"What are they?" asked the earl.

"Gargoyles. The sentinels' power is all that's keeping them at bay," Alannah guessed. "Without them, your house would be overrun again. The Door of Souls is still open."

"Actually, that's not entirely true," said a familiar voice.

Inspector Flhi Swift popped up from beneath the floorboards. She smiled at the earl, who nodded a gracious greeting; the old man was clearly getting used to welcoming new inter-dimensional visitors.

"Access to the vortex is open in the Dark Dimension, but closed here on Earth. The Malevolents keep sending attack parties to see if they can break through. Our sentinels are reinforcing the seal. As long as they're here, nothing can get past."

"So why do you need me?" asked Alannah.

"Because it needs to be closed for good and apparently only you can do that," Flhi explained. She nodded toward the earl, who was edging closer to the sentinels' light once again. "Sentinels can't stay here for longer than twenty-four hours—Fleshies find their energy addictive."

"What, like some kind of fountain of youth?"

"Yes, I've heard it called that before," Flhi acknowledged. "But apart from that, they need to retreat to Evan City and create a line of defense. It will probably buy our dimension some time, but I can't say the same for yours."

"I know, I know. That's why *I'm* here," said Alannah.

Flhi buzzed her wings and hovered close to Alannah's left ear. The wind from her wings tied Alannah's red hair into knots.

"But there's also the other matter we discussed," Flhi whispered. "Meet me in the cellar in five. Come alone, and make sure you aren't followed!"

"Is she here?" Rage asked curtly.

"She's on her way down," Flhi told him.

The little inspector realized how much her commander was suffering, and suddenly pitied him. All those centuries of persecution and bullying faded into history; no A.N.G.E.L. deserved what Rage was going through. "What are you going to tell her?"

"As little as possible," said Rage. "And just enough to guarantee her help."

"Alannah's strong again," warned Flhi. "A sentinel gave her an ecto-surge."

"Good." Rage nodded.

A sharp knock on the cellar door startled them both. Rage immediately retreated into the cellar's darkest shadows and Flhi drew her blaster.

"You down there, A.N.G.E.L.?"

Flhi expelled a sigh of relief and slipped her weapon back into its holster. She held up her hand, telling Rage to stay hidden.

"I'm here," Flhi confirmed. "Are you alone?"

"No, I brought a couple of sentinels for company," Alannah lied, stepping gingerly down the slippery cellar steps. Her feet eventually hit the hard stone floor. "Of course I'm alone. Now, I assume we're here to talk to your ex-commander? You said he was hiding out here."

Flhi flew to Alannah's side and piloted her into the middle of the cellar. "Can you keep a secret?"

"I'm a girl. Keeping secrets is what we're good at," Alannah pointed out. "But I'm not too good with this whole patience thing."

Flhi took the hint. "Commander?"

Rage stepped out from the shadows.

Alannah gasped. He was even uglier than she remembered. Bigger, too.

"Nice teeth," she said.

"What is it about females?" Rage snarled. "Does everything have to be a joke?"

"Only when dumb males are involved," said Alannah bitterly. "Especially those who've tried to kidnap us."

Flhi stepped between her commander and Alannah. "How about a truce?" she suggested. "There are more important things at stake."

Alannah and Rage continued to glare at each other but said nothing.

"That's better," Flhi said. The atmosphere was thick enough to slice. "Commander, why don't you tell Alannah the plan?"

The words seemed to be stuck in Rage's throat. What he was about to ask was against everything he had ever believed in. Had it really come to this?

"Commander?" Flhi urged.

Rage flinched. "Okay, okay! I need your help to rescue Yell and Gloom."

"*You* need *my* help?" teased Alannah.

Flhi explained why. "Commander Rage wants to take charge of the rescue operation himself, like I said, but he can only do that if he's no longer a Gargoyle. He thinks you can change him back."

"Me? But how?"

"From what I gather, your powers should be strong enough to reverse the foulness." Rage softened his voice. "You're my last hope. You're Evan City's last hope."

"You agreed to help. Will you do it?" Flhi begged.

"No," Alannah said. "Not until he's earned it."

Rage exploded with fury. "This is no time to play your petty games!" His horns swelled aggressively. "Lives are at stake!"

"Your life, not mine," Alannah pointed out. "Besides, I don't trust you."

"I saved your life!" Rage couldn't believe that wasn't enough.

"You saved the Higher Dimension. Saving my life was a fortunate coincidence."

"What more do I have to do?" asked the commander.

Alannah smiled. Now she had him just where she wanted him. "Keep your promise and find my parents. If they're alive, I'll help you."

Rage knew he'd just been rumbled. Alannah had called his bluff and if he didn't find a way to worm out of the situation, everything would end in disaster. He was being outsmarted by a Fleshi and, to make things even worse, a female Fleshi, too!

But he didn't panic. All he had to do was turn the tables on Alannah, and one more teensy-weensy little white lie should just about do the trick.

"I could take you to your mother and father right now," he calmly told her. "We could have a touching little reunion with lots of hugging, kissing, and a bucket-load of salty tears thrown in for good measure. But by then it will be too late for us. The sentinels will have retreated to the Evan City borders and ten thousand bloodthirsty Ghouls will be massing. Even you wouldn't be able to repel an army of that size. So what's the point? Why should I help you?"

Alannah's fingertips glowed fiercely. It was a clear warning. "Because if you don't, I'll kill you."

Rage just laughed at her. "Compared with living out the next eternity as a Gargoyle, death sounds pretty appealing to me. But what about you? Do you really want to live the rest of your life never knowing what happened to dear Mummy and Daddy?"

"Commander!"

Flhi was appalled. A.N.G.E.L.s weren't supposed to lie, yet Rage was keeping up the pretense he could lead Alannah to her parents. He was behaving more and more like a wretched Gargoyle with every passing minute. She could only hope the foulness really wasn't contagious.

"Keep out of this, Inspector," ordered Rage. "This is between me and the Fleshi." He glared at Alannah. "So what's it going to be, little girl? Are you going to help me? Or are you going to wave good-bye to Ma and Pa forever?"

Alannah seethed. She wanted to destroy him there and then. The sentinel had supercharged her abilities and all it would take was one deadly astral grenade. At such close range, Rage wouldn't stand a chance. But she couldn't afford to take the risk. If he did know where her parents were, she had no choice but to cooperate. And the worst thing was, he knew it.

"What do you want me to do?"

"That's easy!" Rage curled his lips away from his fangs and grinned. "I want you to hit me with everything you've got."

The blast struck Rage in the center of his armor-plated chest and hurled him clean across the room. He felt his scaly ecto-shell crack as he struck the solid cellar wall, but that was the least of his problems. His chest had disappeared. In its place was a gaping hole through which Alannah's powerful energy stream pierced his soul. The astral light burnt like acid. Rage screamed in agony.

"Stop it," pleaded Flhi. "It's not working."

"Nooo!" Rage gasped. "Don't stop!"

He knew it was working. As Alannah's energy pulsed through him, he could feel the foulness leaving his shell.

Flhi was amazed. The commander was being trans-formed before her very eyes. His outer skin was no longer green. His horns were receding and his fangs seemed to be inching their way back into his gums. Even his huge spiky claws were beginning to look more like hands. In seconds, the Gargoyle would be gone.

And that was exactly why Alannah stopped.

"What are you doing?" shrieked Flhi. "Don't stop."

Rage fell to the floor, clutching his wounded chest. When he glared up at Alannah, his eyes were pools of anger. "Why?"

"Think of it as an incentive," Alannah said calmly. "We know it works now, so when you take me to my parents I'll finish the job. But not before."

"Aarrgghh!"

Rage's body was being attacked. He thrashed about on the hard cellar floor with all the frenzy of a freshly landed shark. The foulness had returned and now took its violent revenge.

The horns rose from his skull, bigger and greener than ever. His fangs grew longer and sharper until they resembled vicious Viking daggers. And huge knobbly green warts erupted all over his damaged ecto-shell. He was a Gargoyle again.

"What about Evan City?" he growled. "The enemy is too vast. Eventually, the Malevolents will overcome the sentinels and destroy us."

"You could always try Plan B," suggested Alannah.

"There isn't a Plan B," Flhi said. "You were our only hope."

Alannah laughed. "Oh, I seriously doubt that. Military masterminds always have a fallback plan, isn't that right, Commander?"

Rage grunted painfully as he struggled to his feet. Instinctively, he plucked a slug from the cellar wall grouting and popped it into his mouth. He crunched once, then swallowed.

"Flhi," he said despairingly. "You're not going to like this."

Wortley drew the line at three sweet treats. The strawberry tart looked extremely tempting, but after one delicious chocolate éclair, a slice of pineapple cheese-cake, and an apple turnover, the young burglar knew he'd reached his limit. Besides, his churning stomach was telling him that you really *can* have too much of a good thing.

"Where did the young lady say she was going?" asked Samson.

"To meditate," Wortley reminded him. "It helps with the . . . um . . ."

"Ghosts?" suggested Samson condescendingly.

"Yeah," Wortley agreed. "And other things."

"Other things?" Samson sounded a little worried.

"Don't ask," warned Wortley. "You wouldn't believe me anyway."

"You actually do see them, don't you?"

"I'm afraid so," affirmed Wortley. "Ghosts, Ghouls, Gnarls . . ."

The footman sank into a chair. If other people could see spirits around Pittingham Manor then perhaps the old earl wasn't going crazy after all.

"So your little friend really is a ghost hunter?"

Before Wortley could reply, a girl's scream raced up the corridor, hotly pursued by the sound of running feet.

"GARGOYLE!"

Alannah appeared from around a corner, red-faced and clearly afraid.

"They're here!" she yelled. "Help me!"

She crashed to the floor and slid along the polished wooden floorboards on her belly as a powerful ecto-blast exploded just behind her. A second explosion blew a door open and knocked a couple of antique portraits off the wall.

"Summon the sentinels!" Alannah gasped as she struggled to her feet. "We're under attack."

Wortley didn't move; he didn't have to. The door to the library flew open and the long barrel of a huge elephant gun poked out into the corridor. The earl, who was clearly struggling to hoist the huge weapon onto his frail shoulder, quickly followed it.

"Let's see how they cope with some good old-fashioned

English lead," he bellowed as Flhi zipped around the corner at full wing speed.

Boom! The earl pulled the trigger and filled the corridor with a mixture of acrid smoke and red-hot shot. Wallpaper was ripped off walls, centuries-old plaster disintegrated into powdery clouds, and half the ceiling seemed to cave in on top of them. Miraculously everyone was unharmed.

"Oops," coughed the earl as he fished about in his trouser pockets for another cartridge. "Almost shot one of those little angel thingies."

Alannah was shocked. She hadn't expected any interference from the old earl and now Rage's Plan B was in jeopardy. If this was going to work, they couldn't afford any complications.

Luckily, Flhi had spotted the danger, too. Before the old man had a chance to duck out of the way, she placed her tiny hand across the earl's nose and squirted astral gas straight up his nostrils.

"Sleep!" she ordered.

After sneezing twice, the owner of the house fell into a trance and obediently obliged. It took a second squirt to subdue the footman fully, but soon he, too, was slumped on the floor, snoring gently beside his employer.

"There should be laws against that," said Wortley.

"There are!" growled an angry voice, just as an enormous ecto-blast detonated above their heads.

Rage rounded the corner and immediately sent a dark magic spell bouncing across the wooden floor. As planned, it discharged early and exploded harmlessly out of range. But it had the desired effect.

A dozen shimmering sentinels poured through the walls of the corridor and hovered menacingly in front of him. Each one was in full attack mode. Their thick golden halos had descended across their foreheads to act as shields. Both wings stood at attention like giant ax blades, clearly ready to strike or defend, and their ecto-rifles were all pointing straight at Rage. They closed ranks quickly, stepping shoulder to shoulder with the discipline of well-trained soldiers, before crouching and attacking.

They showed no mercy—a dark side to their character that they reserve especially for Malevolents—and swarmed toward the Gargoyle in front of them, firing blast after blast of supercharged ectoplasm. Rage knew what was coming but his assailants' speed caught him by surprise and he stumbled backward, only just managing to avoid the blasts. The sentinels attacked again, this time slashing their ivory wing tips mere inches from Rage's own wings as he turned and fled, scurrying up the walls and across the ceiling in a frantic attempt to escape. He disappeared back down the corridor and the sentinels swooped after him.

Phew! Flhi and Alannah sighed together: The plan was working.

"How many?" asked Alannah.

Flhi poked her head through the wall and peered into the almost empty library. With her head still hidden, she signaled to Alannah with two raised fingers.

"Where I come from, that's an insult," joked Alannah.

"That's funny," said Flhi, pulling her head back through the wall. "It is where I come from, too."

They smiled at each other.

"Can someone please tell me what's going on?" asked Wortley.

"That was Commander Rage," Flhi quickly explained. "He's . . . um . . . ill."

"Oh, really?" Wortley didn't believe her. "He looks a lot more than ill to me. He looks like the enemy. Are you sure we can count on him?"

"Trust me," said Alannah. "We know what we're doing."

"And what exactly is that?" asked Wortley suspiciously.

"We're going through the Dark Dimension," Flhi admitted.

"Hell?" spluttered Wortley. "You're going through hell?"

"Well, it's actually the Dark Dimension . . . but I suppose you could call it that. I've got two A.N.G.E.L.s missing and I want them back. Rage and I are mounting a rescue mission. Alannah's job is to simply reopen access to the vortex and then help hold the Gargoyles at bay."

Wortley opened his mouth to speak but Alannah stopped him.

"Don't worry, Wortley, it's not dangerous," she assured him. "I've got everything under control."

Just how do you overpower a sentinel? Flhi didn't have a clue; for some reason attacking your allies wasn't something they'd taught her at the academy.

Naturally, Alannah wasn't worried. "How much trouble will I be in if I hurt one of them?"

"They're invincible," Flhi said. "If you want to get past them, it's going to take brains, not brawn. How's your cerebral cortex?"

"Underdeveloped," Alannah said. "I haven't been to school in more than two years."

"Make them doubt themselves," Wortley suggested.

"They're sentinels, Wortley," Alannah snapped. "They've never had a negative thought in their lives and they certainly don't know what self-doubt is."

"Exactly." Wortley seemed pleased with himself. "Just think how lousy you feel when your confidence is low.

Inflict a bit of negativity on them and they won't know what's hit them."

Flhi thought for a moment, then excitedly fluttered her wings. "He might be onto something. Can you think negative thoughts?"

Alannah instantly thought of her mother and father. She pictured their faces peering back at her from the window of a tiny jet. They waved and she waved back as the plane taxied along the runway. It had been the last time she had seen them, yet the moment seemed fresher than yesterday. Her sense of loss and despair was never stronger than when she closed her eyes and remembered that day. Deep down, she doubted whether she would ever see them again.

"It's working," cheered Flhi. "Look at them!"

Something was happening to the two sentinels. They had begun to cough and, as Alannah projected more and more misery into the room, the coughing steadily became worse. In seconds, great rasping barks were spewing from their mouths and the sentinels were reeling backward, desperately trying to escape whatever was attacking them. And then they saw the Fleshi.

Alannah stepped into the room and solemnly moved toward the magnificent spirits. Tears of sadness rolled down her freckled cheeks and spasms of negative emotion rocked her shoulders, pouring more and more despair into the room.

The wave of distress savaged the sentinels. They couldn't bear it and did the only thing they could: They fought back.

Desperate to stop the attack, they switched their positive energy streams from the Door of Souls and aimed them directly at Alannah. It was two against one—a pair of the Higher Dimension's revered saviors versus a girl with abandonment issues—but there was only ever going to be one winner.

Alannah's doubt surrounded her, acting like an invisible shield. And the more she filled her mind with negative thoughts, the more powerful her shield became.

Soon the sentinels had a choice: flee or roast. Flhi could hardly believe what she was seeing. A single sentinel had been known to defeat hordes of bloodthirsty Malevolent soldiers with just one blast of energy, yet a Fleshi schoolgirl had just sent two of these great warriors running for their lives using nothing more than human doubt. If they could just harness Alannah's powers . . .

Wortley screamed. "The mirror!"

Alannah and Flhi both turned toward the vortex as a snarling Ghoul sprang into the room.

The A.N.G.E.L. drew her ecto-blaster but it was Alannah who fired first. She hit the Ghoul in the middle of its chest and sent it spinning back toward the Dark Dimension. Flhi shot a second Ghoul as it somersaulted toward her. And the carved wooden butt of a hunting rifle, expertly wielded by Wortley, repelled a third growling specter.

"Quick," ordered Flhi. "Close access to the vortex."

"Don't you dare," yelled a voice from out in the corridor. "We're going in!"

Rage crashed through the doorway as a violent ecto-blast erupted just behind him. He left a trail of smoke in his wake as he bounded toward the open Door of Souls.

"Seal it behind us," he told Alannah, grabbing Flhi by her tiny wrist and yanking her toward the swirling gateway.

"Yikes!" was all Flhi could say as she and Rage crashed into a gaggle of surprised Ghouls and Gargoyles, then disappeared toward the Dark Dimension.

Alannah wasn't about to take any chances. She quickly fired a burst of energy toward the Door of Souls, hoping to slam it shut. But something went horribly wrong.

The second the vortex was assailed by Alannah's astral light, it heaved and swirled violently. Attracted by the despair that still filled the room, it reached out a great churning finger that began hunting for the source. Unintentionally, Alannah was drawing it toward her and before she could even think about escaping, it had coiled around her body and squeezed tight.

"Alannah!" gasped Wortley. "Do something."

But Alannah was powerless. And as the vortex began to retreat back toward the Dark Dimension, she felt an all-too-familiar sensation. Her soul was being ripped out of her body.

In all the hullabaloo of Alannah being dragged through the vortex, everyone missed the little creature traveling in the opposite direction. Everyone, that is, except Wortley. He spotted the Ghoul as it slipped out of the swirling vortex and immediately buried itself under a pile of discarded Sunday newspapers. There it lay, as still as a sleeping cat, while the rest of the room erupted in a mixture of panic and excitement.

Angry sentinels burst in from all angles. Within seconds, a platoon of the huge entities stood shoulder to shoulder, weapons drawn. Some fired their triple-barrel rifles straight at the mirror, resealing the vortex so that no enemy could invade the manor house. Others turned their attention to Wortley, aiming their guns at his head.

"Don't shoot," shouted Wortley, raising both arms into the air. "I'm just a kid."

"So is the psychic," snapped a sentinel. "And look what she just did."

Wortley glanced across at the figure lying beneath the mirror. Had Alannah left her body again?

"I don't think she'll be much of a threat to you now," Wortley said.

"Do you think we're fools?" snapped a sentinel. "The psychic has gone astral, and that makes her extremely dangerous."

"Astral?" Wortley didn't understand.

"Yes, look!"

Wortley studied Alannah's body closely. Thinner than a strand of spiderwebbing, a cord seemed to be growing from between her shoulders and rising through the sealed vortex. As he stepped toward it, Wortley could feel the cord buzzing with energy. Strangely, his own body was resonating in an almost identical way, as if the cord was part of him, too. Was that possible?

"It's her lifeline," confirmed the sentinel. "And it's strong. Your friend is very much alive and I'd say that makes her Evanescent enemy number one."

"Enemy?" Wortley snapped. "She's on *your* side."

"Your friend helped the Gargoyle trick us," the sentinel growled bitterly. "She's conspiring with Malevolents and that makes her a threat. You probably planned this together."

A trio of sentinels stepped closer, jabbing Wortley with the ends of their rifles.

"Flhi was with her," he reminded the sentinels. "Does that make her a traitor, too?"

"Inspector Flhi Swift is a trained combat A.N.G.E.L.," the sentinel snapped. "And an Evan City hero. She was probably deceived just like us. We all know that Fleshies like you cannot be trusted."

"Innocent until proven guilty," called a familiar voice. "Now back away from the boy, soldiers. This is his dimension, remember?"

Mayor Cheer waddled through a brightly lit doorway that had suddenly appeared right in the middle of the room. It snapped shut as soon as his camera crew had followed him through, no doubt beaming live to some Evan City broadcast center.

"This boy is no threat to us," Cheer pointed out. "He's far too dumb."

Wortley didn't know whether to be pleased or offended. He finally settled on being pleased as the sentinels lowered their weapons and stopped being quite so menacing.

"Thanks."

"Don't thank me, Fleshi," Cheer hissed quietly. His friendly demeanor had vanished. "If your friend doesn't return with Inspector Flhi Swift soon, I'm going to let my sentinels lock you in a Level Five dungeon for an eon or two. You'll never see another Everlasting Gobstopper for as long as you live!"

Gulp! Why was Wortley always the one left to clean up after Alannah? He really did need to review his career options, and soon.

"Don't get any fancy ideas about running away," the mayor told him. "We know where you live, don't forget."

Cheer threw Wortley an icy glance before shuffling across the room to join the sentinels. Together they studied the mirror, ignoring the boy completely.

Wortley sighed, and was wondering what to do next, when something small moved in the corner of the room. The sentinels were all far too preoccupied to notice. The little Ghoul was slowly belly-crawling its way toward the door. With all those yellowing newspapers piled on top of it, it resembled a badly deformed tortoise. It was going at about the same speed, too.

Acting as casually as he could, Wortley began to follow the heap of magazines as it edged toward the door. Thankfully, neither the sentinels nor Mayor Cheer paid any attention, and both Wortley and the Ghoul were able to escape out into the corridor.

With the sweet taste of freedom dancing across its taste buds, the Ghoul shook off the magazines and started to run across the polished floorboards.

"Not so fast," Wortley said, and he grabbed the little creature by its thick and bony shoulder ridge. Urgh, it was slimy.

"Wet me go!" the Ghoul hissed. It twisted and strained, lashing out with its pointed talons and kicking at Wortley. "Don't make me hurt you."

Wortley tried hard not to laugh. The Ghoul was no larger than a hare, and probably not much stronger.

"Wet me go, I say," the Ghoul pleaded. "If they catch me, I'm dead."

"Give me one good reason why I shouldn't hand you over," said Wortley. He studied the Ghoul closely and saw something rather strange. The creature seemed to be wearing a pair of tweed trousers.

"'Cos it's my house," said the Ghoul. "I wiv 'ere."

"Impossible," said Wortley. "I saw you pop out of that vortex thingy. You're probably an enemy scout or something."

"I'm not a scout," the Ghoul protested. "I just had to escape. That Dark Dimension is cold and scary and those nasty demons are howid. So when I sawed my chance to come back here, I did. Now wet me go, I've got poachers to catch!"

Was this little beast actually the manor house ghost that Alannah had told Wortley about?

"You're the gamekeeper?" Wortley asked.

The Ghoul finally stopped struggling and turned to look at Wortley. It actually tried to smile up at him. "You wecognise me?"

Wortley shook his head. "Not really, it's just that those trousers are a dead giveaway. But weren't you . . . ?"

"Banished to the Dark Dimension? Yes," the Ghoul lamented. "But now I'm back. So take your hands off me!"

Wortley never saw it coming. The little Ghoul twisted its head all the way around like an owl, then sank two rows of pin-sharp teeth deep into his thumb.

Wortley let go immediately and gasped in pain. Blood dripped across the wooden floor, but Wortley had no time to worry about that. The Ghoul was scampering down the corridor, so Wortley set his legs in motion and quickly gave chase. He was going to make the game-keeper pay.

Alannah feared she would never land. She tumbled
head over heels for an age, spinning and twisting like a
sock in a dryer as the vortex propelled her through its
loops and turns faster than the wildest theme park ride.
Light faded, replaced by an almost suffocating darkness,
and, as she desperately gasped for lungfuls of thin air,
the atmosphere became so unbearably cold that she
was afraid she might freeze. Panic gripped her until
she spotted a small shimmering speck up ahead. As
she hurtled toward it, the speck grew larger and larger
until eventually she could see what seemed to resemble
a small floating puddle.

By now she had lost her bearings entirely. She didn't
know whether she was upside down, back-to-front, or
inside out. It was only when she passed through the

puddle and landed on something soft that she realized she was actually the right way up.

"Gerroff me!" mumbled Rage.

Flhi had been knocked to one side but quickly ninja-rolled to safety and bounced to her feet, blaster at the ready.

Rage squirmed free and glared up at his attacker. "You!" he said. "This is no place for a Fleshi."

"I'm not here by choice," Alannah told him. "The vortex dragged me in." She looked around. They were in a passageway. The damp walls were covered in moss and there was an unpleasantly stale odor in the air. The only light came from a handful of burning torches lining a very long and ominous tunnel.

"Where is this, anyway. Hell?"

"The Dark Dimension," Rage automatically corrected her. "No, we went through that. I think we've traveled through another portal to somewhere else."

He peered along the tunnel. Every fifty paces or so, heavy wooden doors were cut into opposite sides of the thick stone walls. He counted four pairs before the passage faded into blackness. Well, they certainly weren't in Evan. "I guess we might be back in the Earthly Dimension."

"Earth," Alannah whispered to herself, wondering exactly where on Earth they were. "Well, we won't find out by standing here. Let's go and explore."

"Thtop right there!"

A clawed hand clamped itself around Alannah's neck. She would have struggled but quickly decided against it as a stinging blade came to rest against her throat. Stinking Gargoyle breath washed across her shoulder.

There were seven of them: large, heavily battle-scarred, and snarling like hunting wolves. Glowing scimitars hung from leather belts tied loosely around their waists and their ecto-shells had been reinforced with an extra layer of thickened scales.

"Thtay thtill, little Fleshi," the Gargoyle lisped into Alannah's ear. "You're going to get me a very big reward."

Wallop! Rage slammed the back of his thorny fist into the face of Alannah's abductor and sent the Gargoyle spinning into the stone wall. Before any of the other Malevolents had a chance to react, he seized the Fleshi girl around the waist and grabbed hold of Flhi.

"What do you think you're doing?" he said to the Gargoyles. "These are my prisoners."

"Prithonerth?" asked a particularly menacing three-horned Gargoyle.

"He'th lying. The prithonerth are all locked up. There'th thomething fishy going on here. Theithe them all! We'll thee what Krot hath to thay about thith."

When four Gargoyles raised their scimitars and stepped forward menacingly, Rage realized he had to surrender, but not to them. Instead, he momentarily yielded to the foulness. The disease had been straining to take over his body for hours and now he allowed it to surge through him like an overdose of snake venom. His ecto-shell pulsed with fury and aggression, bristling with angry ridges. And when he raised his head and glowered at the enemy he did so through the eyes of a temporary alpha Gargoyle.

"RAARRGGHH!"

Six of the Malevolents instantly scurried backward, but Three-horn stood his ground. He was their pack leader, an alpha himself, and he wasn't about to back down from a challenge. He answered Rage with a battle screech of his own.

"WHOORRRGGHH!"

It was just what Rage had been hoping for. Dropping Alannah and Flhi, he sprang forward and struck Three-horn in the middle of his chest. The Gargoyle staggered backward and crumpled to the floor. The fight was over in an instant.

Rage dragged the defeated Gargoyle off the floor and held him in the air like a macabre trophy.

"This is what happens when you challenge an agent of Krot," he hissed at the six remaining Gargoyles. "Now tell me why I shouldn't kill you all."

"You're an a-a-agent of K-K-Krot?" stammered one of the six.

Another one bowed its ugly head. "Oopth, w-w-we didn't know."

"Why would you?" growled Rage. "Krot doesn't share his plans with miserable Gargoyles like you. Only the elite can be part of his militia. If it weren't for us you'd still be scratching around in Fleshi mud looking for slugs, not preparing to conquer the Higher Dimension. How dare you even look at me?"

All six Malevolent soldiers dropped their heads and stared meekly at the ground. They had never heard of Krot's militia, but they were far too stupid and much too afraid to question Rage. Besides, he'd just defeated their leader with one single blow and none of them wanted to tangle with a being as powerful as that.

"We're thorry," said a Gargoyle. "We jutht heard a noithe and came through to invethtigate."

"Came through from where?" snarled Rage.

"From the Dark Dimension. We're on guard duty by the portal."

"Yeah," began another. "We thought the A.N.G.E.L.th were invading."

"The A.N.G.E.L.s *will* invade if I don't deliver these prisoners for interrogation soon," he told the Malevolents. A couple were eyeing Flhi suspiciously. Rage knew he had to get rid of them, fast. "Now get back to your post, before I tell Krot you deserted."

It worked!! The thought of upsetting Krot sent the

beasts scuttling back through the portal faster than star-tled rabbits, dragging their fallen comrade with them.

As soon as they'd disappeared, Rage unclipped a small piece of hardware from his combat belt.

Flhi recognized it immediately. "You stole the track-ing system?"

"You can't steal something you already own," Rage replied. "Besides, can you think of a better way to find your missing soldiers?"

Without waiting for a reaction, he activated the tracker and started walking slowly down the tunnel.

The system took a few seconds to whir into action. The stone walls were almost three feet thick and scan-ning through them was difficult. When the holographic readout finally appeared, it was grainy and weak. But it was enough. Two red dots flashed behind the third door. Yell and Gloom were inside the cell, and they were still alive. Thankfully, they were also alone.

Alannah looked closely at the readout. It also dis-played the cell opposite the one holding Yell and Gloom. And inside that cell were two more dots, only this time they were a different size and color.

"What's in there?" Flhi asked.

"Couple of Fleshies," Rage said. "Weak ones, too."

"We should take a look," Alannah suggested. Instinctively, she was being drawn toward the opposite cell. "They could be in trouble."

"No!" snapped the Gargoyle. "There isn't time. There's every chance that we're about to be surrounded by an army of angry Ghouls. Do you really want one of them to find us?"

Of course Alannah didn't. But she simply couldn't ignore what her instinct was telling her. "I'm not leaving here without checking out that cell," she told Rage defiantly.

"Fine. We'll take a look on the way out," he conceded. "Just help me rescue my troopers first."

Alannah looked across at Flhi for support. But the little A.N.G.E.L. was far too preoccupied with finding her own missing troopers.

"What are we waiting for?" asked the A.N.G.E.L. as she moved purposefully toward the door.

The door was made from wood, just like every other Fleshi-built door Flhi had ever encountered, so when she struck it with a thud and bounced away, she was more than a little surprised.

"Ouch!" She reached out to touch the door and her hands pushed against an invisible shield. It flexed under pressure but didn't yield. "There's something protecting the door. It feels like a rubber barrier."

"A dark enchantment," sighed Rage. "Krot always was good at those things. And it's probably alarmed."

Flhi looked at her commander. Her eyes were wide with horror. "Does that mean . . ."

"They'll be on their way already," he nodded. "It's over."

"Not necessarily." Alannah had other ideas.

She reckoned her abilities were more than a match for Krot's powers any day. And now seemed like a good time to put her assumption to the test. Heat licked across her palms and she told her companions to stand aside.

The enchantment was extremely strong. Alannah could feel the dark magic at work as soon as her own astral light struck the shield. After a few seconds of struggle, she managed to force the shield apart, but only by a fraction of an inch. It wasn't enough to enable Flhi or Rage to squeeze through. More effort was required.

"I need your help," she told Rage. "Try using your own dark magic to widen the hole. It might just work."

Rage didn't like the thought of calling on the foulness to help once again, but he realized he had no choice if Yell and Gloom were going to be rescued. He retched as the disease took ownership of his arms, and his talons tingled. He could see a rip in the shield and he aimed straight for it.

At first nothing happened. But then Krot's enchantment began to buckle. Eventually, there was more hole than shield. Moments later, the entire enchantment disintegrated.

Flhi dashed forward and this time passed straight

through the wood. Alannah and Rage were quick to follow.

Yell and Gloom looked terrible. Cuts and bruises decorated their faces and great holes had been burned into their combat suits. It was clear that they had both been tortured.

"What have they done to you?" Flhi was horrified. With single shots from her blaster, she cut through the bindings that tied her troopers to the wall and gingerly lowered them to the ground. They groaned miserably.

"I knew it would come to this," moaned Gloom. "I'm a lousy combat A.N.G.E.L."

"It's my fault, not yours," Flhi said softly. "You'll both get a promotion for this."

Yell didn't even have the strength to speak. It took all his effort to raise his finger and point at the menacing figure that had just stepped into the cell to join them.

"Oh, how touching," snarled Krot. "I do likes it when loved ones are reunited."

Blast it! The gamekeeper had escaped around the corner
and disappeared behind a solid stone wall. Wortley
kicked the baseboard with frustration. After a few seconds spent fumbling in the dark, his hand brushed
against something cold and metallic. It turned in his
hand and the heavy wooden door opened inward without a noise. Quietly, he stepped into a room. It was heavy
with silence.

At first, all Wortley could see were the soles of the
gamekeeper's feet poking out from under a solid wooden
bed and wiggling.

"Ugh . . . umph . . . come on!" gasped the gamekeeper. It looked as if he was fighting something big, or
struggling to tug a heavy object.

Wortley hoped it was the heavy object.

". . . eeeeaaave!" wheezed the Ghoul. He seemed to be

winning his struggle because inch by inch the creature was reversing into the room.

"Gotcha!" the Ghoul finally cried in triumph as he emerged from under the bed clasping a large wooden box.

"Mine, mine, mine." The gamekeeper showered the top of the box with loving kisses. "I've been missing you."

Wortley's stomach flipped like a pancake. He was bubbling with excitement. Now he knew why Alannah always got so giddy when she caught the scent of something valuable. The feeling was addictive.

"Why don't you save us both a lot of trouble and hand that box over to me," he suggested.

The poor Ghoul almost jumped out of his skin. "Aarrgghh!! Bwoomin' Fweshi. Why won't you weave me awone?"

Wortley plucked a silver candlestick from a bedside table and waved it as threateningly as he could. Demanding treasure with menaces was Alannah's forte, not his. He only hoped he looked convincing.

Thankfully, he did. The gamekeeper didn't fancy going head-to-head with five pounds of solid silver and decided to beat a hasty retreat instead. The Ghoul sprang off the box and immediately began pushing it back beneath the bed. He had almost disappeared completely when Wortley grabbed the little creature by the leg and hauled him up into the air.

"Gerroff me," the Ghoul wailed. "You nasty, thieving Fweshi."

Taking care to keep the flailing claws as far from his skin as he could, Wortley held the Ghoul at arm's length. With his free hand, he reached beneath the bed. "Score!" whispered Wortley as he hauled the box back into view.

Wow. The metal fixings were gold. Solid, too. Alannah would get thousands for it on eBay. But that wasn't what interested Wortley. Instinct told him that there was something far more valuable stashed away inside, and he couldn't wait to see what it was.

"Where's the key?" Wortley asked the Ghoul.

The Ghoul shrugged and blew a raspberry. "Not telling."

"Okay," said Wortley, raising the candlestick above the Ghoul's head. "You asked for it."

With a whoosh, the candlestick cut through the air and smashed against the solid gold lock. Wood splintered and shattered, precious metals bent and buckled and the lid fell to pieces. Three hundred years of history scattered across the floor like a broken matchstick model, but Wortley couldn't care less. Because there, sitting on a cushion of the finest red velvet and glistening up at him with all the sparkle of royal jewelry, was the most beautiful artifact he had ever seen.

"It's worthwess," insisted the Ghoul. "Nothing but a cheap twinket. You might as well just thwow it away."

Wortley knew the creature was lying. Nothing cheap could sparkle in such a spectacular way, and when he snatched the precious brooch off its cushion he could feel its value lying heavily on his palm. Alannah would be so proud.

Only Wortley didn't feel like sharing. He wanted it all to himself. Just gazing at it made him feel special, and he swelled with pride at the thought of owning it. As big as an ostrich egg, the precious stone shone like a diamond, then like a ruby, an emerald, an opal, and finally a beautiful cobalt sapphire. It seemed to be alive, switching colors and even shapes as often as Wortley blinked. Its appeal was almost hypnotic.

Wallop! The bedroom door crashed open and a breathless Mayor Cheer fell into the room. He was followed by three fully armed sentinels and Sergeant Stickler.

"Found you," Cheer panted. "Thought you could hide from us, did you?"

The fat politician was about to grab Wortley by the arm when he spotted the snarling Ghoul. He suddenly thought better of it, and slipped behind a much larger sentinel.

"Get him, Stickler," he said, pushing the sergeant forward. "You take the boy, the sentinels can deal with the

Ghoul. Let's get everyone downstairs where we can keep an eye on them."

The little Ghoul gazed up at the three loaded ecto-rifles and knew he had met his match.

"This isn't finished, Fweshi," the gamekeeper hissed. "I'll have it back, you'll see. I'm gunna get you."

Before the sentinels could fire, the Ghoul somer-saulted up into the air and disappeared through the ceiling. Supercharged ectoplasm shot from the rifles and followed the Ghoul, but it was too late; the little creature had escaped.

Alannah saw Rage spin to launch an attack but he was too slow. Krot hit him with a powerful dark spell that slammed the commander against the cell wall and pinned him there.

Fascinated, the Gnarl studied Rage. "Interesting, the foulness looks pretty advanced, Rage. How do you likes being a Gargoyle? Gots a taste for those juicy sluggsies yet?"

Rage grunted as he struggled to free himself. It was no use. He was stuck fast.

Alannah had always hated bullies. Her last school had been full of them, and for some reason they had always made a beeline for her. Perhaps it had something to do with her bright red hair and freckles? Or maybe it was because she scored perfect marks on every test she ever took. Whatever the reason, Alannah always had her own way of dealing with them: She socked them straight between the eyes.

She stepped between Flhi and Krot just as the Gnarl unleashed his powerful dark magic spell. It would have killed the A.N.G.E.L. stone dead in an instant but simply bounced off Alannah and crashed harmlessly through the dungeon ceiling.

"You don't scare me, ghost," Alannah said scornfully. "You can't hurt me, either. So why don't you just scuttle back where you belong? Or better still, DIE!"

Krot knew his fate was sealed. The focused look in the Fleshi girl's eyes told him everything, and from the moment her deadly spell fizzed from her hands he understood that his existence was at an end. He had failed. The A.N.G.E.L.s would win again.

Krot exploded into a trillion sticky droplets of ectoplasm. The detonation was so violent that his remains struck the dungeon walls like a hail of shotgun pellets, driving holes deep into the ancient granite.

Rage quickly reached for a button on his belt and deployed his astral shield. It sheltered Alannah and the A.N.G.E.L.s, keeping them safe, but nothing else could have survived and Krot was no exception. The feared Gnarl was finally dead.

"Remind me never to tangle with you again," Flhi said.

"We should all get out of here, but there's one more

thing we need to do," Rage said. "That portal we came through needs reversing. This place is teeming with Malevolents; I can smell them. And the only way to drive the Ghouls and Gargoyles back into the Dark Dimension is to somehow close it."

He and Flhi both looked at Alannah. The Fleshi's work wasn't over yet.

Malevolents were already streaming into the dungeons. They dropped from the ceiling, tumbled through the walls, and even took the more conventional route of falling down the steep stone steps. Many were trampled in the rush to find their leader. Others were blasted into oblivion by well-aimed bolts from Flhi's ecto-blaster.

"I'll clear a path to the portal," Alannah yelled to Rage. "You should have just enough time to reverse it."

He shook his head. "I can't. The amount of dark magic required would turn me into a Gargoyle forever. I'd rather die than let that happen to me."

"I could change you back," Alannah insisted.

"The foulness is too strong now," he told her. "It would drain all your power just to bring me back."

Alannah sprayed the tunnel ahead with a shower of darts, obliterating dozens of enemy solders. Rage bounced a dark spell off the walls and took out a handful more. They were working well together.

"Concentrate on reversing the portal," Rage bellowed into Alannah's ear. "It's the only way!"

Ghouls and Gargoyles stood shoulder to shoulder, waving their glowing scimitars in the air like flags at a soccer cup final; a seething wall of mean reptilian eyes stood between Alannah and the portal. There seemed no way through it.

Rage must have spotted a gap. He dipped his shoulder, straightened his horns, and charged headfirst at the bulging wall of Ghouls.

"No-o!" wailed Flhi, as the seething mass of Malevolents swallowed her commander.

Alannah could hardly believe what she was seeing. Rage's action meant certain death, and now they were all doomed. How could he do that?

Then she heard a Gargoyle howl. It wasn't a scream of pain, or one of fear. It was the sound of triumph, and seconds later Alannah understood why.

Rage had lured the Malevolent soldiers toward him, attracting them like ants to a picnic. It was a cunning ruse, and as the swarm of murderous Ghouls and Gargoyles dived in for the kill, Rage allowed an eruption of dark magic to surge through his body. Malicious bubbles rolled across the enemy, burning through their ecto-shells faster than acid. The Ghouls' battle cry suddenly turned into a shriek of agony as the dark magic flooded through their ranks, destroying everything it touched.

Rage raised himself up from the ground and whooped for joy; there was still an Evanescent commander lurking somewhere inside that hideous green shell.

The commander looked across at Alannah and gestured toward the shimmering threshold. "Your turn, Fleshi. Quick, before they come back."

Alannah knew what she had to do: Think dark thoughts. Wherever they were, it was already awash with evil, so once the gateway was reversed, it would feed off the dark energies and suck every last Malevolent soldier straight back into the Dark Dimension. All it needed was a little psychic kick start from Alannah. Only she never got the chance.

The air around her suddenly ignited and she was pitched head over heels into a gaggle of startled Ghouls. Something had attacked her, something exceptionally powerful.

Horrad didn't look human. His brief journey from the Manor had taken him through the Dark Dimension and transformed him into a hybrid creature that no longer belonged on Earth. Huge green warts covered his skin, thick ugly horns twisted down the side of his face, and a tumor covered in pointed teeth was forcing his lips into a permanent snarl. One eye was still almost human, but the other clearly belonged to a Ghoul and, behind his back, a thin, scaly serpent tail lashed the ground angrily.

"Welcome to my castle," he said.

Horrad's castle! So they *were* on Earth.

"And the little A.N.G.E.L.s, too," he sneered. "I suppose you came to rescue your companions. How touching. But completely pointless."

"You're deluded," Rage insisted. "Krot's dead and I've been killing your army of Malevolents for fun. What makes you think you have any chance of victory?"

Horrad flashed Rage a cold smile. "Just this," he said, tugging on a couple of ropes that were attached to his wrists.

Two figures stumbled weakly forward. They were Fleshies and the ends of the ropes were tied tightly around their necks. When Horrad pulled a second time, they fell to the floor at his feet. Then one of the Fleshies spoke.

"Lanni?"

Alannah could only stare in disbelief. For the first time in more than three years, she was gazing at her mother and father. Her eyes filled with tears. It was the moment she'd dreamt of since their disappearance, and she wanted to rush down the tunnel and hug them both. But something was stopping her. Something about her parents didn't look right.

"I have a choice for you, little girl," Horrad said coldly. "Save the world, or save your parents."

"Let them go," Alannah demanded. "They've got nothing to do with this."

"Don't be naive, Alannah," said Horrad. "Your parents have everything to do with this. It was they who wanted to stop me from contacting the Dark Dimension. It was they who tried to thwart my plans and have me removed from the council. Why do you think I abducted them?"

"It was you?" Alannah was horrified. "You took them?"

Horrad bowed. "Guilty as charged."

"And they've been here all this time?" She couldn't believe it.

"We couldn't escape," Ben Malarra croaked. "We tried, sweetie, you have to believe us. We tried every day."

Horrad tugged the restraints and silenced his two prisoners.

"Don't feel too sorry for them, Alannah," he chuckled. "I gave them their own room. Right here, buried sixty-five feet below ground and carved from solid granite. Bed and breakfast, too. And they've been very helpful. Their energies are so potent. If I'd known how powerful they were, I would have kidnapped them years ago. I could never have opened a gateway to the Dark Dimension without their help."

So that was why Ben and Sadie looked odd. Horrad had been sucking the very life out of them. Without Alannah's parents, he was nothing.

"Save the world!" Ben Malarra urged his daughter. "Don't worry, we're safe. He can't kill us."

"It's true," Sadie confirmed. "We're bound together as a family and our psychic attachments are too powerful for him to break. Look at the light."

Sadie showed Alannah her palms. There, barely visible, was a swirl of milky astral light. Alannah looked down at her own palms and at her own churning light. Her mother was right. They shared the same life forces and that was why Horrad couldn't kill them: Alannah's own powers had been keeping her parents alive all this time. She had saved them.

A bolt of dark energy erupted from Horrad's fingertip and burned its way across Sadie's forehead. Alannah's mother writhed in agony as blood poured from the split in her skin.

Horrad laughed wickedly. "Torture is so much fun, Alannah. Can you really live the rest of your life knowing you were responsible for the pain I'm going to inflict on your parents?"

"We'll come back for them," Flhi whispered to Alannah. "You have my word. He won't kill them, because he needs their astral powers too much."

"I can't leave them," Alannah said. "They need me."

Her fingers itched with psychic energy. All she needed was one clean shot at Horrad, but the psychic was clever, very clever. He was using her parents as a human shield and he knew she would never shoot.

"We all need you," Rage reminded her. "If we don't

stop this maniac, your world and ours are both going to end. Do you really want to see a universe ruled by Ghouls?"

"It will be ruled by me!" boasted Horrad. "It's my destiny."

But Alannah had a destiny of her own, and suddenly she knew exactly what she had to do.

Her palms sizzled with energy. She turned toward the portal.

"No-o!" wailed Horrad. But it was too late.

The shimmering surface shook as Alannah's focused gust of psychic energy crashed against it. Violent swirls seemed to be turning the portal in on itself, twisting and tugging until it began to churn like a whirlpool. Whistles echoed loudly through the castle as a gale of dark energy was immediately dragged toward the gateway.

Ghouls and Gargoyles crashed through walls, doors, floors, and even ceilings as they were hauled violently back into the Dark Dimension.

Soon, a river of Malevolent soldiers was flowing through the castle. Thousands of bodies were being swept through the portal. Nothing evil was immune, and that included Horrad. He had been pulled off his feet and was being sucked toward the angry hole. The only things stopping him from plummeting into the Dark Dimension were Ben and Sadie Malarra. He was anchored to them by their psychic restraints and, as long as they were attached, he was safe. Alannah's parents fought desperately to free themselves, but it was a futile effort. The restraints were unbreakable.

Rage, too, was in trouble. He had nothing to hold on to. All he could do was dig his claws into the crumbling cement of the tunnel masonry and hope it would bear his weight.

"Grab my hand," screamed Flhi, reaching out to grasp her former commander.

Unaffected by the pull of the portal, she stood in what felt like an oasis of calm as the swollen torrent of enemy fighters tore past her.

Rage wrapped his talons around Flhi's tiny hand. The energy pulled him off his feet and he dangled loosely in the air. He could feel Flhi's fingers slipping free from his claw. There was nothing he could do to stop their grip breaking apart.

Alannah caught him just as he was about to plummet through the portal. She seized his leg and hauled him to safety, clutching him tightly so he couldn't be dragged away.

"Does this mean I'm forgiven?" he wheezed.

"Not even close," Alannah said sternly.

She tried to move to safety but something was wrong. She seemed to be glued to the floor. "I can't move. We're stuck."

"It must be the Dark Dimension," Flhi yelled. "Your bitter thoughts are attracting it. Can't you think of something else?"

Alannah couldn't. She was boiling with fury. All that raced through her mind was the idea of revenge: Horrad had to die! And that was just the kind of wicked thinking that fueled the Dark Dimension. Alannah was directly in its sights and she could feel it beginning to pull.

"Do something," she begged Rage and Flhi. "It's too strong."

Her feet were slipping across the stone floor. She tried to dig her heels into the ground but it was no use. The floor was covered in slippery ectoplasm and Alannah couldn't get a grip. She was sliding toward the darkness and she couldn't stop.

"It's closing!" Flhi screamed.

The portal was beginning to shatter. Great chunks of swirling matter were breaking off and falling into the whirlpool. It looked as though the hole was actually devouring itself. Anything that was pulled in now was unlikely to get out. Ever.

Rage and Alannah were just seconds from oblivion.

It was time for Rage's exit strategy. He frantically unclipped the tracking system from his belt and quickly switched it on. Provided it worked, the homing button should take them straight back to their previous coordinates on Earth—to the manor house and a welcoming committee of angry sentinels. It would also leave Alannah's parents at the mercy of Horrad. But what choice did he have? It was that or an eternity in the Dark Dimension. He pressed the button.

28

They were back. A temporary homing portal had opened up right in the middle of the library. Alannah, Flhi, Yell, Gloom, and Rage all tumbled through it.

Still desperate to save her parents, Alannah turned and channeled all her fury into one final astral weapon. As the boiling bolt of energy left her palms, she willed it to reach Horrad. But she was back at the manor house now, hundreds of miles from his castle, and her psychic nemesis was safe. For now.

It was a shame the same couldn't be said of the Door of Souls. Alannah's powerful blast scored a direct hit. At first, the sentinels' seal around the ancient portal seemed to absorb the energy. But then it sparked and began to burn. Seconds later, it was absorbed by a twisting tornado of hail and snow as a gateway to the Dark Dimension opened wide. An icy blast licked the walls and ceilings, coating the room with frost. Howls of anger and fury reached through the portal as what was left of the Malevolent army saw a final opportunity to cross back over into Earth.

The sentinels powered up their weapons and prepared for one last stand. But they weren't needed. Alannah's blast had damaged the portal and its unstable surface buckled and warped. Then, as the demons' battle cry grew louder, the portal spewed out one final cloud of snow before slamming shut with a loud crack.

The old manor house shook so violently that the shiny surface of the antique mirror cracked, then shattered, exploding outward. Thousands of tiny glass shards hailed down on to the floor, covering the ground and glistening brighter than the frost.

For a second, the room fell silent. It was over. The Malevolents had been defeated.

Alannah gasped as she was forced back into her body. As usual, pain tore through every muscle and fiber, but this time she didn't care. She had other more pressing things on her mind—like returning to Horrad's castle.

"Take me back!" she ordered. "I need to save them."

"Back where?" asked Wortley. "To hell?"

She ignored her friend and looked frantically around the room. Flhi was in a corner, tenderly cooing over Yell and Gloom. Rage was pinned up against a bookcase by a group of angry sentinels, while he frantically tried to explain who he was and why his captors shouldn't banish him. And Mayor Cheer was standing in the middle of the library, glaring first at Alannah and then at a Gargoyle that looked strangely familiar to him — horribly familiar, in fact.

"It's me!" the Gargoyle yelled. "Commander Rage."

The sentinels attacked the Gargoyle with surges of positive energy, pouring it across him in waves until he was too dazed to struggle. Eventually, Rage slumped helplessly to the floor. He was a prisoner.

Confused and bewildered, Mayor Cheer rushed to Flhi Swift.

"Are you crazy?" he babbled. "Bringing a Gargoyle back to the Fleshi dimension is an act of war. Do you want the Fleshies to attack us next?"

"It's not a Gargoyle," Flhi attempted to explain. "It really is Commander Rage."

"But . . . What? That's impossible!" Cheer spluttered. "The creature looks nothing like our commander."

"That's because he's . . . um," Flhi began. "He's a bit under the weather, sir."

Cheer glared nervously at the Gargoyle. His eyes widened in horror. Now he understood everything.

"He's got the foulness," Cheer gasped. "Kill him!"

"NO!" screamed Flhi, jumping to her feet. "He just saved Evan City yet again."

"We owe our lives to a Gargoyle?" asked a disbelieving mayor.

"It's true," Flhi nodded. "Krot's dead, the Malevolents have all been banished to the Dark Dimension, and the war's over. Thanks to Rage and Alannah, we're safe!"

Mayor Cheer didn't know what to say. If Inspector Flhi Swift was telling the truth, then a disease-ridden Gargoyle and a smart-mouthed Fleshi schoolgirl had just defeated the entire Malevolent army single-handed. Was it really possible?

Stickler stepped forward and whispered something into Cheer's ear. They both glanced down at a piece of hardware nestled in Stickler's hand. It looked almost identical to the commander's tracking system.

"Aarrgghh!" growled Rage. "So that's where my budget surplus went. You commissioned a second unit."

"You didn't think I'd let you spy on everyone alone, did you?" Cheer said. "Politicians like me need to know everything."

"Look, sir, it's true." Stickler pointed to the tracking system's screen. "No trace whatsoever. There's not a single Ghoul or Gargoyle in the Earthly Dimension. They really did it."

"We won!" Cheer smiled. "Evan City is safe. Let everyone know. I want a huge celebration: street parties, ticker-tape parades, a reception at city hall . . . and let's have a national holiday. This will do wonders for my ratings."

Stickler looked puzzled. He pointed at Alannah, Flhi, and Rage. "What about these three, sir? Should I commission some medals?"

"A medal?" Alannah snarled scornfully. "You owe me a lot more than that."

"Don't worry, you'll get everything I promised you," Cheer assured her. He looked slightly disappointed. "Are all Fleshies as mercenary as you?"

"I'm not interested in treasure," she snapped.

Wortley raised his eyebrows and gave his friend a worried look. Perhaps now wasn't the best time to tell her about the brooch that was nestled snugly inside his pocket. "Are you sure you're all right?"

"Two minutes ago I was talking with my parents," she explained. "They're alive, Wortley, they really are! And I need to find them again. I have to save them."

Wortley was even more confused than he looked. How had Alannah managed to contact her parents? Hadn't she just been battling Gargoyles?

"I don't understand," he admitted. "How can your mum and dad be involved in all this?"

Alannah seemed unusually excited. "They were in a castle, Worts, locked in a dungeon. It was Horrad's castle. And it's in Scotland, I think."

Suddenly, everything made sense, and Alannah's eyes

sparkled with happiness. "Don't you see? That must have been where they went before they vanished. It wasn't a Scottish baron's castle at all—it belonged to Horrad. He must have tricked them."

She grabbed her friend by the shoulders and squeezed him tight. "I know where they are, Wortley. They're in Scotland. We've got to go to Scotland!"

Wortley was stunned. He'd never seen Alannah so giddy, and she was talking so fast that his head was spinning.

"Are they okay?" he asked. "I mean, has he hurt them?"

"They're alive," Alannah said. "And Horrad has been draining them of their powers. But he can't kill them. I'm protecting them, Wortley. Can you believe it? I've been keeping them alive all this time. And I still am, but they need my help. They need me to rescue them."

She turned to look at Cheer. "We had a deal. I kept my part of the bargain and now you A.N.G.E.L.s owe me. Send me back to Horrad's castle and I'll consider the debt settled."

Cheer shook his head. "Impossible."

"I'm not asking for a lot," Alannah pleaded. "Just open one of those clever portal thingies. It's easy. I've seen you do it before."

"It's not that simple," Stickler said sadly. "We need to know where your parents are before we can open a gateway."

Alannah suddenly looked excited. "But we were just there. Ask the commander. His little box brought us all back. Surely, it can send me the other way."

Rage shook his head. "I don't have the coordinates. The tracking system was able to bring us back because its hard drive remembered creating an earlier portal right here. It never took us to Horrad's castle, so it can never take us back. It doesn't know the location."

"Are you saying you don't know where this castle is?" Wortley asked.

Flhi and Rage glanced nervously at each other. After a few seconds of silence, Flhi admitted Wortley was correct. They didn't have the foggiest idea where Ben and Sadie Malarra were being held.

"So you lied," Alannah said coldly.

Rage looked sheepish and a little scared. "Sorry."

Alannah wanted more than an apology. She could feel her palms swirling with anger-fueled energy. She wanted to punish him.

It was Flhi who saved the commander. "We can make it up to you."

Alannah paused for a moment and glared at the little A.N.G.E.L. This had better be good.

Flhi gulped nervously and continued. She was about to take an almighty risk. "We'll find your parents for you."

"What?" choked Rage.

"Never!" barked Cheer.

"Oh dear," muttered Stickler, tugging his halo down over his eyes. He didn't want any part of this and suddenly wished he was back in the precinct, filing health and safety reports.

Alannah relaxed her hands for a moment and folded her arms across her chest. "I'm listening."

"Inspector, what do you think you're doing?" asked Cheer. He sounded desperate.

"The right thing!" Flhi answered. "Alannah might be a Fleshi, but we owe her everything. Helping her seems like the least we can do. And don't even think about trying to stop me."

Cheer shook his head and stomped his feet. "It's impossible. A.N.G.E.L.s don't belong in the Earthly Dimension. What if other Fleshies spot you? The last thing Evan City needs right now is an inter-dimensional incident. No, no, no, I really can't allow it."

"Yes, you can," said Rage.

He climbed to his feet and bustled past a couple of surprised sentinels. They moved to intercept the commander but quickly backed away when Alannah pointed a glowing finger toward them.

"The inspector will be safe," Rage reassured Cheer. "I personally guarantee it."

"Not you as well?" Cheer couldn't believe it. First Flhi and now Rage. Why was nobody listening to him? All that fighting must have scrambled their brains.

"We're a team," Rage said, winking at Flhi.

Flhi blushed. She was used to the commander hating her guts. This sudden warmth was a little unnerving. Nice, too.

"Looks like you've been outvoted, chubby," Alannah told Cheer. "They're staying with me."

Cheer knew better than to argue with the Fleshi girl. If his sentinels couldn't stop her, there wasn't much he could do.

"All right, they can stay. But there's one condition," Cheer insisted.

Alannah raised her eyebrows in amusement. The mayor was really pushing his luck.

Cheer continued. "When you've been reunited with your parents, our debt will be settled in full. I'll get my A.N.G.E.L.s back and we'll all forget that we ever met."

"Agreed."

Alannah spat on her palm and offered her hand to Cheer. Reluctantly, the mayor did the same and the two of them shook on the deal. It was sealed.

The mayor wiped his hand across his jacket, cleaning his palm, then dug into a pocket and pulled out something that sparkled. It sat neatly in the middle of his hand and Cheer studied the object keenly. Finally, almost reluctantly, he handed it to Alannah.

Light danced beautifully across the diamond block. "Hmmm, pretty," said Alannah.

"But that's an A.N.G.E.L. Patrol badge," gasped Rage. "You can't give one of those to a Fleshi. They have to be earned."

"After what this girl has done for Evan City, I think she's more than earned it, don't you?" asked Cheer. "Besides, it's only a temporary trooper's badge, issued for the duration of your mission. After that, she's back to being an ordinary Fleshi."

Flhi snorted. "Yeah, an ordinary Fleshi who can shoot fire from her fingertips."

Alannah wrinkled her nose and smiled at the little inspector. Her new friend.

Cheer tapped the badge with his fingertip. "Oh, I almost forgot to tell you. There's a tracking device embedded into the metal. It'll help us keep watch remotely during your . . . er . . . adventures. So, while you've got this on you, we can chart your progress and keep you safe. Don't lose it."

Alannah tightened her fingers around the badge. She was now an official member of A.N.G.E.L. Patrol. She wondered if she'd ever get a pair of wings.

Cheer turned away and offered Flhi and Rage a final, almost pitying gaze before pulling his golden piccolo from a pouch on his belt. He played three tuneful bars. Almost immediately, two invisible doors opened to reveal the inside of a very plush elevator. It was lined in purple silk and decorated in gold.

"Official mayor's elevator, perk of the job," Cheer boasted as he squeezed in beside his entourage. "Oh, one last thing. Whatever you do, try not to start any wars."

The doors eased shut and with a whoosh he was gone.

Everyone breathed a sigh of relief.

"What now?" asked Flhi, looking to her commander for guidance.

Rage shrugged, just as a thick leather-bound book landed between them with a thud.

"Directory of British castles," Alannah said. She picked it up, turned to page one, and prodded a picture of a fortified building.

"Aberdour Castle. Built around twelve hundred and situated in Fife, Scotland. Says here that it's got a vault. That sounds a bit like a dungeon. Let's start there."

Rage stared at the picture. One castle looked very much like another and he had no idea if the building in Aberdour was Horrad's castle or not. But he had a good feeling about this mission. Something told him that they were going to find Ben and Sadie Malarra and then everyone would be happy. He just knew it.

He tucked the book beneath his wing. He was ready.

Alannah fished into her pocket and pulled out her cell phone. She tossed it to Wortley.

"Call your mum," she ordered. "Tell her to start packing for a long holiday."

"Oh great," moaned Wortley. "Most kids my age get two weeks in Florida. I get a wild-goose chase in Scotland."

Alannah smiled and realized that for the first time in years she actually felt happy. She had found her parents once already and she was determined to find them again. And just like Rage, she knew they would succeed. After all, with an A.N.G.E.L., a Gargoyle, and a cat burglar by her side, what on Earth could get in her way?

ACKNOWLEDGMENTS

Many thanks to my agent, Lucy Juckes, who spotted a seed of potential several years ago and worked hard to make it grow—thanks for believing. Also, a whopping thank-you to my editor, Imogen Cooper, who has shown vast amounts of patience and wisdom, both in equal measure. And of course, a heap of gratitude to Barry Cunningham, Rachel Hickman, and the entire team at Chicken House.

GHOUL STRIKE!

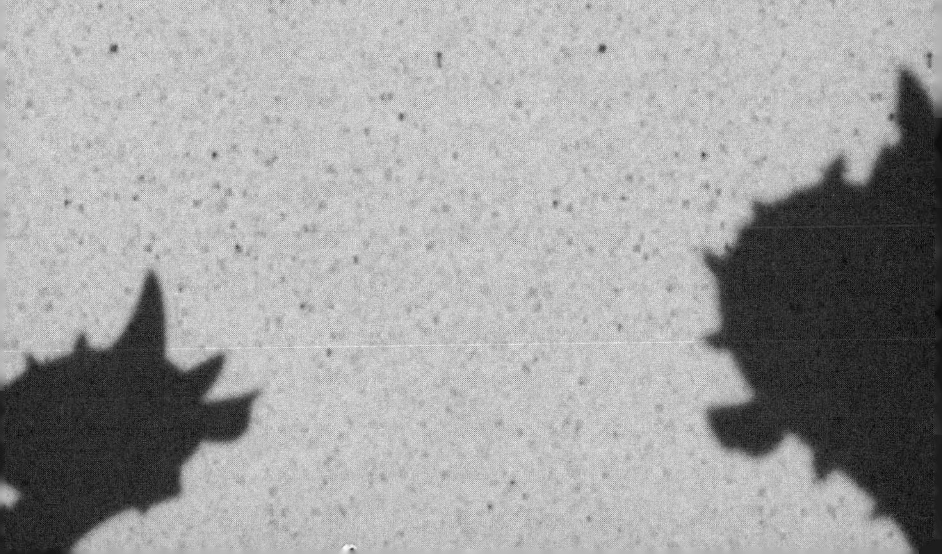